DARLENE

by

Ray Benoit

Dorrance Publishing Co
585 Alpha Drive
Suite 103
Pittsburgh, PA 15238
Visit our website at *www.dorrancebookstore.com*

ISBN: 979-8-89211-268-0
eISBN: 979-8-89211-766-1

This is a love story that weaves into a mystery of violence and suspicion, how a vacation that changed to many situations triggered many events. Steve Mire, a man of integrity and justice, fought for what he believed was right and showed an understanding and compassion for his fellow men.

He met a beautiful redheaded lady in the city of New York and fell in love. But who was she? Where'd she come from? He joined the underworld to be near her, then found himself in position he couldn't get out of. A lady he wanted, but how far would he go to have her, and what must he do to keep her? Darlene, a lady with a heart filled with compassion and understanding. Her lovely smile that captivated Steve's whole being. The love they had for each other will melt your heart. This story has many turns and is full of action about the mobs in New York around the times of the 1950s and sixties.

Ray Benoit comes from Massachusetts. Ray spent four years in the Navy and saw many countries in his travels. He moved to and lived in Connecticut for many years, building and repairing homes. He has three children, who are married and have children of their own.

Chapter One

The Coachman's Bar was dimly lit as I walked in seeing the barroom walls covered with pictures of the Old West. The large mirrors on each side of the bar were engraved with cowboys on horses. The twenty-foot bar was made of dark mahogany with black leather for the armrest. I felt like I was in a friendly place as I sat down admiring this place. I especially liked the brick stairway going down to the basement of that old building, and the iron railing that brought me to the bottom, facing an old castle-like door. It was made with old oak planks, with big black hinges that made the door squeak when I opened it.

Lenny Barker, the bartender, was somewhere in his twenties, with blond hair and blue eyes, along with a smile that made you feel welcomed. But I wondered about his personality, because at times I noticed he changed with certain customers. Lenny brought over the drinks to our table for me and the lady I just met an hour ago. He smiled, then he quickly turned around, going back to the bar with the tray over his head. He was giving a drink to some guy when three men with hoods over their heads stormed in and fired their deadly bullets at the bar.

I saw people yelling in pain as they fell, turning the floor red with blood. Just seconds later they turned their guns to the people sitting at the tables. When I quickly grabbed Darlene, pulling her under the table but I wasn't fast enough, I saw blood coming from her side, and I thought it was all over for the two of us when I felt blood coming down from my left side. I awoke in the hospital, with the doctor looking over me.

"Rest easy," he said in a low voice. "I'm almost through here. I took two bullets out of your right side, now I'm taking your pulse. You had a close call, my friend, you'll be sore for a couple of days. The lady that came in with you wasn't so lucky. She caught three bullets in her left side, but sorry to say four others are dead, and seven others are hurt bad." He smiled and pointed to a man standing by the door, saying, "He's a cop and wants to talk to you."

"Yeah, sure, Doc, and thanks for your help," I said, feeling a little groggy.

"Sorry to bother you. I'm Lieutenant Miles Cretchen," he announced seriously, without any expression. "You're Steve Mire, according to the record that the doc has here."

The lieutenant talked slowly and seemed to be careful of his words all the while watching me. He asked me many questions, and at times he seemed to show some emotion for the pain I was going through. He looked to be around forty years old and in pretty good shape. He was a tall man with black hair and a mustache, looking a little distinguished for his age.

"Sorry, I can't help you, Lieutenant; as you know they wore hoods and came in so fast that it caught us off guard. We had no time to hide or fight back," I explained as I watched Lieutenant Miles taking notes, then he'd look at me and then write something else again. "I wish I could be of more help to you; those damn fools almost killed me and the lady I was with."

The lieutenant got up and smiled, saying, "Get some rest, Steve, we'll talk later."

I was alone now with my mind going back to the night before. I remembered driving out of my friend Ward's driveway when he yelled out to me to stay out of trouble. Well, it didn't take long for me to get into trouble. Here I was in the hospital with two bullets in me, and one of them hitting close to my vital parts in my right side. I felt like I was back in the jungles of Viet Nam again, seeing people shooting at each other.

I left my small town in the Adirondack Mountains for a long-overdue vacation. For the past five years my friend Ward told me to take a month off and go to the big city and relax and maybe meet some people and enjoy life. I worked for Ward for five years after I got out of the service. He was like a father to me. All the time I was in Viet Nam, my wife was having a great time with any man she took a fancy to. When I got home, I found her with some guy in our bed. I felt like a fool seeing them there looking at me. I wanted to kill them both, but instead I went out and took a long walk. When I got back to my house, they were gone with all she owned. It wasn't more than an hour or so later when I heard the news on the TV that they were killed in a head-on collision not far from my house. I remember many times my wife told me she wanted to get away, she wanted to see places. Well, she got her wish in a way, but I felt sorry for her. I was gone almost four years, and I realize it must have been hard for her.

Since that time, I worked without time off or went out with anyone, that was five years ago. I couldn't get myself to trust women. Ward told me many times not to shut myself from the world and not all women were the same as my wife was.

I drove all night trying to forget the past and to try to enjoy the drive and maybe see something good while on my vacation, and maybe enjoy the trip to the big city of New York.

So late the next morning, I got a room at the Standish Hotel after parking my car at the garage. By noontime I walked around seeing things that seemed strange to me. I never saw so many big, tall buildings everywhere, and so many people walking in all directions. It was so different from the small town I came from; I felt like a hick from some farm somewhere. I saw how busy and exciting this place was.

After a while I looked up, seeing a large sign saying "THE COACHMAN'S BAR" in big letters, with a big arrow pointing downward. I took hold of the black iron railing that went downward as I walked over the stone steps. At the bottom under this old brick building, I was looking at a big castle-like door that resembled those ancient days of long ago. The door even squeaked as I entered, I suppose it was to let the bartender know that someone was coming in.

I sat down at the bar when I heard a voice. "What will you have, poison or a drink?"

I called out, "Scotch and soda!" but I didn't see anyone until a man came out from under the counter wiping his hands.

"That's better than poison, huh?" He laughed as he got me the drink. He put his hand out as we shook hands, saying his name, Lenny Barker.

"Steve Mire, Lenny, from the Adirondack Mountains. You got a big city here. I feel kind of lost around here."

After I had a drink, I told him about my being on vacation when a nice-looking woman came in sitting next to me. What I should have said was she was a beautiful-looking woman. I was sure Lenny knew her for some time by the way they talked; he introduced her to me as Darlene Preston. She had red hair that came down to her shoulders, her pretty face showing a natural beauty that never needed makeup of any kind, and eyes that shined showing if she was happy or not. I wondered how old she was but I didn't ask; she seemed to be around twenty-five years old. We talked for about an hour, like we knew each other for years. We changed to a table away from the bar as we talked. I couldn't believe I was falling in love with a lady I just met. The more we talked, the more I liked what I saw. Her smile and soft voice seemed to hold my attention. It was then when Lenny brought us a drink that all of a sudden three men came in shooting.

I opened my eyes seeing the doctor coming in, asking me if I was having any pain. I told him my wounds were hurting some but not like it was before. He gave me some pills and a needle to put me to sleep, then he went out.

I was alone again with the lights out and just realizing how tired I was, being up all night and all that day until late that evening. I was thinking about the shooting now, and the more I thought about it the more I got angry. My muscles were tightening up as my heart was pounding away. I tried to see the face of one of those men that fired their guns without any mercy or caring who they killed. But there was no way I could make out anything to help the lieutenant.

I could feel some pain now as I tried to relax and sleep, but it wasn't easy; my mind wasn't letting me sleep. I could still see the blood on Darlene's clothes and the blood from my side that felt like a hot iron rod going through me. Why would anyone go into a place and just open fire on people, and for what reason? I wondered about many things that night before going to sleep.

Lieutenant Miles came in the next morning after breakfast with a book of mugshots for me to go through. "I know they wore hoods, but look through this book, will you, Steve? You might see something that can help me," he asked in an apologetic way.

I smiled, accepting the challenge, and went through the book, but there was no recognition of anything I could see.

"Steve, I just left Darlene a little while ago. She asked how you were doing, so go see her when you can; she's heavily sedated and worried about you, my boy." He smiled and left.

I watched him go out as I slowly moved myself to the edge of the bed, to get my feet on the floor and holding on to the bed. My side was hurting a little as I tried walking to the bathroom. It took some time getting there between pains and groans. After that, I got to the window seeing people everywhere, with tall buildings in all directions. I wondered if I tried to look for those guys that shot us, where in hell would I look, or what direction would I go in? I hadn't the slightest idea.

The doctor came in later that afternoon telling me I could leave the day after tomorrow and if I was careful walking it would be okay. He changed the bandage and was pleased to see it was doing so well.

So that night I got up and slowly walked to Darlene's room, seeing her asleep but still looking beautiful like when I first met her. I watched her for a few minutes, remembering her smile and eyes that seemed to shine when she talked with that soft voice of hers. As I walked back to my room, my mind went back to the time the two of us sitting in the bar at our small table. I fell in love with her. I wanted to go back to tell her I wanted to take her home with me. But I had to come back to reality that was what I wanted but what about her, what did she want? Here I was thinking about something I had no right to. I didn't know who she really was or if she had someone. I was letting my mind go wild again and I didn't even know anything about that lady, all I knew was what was in my heart. It was what I was feeling at the time I was seeing that lovely woman. But how could that be? I just met her. Funny how things go; I was home for years trying to forget my wife and thinking all women were like my wife. But in just one day, or rather in just one damn hour, I was deeply in love.

The next day was the same routine. I waited to see Darlene that night, only this time she was awake and smiling as I went in. I took her hand while telling her how happy I was to see her looking so well. She was tired and had a hard time to talk, so I stayed just a few minutes. I told her I'd be back tomorrow.

I was released the next day feeling so good just to be leaving that hospital, something about hospitals that seemed to bother me, I didn't like to see people sick or hurt. I walked around slowly until I saw a flower shop. I got a mixture of different flowers for Darlene and took them to her. She was sitting up now, looking a lot better as I handed the flowers to her. She smiled and smelled them as I told her she looked much better than the day before. I was hoping she felt as good as she looked. She smelled the flowers again, taking my hand when I sat down beside her. She put the flowers down on the bed when the nurse came in saying she'd put them in a vase.

Darlene smiled, looking at me, saying, "It was nice of you to come to see me, Steve."

Her eyes seemed to shine as she talked. She was so radiant and beautiful sitting there that I wanted to hug her and kiss her, and it certainly wasn't easy not too. She said she felt a lot better now and wished she could leave the hospital.

I looked at her and asked, "Do your mother and father know you're here?" as I got up.

She turned away and I saw a tear coming down her cheek. It took some time before she answered.

"They're both dead, Steve." Then she picked up the flowers and smelled them again, holding my hand tightly, saying, "They were shot one night three years ago. I had to get something from the store and when I got back I found them dead, and I've been looking for them killers for the last three years."

I felt bad for opening old wounds. "Sorry, I didn't know," I told her as I sat down again. "I talked to the doctor a while ago. He said you'll be ready to go home in another three days, maybe. I hope you will show me around this big city of yours; I'm just a hick from the farm, you know," I said, smiling.

"If you come back to see me, I will be happy to. I can't wait to leave here, Steve," she said in her soft voice and looking sadly. "Yes, I'd be happy to show you our city; it's a big place and much to do here," she said with a smile, showing that sparkle in her eyes now. She seemed to like the idea of showing me the city of New York. I told her I would come to see her every day so she wouldn't forget.

We talked for a while and I really didn't want to leave, but it was best that I did because she was getting tired, so I left her with that smile she always had that showed her beauty. I told her I would see her the next day. I walked around until I was getting tired when I spotted the sign I saw the first time I got to this city: "THE COACHMAN'S BAR."

I wondered as I stood there if I should go in or not. I felt kind of funny about it, maybe because I was shot in that place. I lit a cigar, then I slowly went down the steps to the old castle-like door. Inside I sat down at the bar with Lenny looking at me, then he looked at me again and smiled.

"Holy shit, Steve! Glad to see ya, man! How ya doing? I heard ya had a hard time of it; Miles came around telling me about you and Darlene."

Lenny talked while showing some emotion to our getting shot like we did. He also seemed happy that I was doing okay.

He took out two glasses with a bottle of scotch, then he filled the glasses, saying, "Have a drink, Steve; I think you need one. You know, I'm sorry as hell ya got hurt like you did, and right here in my son-of-a-bitchen place! It couldn't happen somewhere else! No, it happened right here! Sorry as hell, Steve." He poured another drink and was yelling about the whole matter. He'd find them and kill them! "Ya, I'll get them, Steve!" he yelled out again.

He smiled, saying in a lower tone of voice, "I hope you feel good enough to go with me tonight; it might be worth your while, buddy." He poured another drink, saying he had to see some people and thought I'd like to go along. "It's all free, Steve, the food and the drinks, so you go and rest. I will pick you up around seven right here tonight, okay, buddy?" he asked, smiling.

"Okay," I told him as I went to the door, but then I went back to the counter, taking out some money to pay for drinks when he said they were on him, so I nodded, saying thanks, and went out.

When I got to my hotel room, I thought about the people I met in just a short while. A beautiful woman and a friend like Lenny, he was easy to like, with a pleasant personality, and seemed to be a nice guy.

It was close to seven o'clock when I went back to the bar and waited for Lenny to show up. It wasn't long after he showed up with some guy he said was his friend Tom. He got out of the car as I got in. Lenny told me Tom worked for him and he had things to do. He talked about many things that sounded like a little bragging. We were riding in a new Lincoln that felt smooth as we rode on. He had a bottle of scotch under the seat and drank as we rode on, then later he handed me a Havana cigar.

"Have one, Steve. I have them for my friends. I think you like good cigars." He had a smile on that seemed to be glued to his face, because it was always there.

I lit the cigar Lenny gave me and puffed it a few times when I asked, "Were you always a bartender, Lenny, or do you do it for something to do?"

He turned to me, smiling, then threw his cigarette out the window. "I own that bar, Steve; I do a lot of things to make money. Maybe ya might want in, huh? I can arrange it; I know a lot of the right people," he said, puffing on his cigarette. He started to talk more like he was some bigshot, and the more he talked on the more he puffed on that poor cigarette to death.

We came to the seaside and turned into a driveway that led to a big house that overlooked the ocean bay.

Two men started to come to us when Lenny waved to them, and they stopped. Lenny told me not to worry if I saw people with guns.

"They're friends, Steve, as long as you're with me, buddy, you don't have to worry." He talked like he had some kind of an in with God himself.

"Okay," I said as I went in behind him.

He was right about the guns; they had them in their belts and under their shirts, and maybe in their shoes, for all I knew. But it seemed like it was the fashion of the day, or like it was the thing to do. The women all dressed up like queens, then it finally got to me. I knew then this was no ordinary place. I also knew this wasn't the place I should be in.

As we went in, I was now looking at the big winding stairways on each side of the room going up to the second floor, like I saw in an old movie sometime ago. It was an elegant sight. High above the stairway hung this most exciting chandelier I ever saw, and how beautiful and enchanting it was, casting its rays of colors of the rainbow. The rays of each crystal shined on the walls and ceiling. That made it look all the more magnificent. I wondered what the cost of that wonderland of luxury could be, more than I could imagine, I supposed, as I was thinking as my eyes looked around like a kid in a candy store. I had to hold my breath at the architecture and the stylish manner of some master builder of long ago that worked to construct this exquisite building. Whoever built this mansion knew what he was doing. The finished lumber chosen for the staircase was dark mahogany throughout with a high-gloss finish that shined like a mirror. The high ceilings with hanging lights enhanced the beauty of each room. Each door was made of dark oak and was double thick with solid brass hinges and doorknobs.

The builder chose the right spot, or site, I should say, to build that magnificent structure, standing on a knoll overlooking the bay, and just beyond the bay was the open sea, the Atlantic Ocean. Trees and shrubbery, along with flowers that filled the landscape with great beauty, made it look truly like a fairytale.

I remember reading about such places in books, but never did I see such a place in real life. I guess as far as I knew I would never have seen a place like this if I didn't come here with Lenny. After all, I came from a small town, almost at the top of New York State, where buildings such as this just didn't exist there. But there was something wrong about this wonderful place; it belonged to the wrong type of people. A place such as this magnificent piece of expensive real estate should belong to those that deserve such beauty, as this big mansion by the bay.

Lenny was pulling at my arm as I turned around to see a big man standing next to me. He made me feel like a child that never saw anything before, and he was right; I never did see anything like this mansion before.

"Sorry, sir, I was caught up in a land of beauty here. I'm overwhelmed, sir; this place was built with an exquisite taste," I told the man as he put his hand out to me, and I noticed the look of satisfaction on his face because of what I just said.

"I see I'm going to like you, Steve; you appreciate beauty as I do. Lenny told me you're a friend of his, and I'm happy you approve of my home. I pride myself to the best of everything and anything. You get acquainted with my people here," he said as I heard him talk with every word precise and meaning what he said. "Lenny gave me the idea that you might join us. I need good men. I'm Leo, Steve, I own this place and all that's in it. I run a big organization here, and I'll be talking to you sometime later." The big man turned around, walking toward the big doors where two guards stood.

I watched several other men following him like he was God himself. Lenny turned to me and smiled, like he approved of me, as Leo just did.

I walked to the next room where the bar was, with two bartenders looking at me. Just behind the bar were two big windows from the ceiling to the floor, with drapes that enhanced the rest of the picturesque décor. Looking around I was seeing what I despised the most, hoods, the underworld, and all it stood for. Here I was right in the middle of these sorry-ass low-class animals who called themselves people, but I always called them misfits of the world.

I got to the bar for a drink when the bartender told me he knew what I drank. He said Lenny told him to take care of me. I had to smile over that. He also told me his name was Marty, a young man of twenty-two years old that seemed to be a little nervous, and I could see why with all the guns those people were carrying in that place.

I walked through two big doors that led me to the outside porch. Just beyond the porch was a seventy-five-foot yacht tied to the dock, which was as elegant as the mansion was.

Lenny came out saying that he had to leave for the night and hoped I could stay there and he'd pick me up in the morning. He said to find someone there to keep me company.

"You'll be alright there, okay? I'll see ya, Steve."

I told him, "Alright, if it's okay with Leo."

"It's okay, Steve; you're with me, buddy, so enjoy yourself."

I watched him drive off as I finished my drink and wondered about what Lenny told me before, how he made his money. Now I knew.

I was about to go after another drink when I heard a woman's voice behind me.

"I see Lenny deserted you. I'm Marie Steve, can I show you around?" she asked, smiling.

I turned to see a tall brunette with a sexy voice and very pretty. She also had a great shapely body that wasn't hard to notice.

"Thank you, if you don't mind. I see everything here is either attractive or beautiful."

She smiled when Marty came with a drink for the both of us.

"I took the liberty that you might want one, Steve. Leo asked me to keep you company because Lenny had to go for the night, like he does at times." She took a drink and commented on what I said. "That was a nice thing you said, thank you, Steve." She took another drink and looked at me again, saying, "At first I thought you were Lenny's brother, you look a lot like him, but a lot different in character, I noticed." She smiled, walking toward the big mansion, taking out a cigarette as I held a light for her. Then she talked about Leo and his house.

We walked around the place slowly as she told me about many things that went on and who was who.

I noticed something else about her. Not one person said anything to her or even looked at Marie, like she wasn't even there. It seemed strange and made me wonder, who the hell was I with?

We stopped at the bar for another refill and walked some more. She then stopped and looked at me, saying I was different from the others there.

"You don't fit in with this bunch of misfits, Steve. I guess what I'm trying to say is I like you, you're more reserved, you seem to have some care for people. The men here couldn't care less about anyone but themselves, that's why I said you don't fit in here, and I'm glad you don't act like the others here either. I don't know how well you know Lenny, but be careful, Steve, he's no one to fool with. Never trust or underestimate him. He's not only crazy, but a very dangerous man," she told me with a serious expression on her face.

I didn't let on I knew him that well or I just met him. I just let her think he was my friend from long ago. I listened and pretended I was part of this place, or part of what it represented.

She motioned to the guard to bring another drink. I noticed he moved quickly, like he had to. Who in hell was this lady I was with? I was wondering. Was she a boss or Leo's girl? I knew one thing for sure, she was no ordinary lady that just hung around the place. No, she was more special than that.

We walked to the water's edge, letting the waves come close to our feet. There was a slight breeze that felt cool as the sun was just going down. After a while I looked up, seeing the stars starting to light up the heavens above. It wasn't long after when the moon came out from under a fastmoving cloud, showing our shadows on the sandy beach as we slowly walked in that cool summer night.

I could smell her perfume as we talked like old friends, but after a few moments of silence she asked if I was married.

"No, I'm very single, Marie. What about you? You're a beautiful lady. I would think you'd have many men after you," I told her when she looked at me.

She turned around again, looking out at the water, saying, "I never found anyone I liked. All I know are the men here at this place, Steve. I'm tired of seeing the type of men we have here, killers and drug addicts, you name it, we got it here."

She threw her cigarette away and asked if I would go to dinner with her. I agreed I would like that. She looked happy, saying she knew of a great place, so we got in her car and drove to a place that was, in every meaning of the word, elegant.

After dinner we had a drink and danced until midnight. It was a nice, quiet, and enjoyable place. Then when the place was closing for the night, she went to pay the bill. I told her I'd pay it, but the owner came saying he would pay the bill, all the while looking at Marie, like he was in love with her. He said he would be honored if she would come back again.

I looked at her when she said to the man, "Thank you for being so good to me. I'll do you a favor sometime, just let me know, Sal, okay?"

Sal smiled as we went out.

Going to her car, I knew she was something special. She drove and talked about the organization, then stopped at her place.

We went up to the second floor to her apartment, with glass sliding doors that led to the outside porch. We stood there at the rail, looking out at the open bay below. It was a beautiful sight to see at that hour of the night with the stars and a full moon, giving enough light to see the rolling waves coming in and softly hitting against the sandy beach just below us. Far to the horizon I could barely see a ship, in the dim light from the moon shining down on the waters. I watched a big ship slowly making its way toward the horizon, until it went out of sight.

"It was a great evening, Steve. I haven't danced since I don't know when, I forgot how it felt. I hope we can do this again, Steve," she said, looking at me.

"I look forward to it, Marie," I told her as I sat down. I was getting very tired now. It was a long day and my wound was starting to hurt me.

She sat next to me and took my hand. "We shouldn't have danced so much, Steve. Lenny told me about you being shot. I hope you're alright. I'll get the bed ready while you freshen up. I have some pajamas for you." She left me as I got washed.

I noticed my bandage was soaked with blood when Marie came in seeing it. She told me to sit down and she'd change the bandage, with a sympathetic tone in her voice. It wasn't long after that we went to bed. I was overtired, making it hard for me to sleep. I thought of many things that night, wondering what would happen next, and I was also wondering, how did I get with these people in the first place? It was kind of funny in a way, how I was drawn into things so easy and not realizing it.

The next morning came with a bright sun, warming the morning air with a gentle breeze. We had breakfast before going back to the mansion. I told her what we said would never be mentioned.

She smiled, saying, "I know that, Steve. Like I said before, you're different than the others we have here."

Just as we pulled in the driveway, Lenny came by saying how busy he was all night. He told me to wait a minute for him as he went in the mansion. Marie said she'd see me later as I watched her walk away.

I was still wondering who in hell she really was. What did she really do there at that place? But it didn't really matter; she was very nice and we got along pretty well, at least we were friends.

Lenny came out with some guy, introducing me to Gus. "We'll go in my car, Steve, you know, buddy, you should go with us! You'll see how we make our money. I got everything under control, Steve, you just watch us." Lenny laughed, looking at Gus.

I was wondering what that was all about, and what he had under control.

We took off as I quickly got a cigar out and puffed the smoke all around me so I couldn't smell the terrible stink coming from Gus. He was a short man, about forty years of age, and kind of pudgy with a mustache. If I had to guess, I'd say he never took a bath. The odor was so overpowering, and I don't know how Lenny could stand the smell of him.

We came to an old building that had a sign over head saying it was a barber shop. Gus and Lenny went in the place as I followed from behind, and I had to smile watching them go in like two gangbusters. My side was hurting while I got to the door. Inside the place was set up like a betting station, with two men taking bets over the phone while a fat man was counting money. Lenny went to him with an envelope. The fat man looked at him and went to grab for the envelope, but Lenny let it drop to the floor. I was looking at a different Lenny now. There was no smile; instead I saw a cold, dark look on Lenny's face, giving me a chill. His eyes full of hate and the look of death. I saw that same look in Viet Nam many times.

I noticed Gus slowly going for his gun as I stayed close to the door. Then Lenny gave a loud yell at the fat man to pick up the envelope, but the fat man yelled back, telling Lenny to go to hell. Lenny stared at him and hit the man with his gun's butt with such a force, I knew then the fat man was dead. Lenny was looking down at him on the floor, and laughed like a sadistic madman. I was about to leave when two other men went for their guns, but they fell in a hail of bullets that Lenny and Gus fired quickly as I ducked behind the door. Lenny was about to turn and leave when two other men came from the back room, shooting at Gus and seeing him turn to shoot back, but he fell, hitting the floor, as his gun slid over close to my foot. Lenny fired back, getting one of the men, but the other man shot Lenny in the leg.

I bent down, grabbing the gun that Gus had, and I fired as quickly as I could at the man, hitting him three times before he fell. I put the gun under my belt and got to Lenny before anyone else came in. He tried to move when I saw blood coming from his leg.

I ran to him and tried to get him up when another man came in, pointing his gun at us, when I quickly fired twice before the man could shoot back. I put the gun back under my belt and tried to get Lenny up again to get him to the car.

"Hell, man! You glued to that damn floor? Better stop eating for a while, buddy, you're heavy as hell," I told him as my side was hurting more now, and seeing some blood coming out showing through my shirt.

Then Lenny started to laugh going through the doorway when I looked at him.

"This isn't the time, Lenny, you're bleeding and my side is killing me! Now move the good leg to help me a little!"

After a while I got Lenny in the car and drove away from there. When we got far enough away I let out a sigh of relief, feeling a lot safer now. Lenny lit a cigarette as I took out the bottle of scotch from under the seat.

"Yeah, Steve, I need a long drink. I didn't think things would go so wrong like they did."

Yes, it did go wrong; they should have known anything can go wrong if you don't check things out before. I thanked my lucky stars we didn't all get killed.

He started to laugh and repeated what I said about him being glued to the floor. I looked at him, taking a puff on his cigarette. I had to laugh myself because it was kind of funny, but not at the time I said it.

Lenny's expression changed as he turned to me, and he wasn't smiling now, or was he laughing? No, he was serious. "You saved my life back there, Steve. I'll never forget that, my friend." He sat back, taking out another cigarette and lighting it, then looked at me again and smiled.

I drove as fast as I could without getting a ticket for speeding. I glanced down, seeing the blood coming out of his leg, so I pulled over and tightened my belt around his leg to stop the bleeding. It took about another half-hour later before we got to the mansion. I yelled out at the guards to help me, then they came running and quickly took him inside the mansion while I slowly followed behind, holding my side. The doctor started to work on him when I went to the bar for a drink; I needed one with my side hurting like it was. Marty was watching me as I took a drink, wondering what happened to us.

I had to smile by his expression on his face. "No, Marty, it didn't go that great, but he'll be okay; it's just a leg wound."

Marty went back to his work when Marie came in.

"You okay, Steve?" she asked, then she saw the blood coming through my shirt. "Oh, Steve, you hurt your side again. I'll get the doctor, so don't move."

When she left, I took out the envelope from my shirt I got from that betting place and left on the bar counter. Marty handed me a towel to put over my wound, then I finished my drink. I felt the pain more now as I sat there thinking how fortunate I was to be there at all.

Marie came back, saying the doctor would be here in a few minutes. She got another drink, then sat down said, "I told you to be careful! He'll get you killed," being a little excited.

I had to smile because she was so concerned about me. I told her the main thing was the job was done but it could have been done without anyone getting killed.

The doctor came in and fixed my side when Leo walked in with Lenny behind him with his crutches.

"I'm thanking you for your help, Steve. Lenny says you acted quickly and seems to think you two are a good team. I hope so. I know you did all you guys could, but there was an envelope I wanted from those men. We won't worry about that now," he said, looking disappointedly.

Leo started to leave when I asked, "You mean that envelope on the counter there?"

Marty handed the envelope to Leo, and Leo looked at me with a puzzled look. He took out large bills bound with elastic bands around them. "Yes," he said as he took some bills out and handed me several of them. "I take care of my boys, Steve." He puffed on his cigar and went out like he was God over all of us.

Lenny remarked that Leo liked me and said he wanted to go home now. I told Marie I'd see her later.

We got to the car and drove away from the big house, when Lenny smiled, saying he liked having a chauffeur to drive for him. I had to laugh when I looked at him.

"Yeah, son of a bitch, like you said before, we make a good team," I told him when he looked at me, saying, "You're okay, Steve."

Lenny smoked, then threw the cigarette out the window and looked at me again. "I have something for you, buddy. Put your hand under the seat and take out the box that's there, it's yours."

He watched me as I opened the box. It was a thirty-eight automatic with a silencer, along with a box of shells to go with the gun. It was brand new and a beauty.

I looked at him. "Is it my birthday?" I asked.

He laughed, saying it was from him for saving his life.

I took a cigar out from my pocket and looked at him again. "Don't you think I should have a canon? Being with you, I might just need one."

Lenny laughed, saying, "Steve, you're okay in my book."

We drove in silence for quite some time as I was thinking to myself. Here I was with killers and God knew what else. But as I thought about it, maybe I should go along with these people, maybe I'd find those guys that shot at Darlene and me at the bar. Maybe I could get these guys caught or killed.

So I figured I'd tag along for a while and see what happened. After all, I had a month to hang around.

I pulled in to the garage, where Lenny's man Tom was waiting for us. He looked puzzled seeing Lenny getting out of the car with me handing Lenny his crutches.

I was walking slow and bent over some when a smile appeared on Tom's face as he said, "Let me guess, you guys just came back from the war."

Lenny looked at me and laughed. It was funny by the way Tom said it.

I pointed to Lenny, saying, "Whenever you go with him, you have to fight your way out."

We walked to the bar while Lenny was telling Tom everything that happened and added more to it, but I didn't say anything. I had a drink and talked for a while. Tom talked more as he got to know me. It was an hour later when I left them.

At my hotel, I stretched out on the bed and slept until six that evening. I was tired and sore. I showered and changed clothes, then I put my new gun in my belt, thinking it was a good idea since I didn't feel all that safe there after being shot and going through what I just did. I certainly didn't feel like I was in some church.

I went to see Darlene and stayed about an hour. She was doing fine and looking a lot better. I left her and went to dinner and had a few drinks. It was around eleven o'clock now as I went out on the street, looking around, seeing the sky getting darker now, with just a few people at the other end of the street.

I walked slowly toward my hotel when I noticed two young guys following me from the other side of the street. I quickened my pace when they did the same, knowing I was in trouble. I took the gun from my belt and held it in my hand with my shirt sleeve over the gun to hide it. I was now two blocks from my hotel, knowing I certainly couldn't run especially with the way I was feeling.

The taller guy with a knife in his hand had a beard and long hair, looking like a hippy and very skinny as he kept coming toward me waving his knife and telling me to drop my wallet. The other guy had a round hat and baggy pants, looking like a bum following behind, laughing like an idiot. He seemed as though he didn't have a care of what was going on. He acted foolish as he danced around looking crazy when the tall one yelled out for me to stop and drop my wallet.

I told the taller one to go to hell when he got closer, slashing his knife back and forth, trying to scare me. I backed into an alleyway as he got closer to me. He yelled louder and was getting madder at me, saying he was going to kill me. That was when I fired my new gun, hitting him in the chest. He fell to the concrete pavement with a surprised look about him. The other crazy man went for his gun when I shot him also.

I realized the gun with the silencer made just a muffled sound, making it hard for anyone to hear it. I looked down at the two, seeing a small gun on the tall man's ankle, so I knelt down and took it from him and quickly got away from there. I put the small gun on my ankle in case I'd ever needed it sometime.

Back at my hotel I washed myself and lay on my bed feeling sorry for those guys, even though they tried to kill me for the money I had. Young men that could have done something better with their lives. I got up and sat by the window, for the longest while thinking about those two guys. It seemed to bother me for some reason. I sat there by the window looking up at the sky, seeing a few stars and finding myself wishing for Darlene to be there with me. I wanted to ask her many things, like going home with me. I felt lonely now and feeling down because she wasn't here. I was thinking many things now, even about the town I left. I was also missing the woods and the animals I always saw at my place in the woods by the lake. Just beyond that lake was this mountain that looked down like it was protecting what it towered over. I always thought that place was my paradise.

Yes, I was missing all that, especially now as I thought of many things as my mind went on that night sitting there alone like I did at times.

It was six o'clock the next morning when I got up. I didn't feel all that great as I got dressed. I had coffee at the hotel restaurant when I saw Tom coming toward me.

"Good morning, Steve. Lenny wants to see you. He said something about Leo's men getting killed last night."

I looked at him and kind of nodding my head, saying, "Yeah, Tom, I got nothing to do but to rest and enjoy my life."

Tom smiled, telling me Lenny was hurting and was acting very nasty.

Tom drove to the bar where Lenny was waiting for us. He was holding on to his crutches when I asked how he was doing.

"The pain! The damned rotten pain going right through me, Steve, and that asshole Leo can't wait! He wants us to visit someone he thinks killed his two men. They had a lot of money on them, along with cocaine, at the time.

I looked at Tom, saying, "Here we go again, Tom."

He laughed as Lenny puffed on his cigarette like an old steam engine.

We got in the car with Tom driving. I lit a cigar, watching the streets because it looked like a bad neighborhood we were going into and I didn't like it.

Tom stayed in the car as Lenny and I had to go to some old building, but it was about four buildings away. We had to walk slowly because of Lenny with his crutches and me with a sore side that was still hurting some.

We finally got to the old building that was run down and looked like it was ready to fall. Lenny knocked on the door while I looked around. Inside the door was a guard that let us in, when a black man came from the other room, yelling out, "I took over this part of town! Leo gets no more friggen money from me! You, tell that son of a bitch he gets nothing! You hear that?" he yelled out while pointing his finger at us, saying again, "He gets nothing more from me!"

Lenny looked at me knowing only too well what he had on his mind. That was when Lenny smiled, telling the man okay, like he was leaving, but that was when he quickly pulled his gun out and shot the man. I shot the guard that was by

the door as we quickly took the money and the drugs that was there and backed out the door. As soon as we ran out, a man across the street started shooting at us.

Tom jumped out of the car and shot the guy three times before he fell. We drove away as Lenny was counting the money. There was over fifty thousand dollars there. He gave Tom and me each ten thousand dollars, saying he would keep the rest for a rainy day. I'd been with these guys for a short time and I already had more money than I ever had in my entire life. I could see now why people went for robbing and killing, because it paid big money.

"Steve, we're going to see a guy at a bar we know. I have business to talk over with him, we'll have a drink with him. Actually, I don't think you will ever forget this place when you see it; there's no other place like it in all of New York City." Lenny laughed and Tom smiled, and once again I started to wonder what else I was getting into.

We got to that bar and Lenny was right, that damn place was so crummy and filthy, even the floor was sticking to my feet. The owner was so dirty and even the apron he had on was dirty, worse than he was. He was big around as he was tall. He took out three glasses for our drinks that were so greasy, it seemed like they were never washed. In fact, I couldn't even see through them. I got so angry I pushed him against the wall, then I noticed cockroaches and other kinds of bugs running in all directions.

"You filthy piece of shit!" I yelled at him. I didn't want to hit him because I'd get some of his shit on me. I just walked outside to breathe some clean air and calm down.

That place stunk so bad. I don't know how people can sit on dirty stools. And to drink from those crummy glasses, which seemed to never have been washed or even cleaned at least a little bit, anyway.

I waited for Tom and Lenny to come out. After a while they came out, when Lenny started to laugh. "You know, Steve, that crummy shit makes us a lot of money. That's why we put up with him," he explained.

"Is there anything else we're doing today, or should I ask?"

Tom laughed as Lenny took out a cigarette, saying, "There's one more thing to do. I have to see this guy that sets up deals. In fact, he set one up that went bad. Tom knows who I mean, huh, Tom?"

"Yeah, Steve, his men are the ones that shot up the bar where you got shot."

Right then it got very quiet when Tom quickly put his hand over his mouth, but it was too late; he let the cat out of the bag, and I heard what he said. My heart nearly stopped because it hit me so damn hard, I couldn't believe what I heard. When I looked at them with my mouth open and having a hard time controlling myself, I wanted to take my gun out and shoot them both. They knew all the time and never said anything about it, and it didn't bother them if Darlene or I were killed or not. Tom was red in the face with Lenny blasting him, like he was going of control. He called Tom all kinds of names and was threatening to kill him.

Then Lenny looked at me with a red face, saying, "Sorry ya had to hear that, Steve. I wanted to tell you myself, but I just couldn't, Steve. There was nothing I could say to justify ya being shot like you were. The guy I hired to do the job had his men shoot everyone. They were afraid they'd miss the one they were after. They were hired to kill some guy that was ratting on our organization. Okay, buddy? Sorry as hell, believe me, Steve, damn it! I didn't want you to hear it that way," he said, looking badly about it.

"Yeah, I'm okay," I said, but I wasn't okay. I felt ill and betrayed by a guy I was getting to like. I thought I could trust him, and I remembered Marie telling me to be careful. She was right about Lenny; he was a killer and liked what he did.

Tom stopped the car by some guy trimming his bushes by the driveway. The man got red in the face and yelled at Lenny for coming to his house. He was a bad cop that Lenny hired but bungled the job he was supposed to do. The man had done jobs for Lenny before. So why was he here? I was thinking.

Lenny got out of the car and put his arm around the man's shoulder as they walked toward his house, with Tom and me following behind.

"Take it easy! I got something for ya," Lenny explained, "I need you boys for a job. It pays ten thousand now and ten more thousand after the job is done," Lenny told him in a low voice like he was his longtime friend.

The cop, called Cal, smiled when he heard about the money Lenny told him about. Lenny lit his cigarette, telling Cal to call his boys right then and now, and to tell them to meet us at the gravel pit Friday night at ten o'clock. Cal made the call and got the surprise of his life.

When he turned away from the phone, he was looking at Lenny's gun pointing right in his face. "What! Why the gun? I did what you wanted!" he yelled out in a frightened voice and looking very nervous seeing Lenny staring at him like he was.

Cal started to back away in a sweat, seeing Lenny's eyes wide open and staring with a distorted face, then Lenny fired his gun into Cal's face over and over again. Cal fell against the wall, then fell to the floor with blood splattered everywhere. Lenny laughed like a crazy man seeing Cal on the floor with half of his head left. He went all to pieces firing his gun until it went empty.

Cal was a big man with black hair and a long mustache. He was a shifty type that never looked at you straight. A man that seemed to be afraid of nothing until he saw Lenny's gun in his face, knowing it was over for him.

Tom looked at me like he wanted to say something but changed his mind. I noticed he didn't like what he saw. I know I certainly didn't like it either. I wondered, would he laugh when it came time to shoot Tom or me? It was a terrible sight to see, Cal lying there with half of his head gone.

We got in the car and drove away in silence. I smoked my cigar thinking how cruel and rotten Lenny was. I knew Cal was the same kind of rat as Lenny was and needed to be taken care of, and it was no loss getting rid of him. But it was the way he did it.

I'd be happy to see the other three men that shot Darlene and me get the same Friday night; three more rats would be dead. They cared for no one when they fired at us that afternoon.

Lenny smoked his cigarette and took a drink from the scotch bottle. He said nothing until we got back to the mansion and went in to see Leo while Tom and I stayed outside. Tom sat down on the back porch when I told him to forget what was said and done. He smiled and seemed to feel better about it.

"I'm glad you let it slip about those guys that Cal hired, Tom. Now I can rest knowing they will be killed Friday night, and I'll be happy to shoot them guys myself," I told him.

Marie came out telling us we had a meeting to attend, so we went in listening to Leo telling us about some new jobs coming up and who would run them.

Leo said something else that made me feel sick. I already got one shock today, when Tom let it out about the guys that shot Darlene and me, now I was getting another shock. Leo said Darlene was coming back to work soon. I sat there looking around at that bunch of shit they called people; I couldn't believe what I just heard. I was wondering, what in the world was she doing with this bunch of killers?

I saw her eyes that sparkled, her hair that glistened under the sun. I saw her smile and beautiful face that I couldn't forget for one minute. I couldn't understand why she was in with that good-for-nothing crowd! What did she do in that damn organization? She didn't fit in with these people, but I heard she was in with that bunch of killers. What was next? I was trapped in this organization I joined just to help a lady I wanted, a lady I loved, now I found out she was part of what I hated and despised.

After the meeting, Lenny told me he had to go for two days. I got a drink and walked out to the water when Marie came to me saying she talked to Leo about me. She said Leo thought a lot of me and I would be moving up to a higher position. She said she told Leo that she liked me and she wanted me to move up also. Marie took my hand as we walked along the shore.

Later that evening we went to dinner and danced. It was eleven o'clock by the time we got back to her apartment.

We sat on the back porch looking out at the bay. We had a drink when she looked at me, asking, "Steve, do you like me?" in a low voice and with a stare.

I was surprised she asked me that question; I wasn't prepared for that. I took her hand and kissed it while I was trying to find some kind of answer to give her. "I do, Marie, more than you think, but for the time being we should take it slow and see what happens," I told her as she took a cigarette out.

She went on to say, "I miss you all the time when you're not around, Steve. I miss you more and more now that I know you better. You feel that way too, Steve? You know, together we could do so much. We can have whatever we want, I'm in a position to do just that," she said in a kind of excitement in her voice, with a smile.

She got up and stood by the rail, looking out over the water, and she seemed to be looking beyond and far away, saying in a low voice, "I have something I want to tell you, Steve, that I never told anyone else about me never leaving this place. I look out there beyond the horizon and want to go there no matter where it takes me." She turned to look at me again as I got up and kissed her.

"You might just get your wish someday, my dear, I sure hope so, Marie."

I looked up at the moon just coming out from behind a cloud, then the thunder that sounded very loud, with a bright streak of lightning hitting the water in the bay just below us, with the loud cracking sound that made us jump. The lightning kept hitting the water closer and closer to the building, making Marie jump against me. The lightning hit again when she kissed me.

I could feel her body against me as she held me tightly. I told her we'd better go to the bedroom. We made love, forgetting everything else.

I was widely awake about an hour later. I got up, leaving Marie sleeping soundly. I got up with thoughts crowding my mind so much, I couldn't sleep anymore. I smoked a cigar as I stood there by the porch railing, looking out over the bay that had now become calm. The sky cleared to reveal the stars lighting up the heavens as I watched the waves rolling in and splashing over the sandy beach just below me.

I was thinking about Marie wanting to get away to anywhere. She said she never left the city. Marie was a tall lady, and very pretty and very bright with a great smile, but something was missing in her personality. She seemed to be very cold to life, like she didn't care about other people; it was more about herself. I certainly didn't blame her for wanting to leave that place, and I still didn't know who she really was or what she did at the mansion, but I noticed no one bothered her for anything, and I was also wondering why.

My thoughts were now focusing on Darlene. I was seeing her in all her beauty, and it bothered me to think she was connected to the organization of killers, and drug pushers, and all kinds of things that went on there.

I really didn't know what to do about it, but I still wanted to take her away from there. But I really didn't know just how far would I have to go to do that, and what would it cost me? I was also wondering, what in hell was I doing there in the first place? Being in with those rotten people. I was now thinking about Marie and Darlene; there was no comparison between the two women. If I had to choose, it would certainly be Darlene I wanted. Marie was a brunette and very trim and very attractive, but her attitude and thinking was more for herself, and she showed that part of her very distinctly by her actions and the way she talked about others.

As for Darlene, she was very beautiful but also beautiful inside her whole being. She was caring and showed she had a heart. Far different than Marie in every way. And it was the feeling I had when I was with Darlene; I felt relaxed and happy to be with her, the feeling of wanting and loving her, but I didn't feel that way with Marie. Somehow I felt when she got whatever she wanted she won't need me anymore, or anyone else for that matter.

It was eight o'clock the next morning. Marie took me to my hotel. Later I went to see Darlene at the hospital. She was already sitting in a wheelchair. Her eyes sparkled when she told me she could leave the hospital the next morning.

"Will you come for me, Steve?" she asked, being a little excited about it. "Of course, I'll be here. I've been hoping to hear that."

I wanted to hug her but I didn't dare; I was reminding myself her wounds were not that healed up yet, and looking at her now made me want her all the more, no matter what the cost. She looked at me in a concerned kind of look about her, asking if I was okay.

"Yes, I'm okay. I feel great now that I know you're feeling better, and looking so beautiful. Why you ask?"

"You look okay, Steve. What about Lenny and the organization?" she asked.

I looked at her, saying, "Well, as you know, I was there most of the time with Lenny; he's a sadistic killer and Tom is afraid of him. Marie is something else; she seems to be some kind of bigshot there, but I don't really know what she does or why she's even there. No one seems to bother her any; the organization sells drugs and it kills anyone that gets in their way. All in all, I'd say they are a fun group," in a sarcastic way.

She smiled and took hold of my hand. "I guess you know them, Steve. I know them too. I want them caught or killed, I really don't care which. Lenny came by telling me what you guys did." She looked at me, saying she wanted me away from those people, that I didn't belong there.

I was thinking the same thing about her; I wanted to tell her I knew she worked for the gang. I also wanted to ask what she did there, kill or sell drugs, but I let it go for the time being. It was hurting me to know she was part of that rotten bunch.

Later I walked around the city killing time and looking in store windows, and all the time my mind was on Darlene again. I hoped she wasn't in too deep, not only for her sake but for mine as well.

I was thinking selfishly now, because I wanted her so much.

I walked a lot that day with only one thing on my mind, a beautiful lady with red hair, a beautiful smile and shining eyes when she was happy, and that was telling me not to run, because she was worth it.

By eight o'clock the next morning, she was waiting for me by her hospital door.

"Good morning," she said, smiling. She looked so beautiful, like the first day I met her.

I kissed her and said good morning and took her arm. "It's been a long time since I took a lovely lady out. May I take you to your car, madam?" I asked her when she laughed.

Once in the car, I drove toward the ocean beach as she sat close to me. I lit a cigarette for her when she asked me, "Where are we going?" Then she said it didn't matter; it was so nice just to be out of that hospital.

"I thought the ocean air would be good for you, so take it slow and easy," I told her.

She seemed to be happy looking out the window, watching the scenery go by, and I was feeling happy myself just to have her close to me.

"In a few days you'll be getting your strength back, and who knows? Maybe you might even show me the city of New York."

She laughed, saying, "I'll take you through every street and besides, I owe you for seeing me in the hospital." She looked at me, then she turned, looking out the window, saying very softly, "I feel good being with you, Steve." She took a puff on her cigarette, then turned and looked at me again, saying, "I thank you again for seeing me, Steve. I thought I'd never see you again. I thought you were killed that day when we both got shot. Then Lieutenant Miles came to see me, he told me you were hurt but you would be okay, and I was happy to hear that because I was worried about you," with a serious look.

I would look at her every now and then as we drove for the shore. I could see it was difficult for her to let me know how she felt. Her voice soft and low and unsure of what to say, like she was afraid to say anything about her feelings.

"You know, Steve, I used to come here to pray and wish that someday I would find those guys that killed my mom and dad, but my wish never came true." She went silent again as we walked on in the warm air with the sun shining brightly, while her eyes showed a little sparkle as she looked at me.

I knew Darlene was happy to be there, and at times she would squeeze my hand and smile. That made me feel great. Like in some way she was saying she really did care some for me.

Darlene stopped and looked at me again, then went on walking as she said, "I have something to tell you. I know you are just going after the killers and drug pushers. I also know you're not the kind to push drugs or hurt anyone, but I wish you weren't in with that bunch. Some time or other you might get into trouble. I know Steve, I was with them for three years now, I know them well. I joined them to help me find the ones that killed my mother and dad. So far I never did. I joined them for that reason, Steve, to catch those killers."

I was letting her talk because maybe it was good to let this off her chest. I also wanted to know if she killed or sold drugs like the others. I knew now she was doing what I was trying to do, getting rid of killers and violent people.

The sun was warm with a slight breeze that moved the stands of her hair. I could smell her perfume. I liked the smile she always had, that made me happy and fortunate just to be with this beautiful lady I adored so much. I thought now was the time for me to tell her about the men that shot us.

We started to go back to the car when I told her I had something to tell her.

She looked at me and smiled. "You have something to tell me, like a confession maybe? Come on now, come clean," she said.

I had to laugh at the way she was looking at me. "I have something to tell you, my dear, and it isn't a confession. I know who those guys are that shot us and all those people at the bar."

She looked at me and turned away, then looked at me again, asking if I was making a joke.

"No, I don't joke about something like that. I was with Lenny and Tom when Tom let it slip out. Lenny told me about a cop that sets up deals on assassinations. Now this is what he told me. He hired this cop to have his men shoot some guy the organization wanted killed. Now the killers didn't know what that guy looked like, so they panicked and shot at everyone there, including us."

Darlene looked at me with staring eyes and mouth open. She couldn't believe what I told her was true.

"Your mouth is open, yup, there goes a fly, he thinks it's place to live. Yeah, there he goes." She laughed. "Are you crazy? I don't see any flies here, what happened next?" she asked.

"Well, for one thing, Lenny got wild on Tom, calling him names, and wanted to kill him, then Lenny tried to make it look like it was better I didn't know about it. But when I heard it, I thought about killing them both. I almost did, but I had to control myself, Darlene. I didn't care so much about me; it was you who almost got killed, and that bothered me a lot more. I worried about you, beautiful. It hurt me seeing you in the hospital like you were."

I told her how Lenny shot the cop and laughed after Cal lay on the floor bleeding. Tom didn't like seeing Lenny doing what he did. I told her I'd play the game for now, but sometime later the time would come that Lenny and I would fight. I also told her the three men that did the shooting would be killed the next Friday night coming.

"I'm glad to know they will be taken care of, Steve," she said, looking out at the waves coming in close to her feet.

She took my hand, saying in her low tone of voice that she joined the gang to get whatever she could on them and turn them in to the police. She had a job to do, but now that I came into her life it would be harder to do that job.

"Steve, when I met you at the Coachman's Bar, I felt a change in me. I only had myself to worry about, now I have you. When you came in to see me in the hospital, I looked forward to that, but when you had to leave I felt so alone and I'd find myself thinking about you. I wondered, where did you come from, or what kind of man are you really? And so many things I wanted to know about you. Now being here with you, I like you more, but I'm having a hard time about it. I'm not used to being with anyone, Steve. I was always alone and thought only of myself and my job.

"I wanted to find the killers of my parents and to quit this job, but I can't until then. Please don't make it any harder for me, Steve," she said in an unsteady voice.

I put my arm around her shoulder before we got in the car, and in a low voice I said, "It's a tough world, honey. I'd like nothing better than to leave here, my dear lady, but I can't do that until you do. If you're so intent on catching those guys, then I'll stay right here and help you. I have to make sure you'll be safe. I can't help that, Darlene. I want to stay and get those guys too. So, let's see what happens," I told her.

She smiled as we drove to the big city. "I have a lot of money to spend, and I'd like to take you to dinner this evening if you're not too tired." She said she wasn't too tired and she knew of a place if I wanted to go there. "I don't want this day to end, Steve; it's been so wonderful, I haven't been this happy since I don't know when," she said, looking at me with a solemn look about her.

I parked the car at the hotel garage, and we took a cab to the New Yorker Restaurant. It was only two blocks away, but it was too far for Darlene to walk. It was a great place, indeed. It had elegance and was very expensive.

We sat by a large window that showed the lights outside and the people walking in all directions. We sat down to a candlelight dinner and soft music from a six-man band. We danced slowly until our dinner came, then we ate and had some wine. By ten that night we danced again slowly, with her head on my shoulder. I felt like I was in paradise somewhere out of this world. It was a pleasure being with this lady; I couldn't keep my eyes from her. I wanted so much to say what was in my heart and what my feelings were, but I couldn't, not just yet. I didn't want to do anything to push her away from me, because that would destroy me for sure.

We sat down and had a drink, then a little later she went to the restroom. As soon as she left, I told the waiter to bring a rose for the lady. When she returned I handed it to her, and when she smiled and smelled the rose her eyes started to water.

She got up and took my hand, saying, "Let's dance once more, Steve."

She put her head on my shoulder as we danced for the last time that night.

It was close to midnight now when she said in her low, soft voice, "You're making it hard for me. I don't know what to do about it. I never had this feeling before. I think I'm in love with you, Steve. This can't happen, I can't let it happen. I'm not ready to be in love," she said.

I could feel her tremble a little as she wiped her eyes while we danced.

I held her in my arms, going around the dance floor slowly, when I asked her in a low voice, "Is that so bad, to fall in love? To love someone that adores you and has ever since he met you that afternoon in the Coachman's Bar? Someone that will give his whole life to you, and all you have to do is to take it? Yes, my love, I loved you since the moment I met you, and I can't help that. There has to be a reason, maybe it's because I feel wonderful when I'm with you. Just as if we were meant for each other, and I firmly believe that."

I tried to explain my feelings in my own awkward way. It wasn't easy for me either, but all I knew was I wanted her more than anything in the world. What did I know about love? I didn't really know the right words to say to a lady, I just let my heart do it for me because it was the way I felt whenever I was with Darlene.

We sat down as the band took a break. Darlene took the rose and held it to her cheek, saying she never felt this way before. I knew what she felt; it was love that was new to her. She never had time because of what happened to her parents. She was too busy looking for her parents' killers for the last three years.

I looked at her, holding her hand, saying in the best way I could, "You know, my dear, it's love, that's what it is. That's the way I feel, and it's a wonderful feeling but at times it isn't that wonderful. It can be great and it can also be cruel. You can be happy at times and you can be in tears, and sometimes you can feel what your partner feels. Just like when you were in the hospital, I felt your pain even though I was also shot. That didn't matter, because it was you that I was worried about. Yes, maybe it was because I thought you might not make it. I didn't know if you would pass away or live. That was the hardest thing for me, because I was in love with you. I didn't want to lose you, Darlene," I tried to explain.

She took a drink, then took my hand, saying, "I must be dumb, huh? I didn't know. I never met anyone like you, Steve." She turned away and wiped her eyes.

I took her to the dance floor again before the band was to leave and danced away from the other people when I said, "It's what's in your heart, my dear. It's the way you feel about someone. Your heart will tell you in some way about someone, and I've always believed your heart never lies to you. The only thing I know about you is you care about others and you show it. That time we met, I was hoping you would like me. I'm not a man in some high office or some bigshot, no, I'm just a man trying to find my way in this world, such as it is. But I will try giving you whatever I can as long as we are together. I don't know if you have someone you care for, or if you're married or not, or maybe you want something better in life."

We danced slowly with the soft music playing. She was silent as she held her head on my shoulder, then she kissed my ear and put her head on my shoulder again.

It was time for the restaurant to close. We left the restaurant and went outside. Her apartment was two blocks away, so I called for a taxi; I knew she was too tired to walk. She was wondering about her job now and wondering if she could go on like before. It wasn't the same anymore; it wasn't only her now, like it always was. It was the two of us now, well, at least I was hoping it was the two of us.

We got to her apartment and I helped her inside and kissed her. I hugged her, being a little careful because of her wounds.

"I'll see you in the morning, honey," I told her.

She kissed me before I left. I felt good being with her. We had a great time being together.

When I got outside her apartment, I noticed a car coming around the corner and stopping.

"Hey, Steve!" he yelled out.

It was a man from the organization. He got out of the car and asked if I wanted in on a big deal that was going down at two o'clock that morning.

"Yeah, why not? I can use some action, but I need a gun. I don't have one on me; I didn't think I'd need one tonight," I told BeeBee. He was a short man that looked like a lumberjack, built big around and not too much for brains.

Inside the car was another man BeeBee introduced me to as Lon. He was a tall man with a beard. He smoked cigars and grunted more than he talked. BeeBee explained that three men were to exchange half a million dollars in cash for more than that in drugs. It was taking place at the lumberyard on the docks.

"You in, Steve? We sure as hell need you," he asked.

"Yeah, I'm in. I need a gun, BeeBee."

He gave me one of his as I checked it out to see if it was loaded or not. He also told me we had to pick up Micky.

"You know Micky, don't you, Steve?" he asked excitedly.

"Yeah, I know him," I said as he drove to a bar on the waterfront.

Micky walked in smiling when he noticed me sitting at the table. "I know it will be easy with you here, Steve. Shit, man, good to have you with us!"

I had to smile by the way he talked. It was always fast, like he was in a hurry all the time, but he was always right to the point. Micky was a guy that never went to school. He was a mama's boy, and being tall and thin he looked like a nineteen-year-old kid. But he was really thirty-five years old. We had two drinks and went over the job, when I noticed Lon looking at each of us like he had other ideas.

I never trusted anyone that wouldn't look at you straight. He never did look at me straight in the eye; he always looked the other way whenever he talked or answered.

BeeBee drove in through the gate to the lumberyard and opened the office door. The light was on over the door, showing enough light on the driveway and the lumberyard area. There was a toolshed to the right of the office. Micky hid to the left side in some old forklift that was there for years as I hid behind a lumber pile almost in front of the office. I didn't see Lon anywhere and that made me nervous, but at the time I couldn't do anything about it. I smoked my cigar as I looked around for the next few minutes, seeing the sky dark and feeling its warmth with the soft breeze. There was no moon out, making it better for us, then I saw two cars coming through the gate and going by me and stopping in front of the office.

A man got out showing a suitcase full of money to a guy from the other car, then the man laid the suitcase down on the ground, in front of the car's headlights. When the guy in the other car came out, showing two big bags of drugs, he laid them on the ground. So, the man with the money went to look at the drugs to make sure it was what he wanted. That was when BeeBee jumped from the lumber pile and shot the man, then Micky quickly fired at the other two men, getting one while BeeBee got the other man. I was surprised to see those men fall so quickly.

I didn't think those guys were that good of shooters. They both got out of their hiding places and went to see if those men they shot were really dead or not. That was when Lon showed up in front of them. I stood still to see what was taking place when Lon shot both of them point blank, like I thought he would do in the first place. I had the feeling he would try a double-cross. I watched him go for the money when I got behind him, and never once did he turn to look for me. I thought that was kind of odd. I supposed he was too busy going for the money that he just plain forgot about me.

"I guess you want it all, huh?" I yelled out. "Drop the gun or try your luck!" I told him while watching his every move.

He stood there for a second, then he whirled around, firing his gun, hitting me in the left arm, when he must have slipped and fallen backwards, but he was still shooting at me. I fell to the ground and rolled to dodge his bullets. When his gun was finally out of bullets, he got up, looking at me, saying don't shoot when he quickly fell to the ground again, taking out another gun out, when I shot him before he could shoot again. I looked at him as he lay there on the ground, then I checked BeeBee and Micky knowing three more rats wouldn't put drugs out on the streets again. Besides the other three guys lying on the ground, it made it six rats.

I put the money in one of the cars, but the drugs, I opened the bags and threw the white stuff in the water that was close to me. I drove the car at regular speed so as not to get stopped as I smoked a cigar and drove as though it was a Sunday drive. I left the car a block away from my hotel and counted the money on my bed. I knew it was a half-million at least. I checked my arm, seeing it wasn't too bad, so I put three bandages over the wound.

Early the next morning, I went to the bus station with the money in a suitcase. I sent it to my friend Ward, then I got to a telephone and called Ward, telling him to use the money to build my house with. Ward had a friend that was a builder. I told him I might have a wife to go home with sometime soon.

By eight o'clock that morning, I stopped for Darlene and we went to breakfast. I told her about the night before as she listened and would look at me wondering if it was true or not. It wasn't more than a few minutes later when the news came on the radio, saying there was a drug fight at the lumberyard by the docks last night, leaving six men dead. I took some coffee and smiled, looking at her.

"Okay, I believe you," she said, smiling, then she laughed.

As we walked out to the car, I asked, "Where is that trust we are supposed to have? I bet you thought I was having fun with other women, huh? Come on, that's what you were thinking."

She laughed getting in the car. I had to smile watching her laugh with that sly look she gave me at times.

I drove to the mansion, where Darlene was greeted like she was their older sister or something, and Leo took her hand and kissed it. He would even show his teeth, thinking he was smiling. He was reminding her she had to be back there for Friday night's job.

The same night Lenny and I were to meet those guys that shot at us. I watched Leo leave as his men followed him. Maybe he did think he was some kind of God.

I went to the bar seeing a new bartender there; he said his name was Sidney. He was a young man with a mild manner about him. But at the same time, he gave me the impression of being tough and tried to show it like some men did at times. He was slender with red hair. He also looked younger than he really was.

Darlene and I walked out the back door, where the yacht was. She was quiet as we walked in the sand along the shore.

"Something wrong?" I asked.

"I don't know, Steve, but I have this strange feeling that I never had before. I never worried about being shot, and since I've been shot I feel so unsafe. I don't have the guts or the will to go on now. I know I can be killed like anyone else," she told me in a low voice that seemed a little strained.

I took her in my arms. "We both can be killed anytime or anywhere, but you want to find those guys you been looking for that killed your mom and dad. I will watch for you as long as I can, but we should just get the hell out this damn place," I told her.

She kissed me, saying she had to stay and see this through, being a little stubborn about it.

We walked in the warm air as the light breeze moved her red hair that shined in the sunlight. I marveled at her shining beautiful eyes as they looked at me, showing the loveliness of her whole being.

She looked at me, saying, "You're looking at me, why? Do I show how scared I am?"

I smiled, putting my arm around her shoulder as we walked on. "I always look at you, I keep thinking I'm dreaming. I wonder at times if you're real when I look at you, a beautiful lady with something missing, like maybe a crown. You're beautiful as a queen, my dear, and I love you with all my heart," I told her as we walked for a while, then I said, "I can lose you, my dear; the time will come when you or I might be killed if we keep going like we are."

She went silent as the waves came rolling in softly, with the seagulls flying overhead.

"If something happens to you, it would kill me too. I'm part of you now, and you're so obsessed with finding those killers. I doubt very much if your parents would want you to pursue this. They're up there with God now. If God didn't want them there with him, he would have left them right here on earth. They're safe now, so live your life before it's too late," I tried to make her understand.

She turned around and hugged me, then asked, "Will you always love me, Steve?"

"Yes, my dear, until my last day on earth," I told her.

We walked in silence holding hands, and once in a while she would rub her cheek with my hand and she'd stop and stare across the bay. Then she'd look at me, and at times her face would go blank with no expression, as she seemed to be searching the horizon, like she was looking for some kind of answers. Maybe she was thinking about what I said, or maybe we could just go and get away from this charade, before it was too late.

Darlene asked about the three men that Lenny and I were supposed to kill Friday night. "They'll be killed, won't they, Steve?"

"Yes, I'm sure they will certainly die. If I know Lenny, he can't wait to use his gun again; that's something he likes to do," I told her.

She turned to me again, saying, "Maybe we can try something else, like getting rid of these people. We can make things happen, can't we?" She smiled, looking at me.

"Well, it's just a thought, but I know a man just across the border of New Jersey. He always wanted me to join his gang—he's as bad as Leo is, Steve. He runs drugs and many other things. Sam Luchin is his name and he hates Leo. Maybe if we got them to fight each other they might just kill each other off, and maybe we could leave this place, our job will be done."

We sat on a log that was washed up on shore.

"Are you trying to get rid of all the rats on earth?" I asked.

"No, all I want is to quit knowing I got rid of some of them. They know us, Steve, and they will find us no matter where we go," she said, looking at me.

"Okay, I buy that, what you got in mind?" I asked.

"I'd like to talk to Sam if he still wants me to join him. You got any money on you, Steve? I mean a lot of money?" she asked with that sly look on her face.

"Well, I got about four thousand on me, why?" I asked. "What's going on in that pretty head of yours?"

"I thought if you played poker with his men while I talked to Sam, in the same time you can look around as you play poker. Maybe you could find a way to take them. I was thinking if we make it look like Leo's men attacked Sam, then maybe Sam will attack Leo." She smiled, then she laughed.

"Something funny?" I asked.

"Yes, why I asked you if you have a lot of money is because you'll need it. They play for keeps, and they will take all the money you have, and fast; you won't have a chance with them. But I need time with Sam, so at least stay in the game long enough so I can do that," she said, then she started to laugh again.

"Very funny. I'll have you know I'm not too bad at cards. How do you know I'm not some card shark?"

She laughed as we went back to the car. "I like being with you, Steve, you make me laugh. You, a card shark, sure you are," and she laughed again. "Come, my big, strong card player," and still continued to laugh.

We drove over the bridge into New Jersy and turned toward the Bayonne Bay. Sam's place was close to the water like Leo's mansion was. He had a yacht that was bigger than Leo's, but the house looked like it needed a lot of work.

The guards smiled when they saw Darlene and greeted her like she was their long-lost sister or something. Sam took her hand and kissed it like it was made of gold, eyeing me at the same time when his guards took my gun. Darlene told Sam I was her bodyguard and wanted to come by and talk like old times.

"Well, it's been a long time, but all that matters is you're here, Darlene."

Sam looked at me again, saying he missed her.

"Sam, I'd like to talk with you, and do you think Steve could play poker with your men for a while?" she asked.

"It's his funeral. He said if he's got money, go in that door, tell them to let you play," he told me as I looked at Darlene.

She had a smile on like I was being led to the slaughter.

I watched Sam as he and Darlene left me. He was a tall man with a little bend in his shoulders, like he was hurt some time ago. His hair was black, dark eyes, and a little too skinny. I turned and went in the other room, where the men were playing poker.

"Sam said it was okay to come in, mind if I play? I have money."

They looked at me like who cares when a mean-looking man looked at me, saying, "I'm Del, George, Ben, Org, and Whitney."

I sat down, putting my money on the table as the men looked on. I felt like they already thought my money was already in their pockets.

We played for an hour or so as my money was disappearing. Whatever I had in my hand, it seemed they had a better hand. I couldn't see them cheating, but nevertheless I never won. I held my cards close to me so no one could see what I had.

I looked around as they raised the pot until it got to me. I was looking at my hand now to see four tens looking at me, so I asked for one card and raised the pot with all I had in front of me. They all called and for once I won. I even won several games after that, until I had about ten thousand dollars in front of me. Then I got a bigger surprise; for the first time in my life I had a royal flush. I had never seen a royal flush before. I put all my money in the pot, saying I bet everything I have. They looked at me, then they looked at each other, putting their money in slowly, with that look of wonder on their faces if they should or not.

I was feeling the tension building up as they stared at me. I put my cards down as they all looked and showed their distaste, or should I say their hate? Sam and Darlene came in as I was picking up all the money I won. Darlene looked at me, seeing all the money I had, and she smiled, saying we had to leave.

I got up, saying, "Sorry, guys, I hate to leave when I'm ahead, but I'll be back. Maybe you will win it all back," as they gave me a dirty look.

Sam laughed, saying, "Anytime, Steve, if you can beat these mugs then you can play anytime." He laughed again.

About a mile away, I commented that it was like taking candy away from babies. Darlene looked at me, saying I was just lucky.

"Yeah, I guess I was, but I got fifty thousand from them. I suppose it's enough to buy us a meal now and then," I told her.

She smiled, asking if I noticed the girl that was bringing the drinks to us.

"Yes, I did see her. I felt bad for her, the way they treated her, and the way she was dressed and look scared. She's Del's girl and she's terrified of him," I told Darlene.

It was late that evening, so by the time we got to Darlene's apartment I kissed her and was about to leave when she asked me to stay with her. She put her arms around me, saying for me to stay.

"I don't want you to leave, Steve. I don't want to be alone anymore," she said while she was still hugging me.

"Okay, but you know my mother warned me about you women. You should be ashamed luring a nice man like me to your apartment."

She laughed, saying, "Your mother said no such thing," and laughed again. "You made that up."

I had to laugh myself seeing the expression on her face.

We talked for while about many things as we got ready to go to bed. She still had some pain on her right side where she got shot. When she took her dress off, I saw the big bandage she had. She said she had to see the doctor in two more days for him to check her wound. When I touched the bandage, she jumped.

"Still tender, huh? I shouldn't be with you, Darlene. I don't want to hurt you," I told her.

"It bothers me some, but it's getting better," she said and kissed me, then we got in bed. It was wonderful to be with her as we drifted off to sleep.

It was raining the next morning, and it was a terrible day. Darlene told me that Sam had an important meeting all that day and late that night in Texas. He'd be gone long enough for us to get things started between him and Leo.

"You think we could go back to Sam's place and start things moving? I'd like to get that girl away from there. Any ideas?" she asked, looking at me.

"Yeah, I only have a gun, and they have many more guns and more men. Now if I had some dynamite, I could even the odds lot better," I told her.

"I know a place that sells it; they sell anything you want and everything you need," Darlene explained.

We went to a place on the side street from the main road, under a big red-brick building. She was right about having everything I needed. I got some dynamite and an automatic thirty- eight with another clip. I gave the guy two thousand dollars and told him to remember me, I might need more.

I asked Darlene, "Why is it that these people are right in the city selling guns and ammo to anyone that goes there? Why haven't the police stopped them? If they don't, I will."

She explained that the police were watching them; they arrested the ones that bought that stuff, that way they knew who all the thugs were in the city.

I told her I would check it later. "If they don't close that place, I will do it myself."

"I believe you would, but take it easy, Steve; the police know what they're doing," she said.

"No, they don't!" I told her, and I went on to say, "It's too dangerous with all that dynamite they have there. Some time or another it will go off and blow the other buildings that's around there. Young people will buy guns, and you know what they will do with them."

Darlene looked at me and said no more.

We got to the car and started for Sam's place, when Darlene said she would be safer when I got rid of the dynamite; she was afraid it would go off. I told her it had to be lit first, so it was safe and not to worry.

I turned to look at her, saying, "You don't have to worry, my dear; you're safe with me, honey," then I put my hand on her leg.

She looked at me, then at my hand on her leg. "I'm safe, huh? Yeah, I'm safe."

I had to laugh as she lit a cigarette.

We were close to Sam's place now so I pulled over by a big tree, then I looked at her. "Are you ready for this, honey? This is no kids' pray, you know. I got this new thirty-eight, it's loaded and ready for you, and take the extra clip in case you might need it."

I watched her, knowing she was a little nervous, but she was ready. She wanted to get Sam and Leo to fight, and maybe they would annihilate each other, and maybe again, just maybe that would be the time for us to get away.

"Steve, I've never been happier than I am right now. Being with you is wonderful. I never thought I would ever fall in love, but I did and here we are, ready to do a job together, and you know, I'm not worried about it because you're with me." She smiled and kissed me on the cheek, asking, "What would you be doing if we never met? I wonder about that at times," she said, looking at me, waiting for some kind of answer. But before I could answer, she asked, "Why do you love me, Steve?"

I wondered why she'd ask me that.

Then she said, "I just like to know," in her soft voice.

"Well, your first question was about if we never met. I believe we would have met somewhere, and somehow I would have found you, because it was you I was looking for. Why do I love you? There are many reasons why. Your eyes that sparkle when you look at me, your pretty face, your attitude and personality you have. But most of all, it's the way you make me happy, just being with you. What you just said a while ago. You're not afraid to go on this job, because I was with you. You couldn't have made me any happier or proud," I told her and kissed her.

She didn't say anything but sat close to me as the rain came down harder now.

The wind was blowing the rain against the car windows. The sky was dark with a heavy overcast and getting colder now, but we didn't care about the storm because it was warm inside our car. Before we left for Sam's place, we went over the plan we agreed on before. We knew what we had to do.

I looked at her, asking, "You ready, gun slinger?"

She laughed and nodded. "I'm ready, my dear, I'm with you," she said as I lit a cigar. I'd use it to light the dynamite with.

I drove to Sam's place and when the guards came to us, Darlene told them we were there to play more poker. They just said, "Don't let them take your money, Steve." I laughed about that. If they only knew what was going to happen there in just a few minutes from now.

Inside, Darlene went to the office, where another guard was.

I went to the game room, opening the door just enough to see how many men were there. I counted the same five men I played with before. I lit the dynamite and threw it into the room, then ran to the other room, throwing another stick of dynamite in there, and ran like hell out of there. I ran to the bathroom, down the hall at the end of the building, to get under cover.

The shattering blast blew the walls apart, with a terrible rumbling noise. I checked the rooms before leaving to make sure they were dead. I ran out to see where Darlene was, and a second later or so she came running with the girl behind her. I yelled out, "Let's go!"

Just then the two outside guards came running toward us, then both of us shot them. Darlene ran with the girl behind her, but the girl was crying so hard and scared to death. She was slowing her down and holding Darlene back, until Darlene grabbed the girl and ran fast to the car. I stayed behind so I could throw the last stick of dynamite into the back shed. It blew up as I ran for the car.

Darlene was driving and drove out like a bullet, going around the corner on two wheels. "Slow down, honey. I'd hate to die like this, you and Lenny just laugh in the face of death, huh?" She laughed, saying she could handle it.

"Yeah, but I can't; the scenery is rushing by so fast, I can't light my cigar," I told her.

She laughed again, looking at me, then she slowed down. She told me to give the girl a thousand dollars so the girl could take the bus home.

It was over an hour later when we got to Darlene's apartment and freshened up and changed clothes. We put the money we got from Sam's place under the bed and went to the restaurant. Ben, our waiter, had our table ready, along with a rose by Darlene's glass of wine.

"I knew you would come tonight. I wanted you to have the same table by the window, so you could see the stars and the moon when it comes out."

When Ben left we took a drink of wine, then I smiled, looking at Darlene.

"I'm proud of you. I liked the way you acted at Sam's place. You were quick and professional."

"I know," she said and laughed.

"Yeah, just like a gun slinger," I told her as we got up to dance.

She commented on how Ben took care of things so perfectly, like a pro at what he did.

We sat down when Ben came with our food. Darlene asked if he did this with his wife, like he did at the restaurant. Ben looked at her and smiled. He was a black man with white hair and along in his years.

"My lady, if you have something good, then you do whatever it takes to keep it. Sometimes it isn't enough, but you do your best anyway."

Darlene smiled as he walked away. "Nice man, isn't he?" she commented.

It was around ten o'clock that night as we walked from the restaurant to the street. I wanted to see Lenny, to see his face when he heard about Sam being hit.

"What you think, honey?" I asked.

"Good idea, Steve. You know something? We make a good team, don't we? Just like Lenny says to you." She smiled, squeezing my hand.

"Yes, we do, honey," I told her.

As we walked, she said, "Ben said a nice thing about doing for someone you care for. You say nice things to me, Steve. I wish I knew the words to say how much I love you."

"You do, my dear lady, you say it in everything you do. You don't need words for that; you say it by the way you look at me, the way you talk and act, how you hold me and kiss me. You say it in actions, and that means a lot," I told her.

We got to the Coachman's Bar and asked the girl bartender if Lenny was coming in. She said she didn't know. I told her who we were, and we got drinks and talked for a while. Darlene asked me why I came to New York, I told her I came to get away for a while. I told her about my wife and what happened. I also told her how I felt about women, because of my wife.

"But something happened to me, Darlene. I found a lady, a special lady. I found you, my dear. I hope you are as happy as I am."

She smiled and kissed me. "I am happy, Steve."

We left there an hour later and went back to her apartment. I lay there in bed, thinking about my job for the next night. Darlene had to see the doctor to take off her bandage to see how it was healing, and I had to meet with Lenny in the morning.

By eight the next morning, Lenny and Tom were waiting for me at the Coachman's Bar. Just before we were to leave, the phone rang.

Lenny's eyes got big while looking at me as he put the phone down. "Damn! Holy shit! Hell, man! Sam got hit last night! His place got blown up! Eight of his men dead! Now Sam thinks Leo did it, and Leo thinks Sam will hit him."

We drove for the mansion to see Leo. He was there all worked up. He wanted us to have some kind of plan to hit Sam, before his men hit us. Lenny told Leo we would after we took care of the three guys we had to kill that night.

I told Lenny we should go take a look at Sam's place, we had the time. We got in the car and drove over to Sam's place, seeing all the damage that was done. Lenny said whoever did that knew what they were doing. We noticed Sam moved to the other building that was close by. Yes, his place was destroyed, because the house was old and weak; it didn't take much to blow that old rotten wood.

We drove back to the mansion to see Leo. We went over the layout of Sam's new place, thinking when we should hit him.

"I think we should hit him in the early morning, maybe a little before sunup," I told him, but Lenny thought it would be best at night so we wouldn't be seen by anyone.

"One thing about that, Lenny, they can get away in the darkness. In the morning before they get out of bed, we'll have them cold; they won't know what hit them," I explained to him and to Leo as Leo watched us plan this thing out.

Leo was smoking his cigar and chewing it at the same time. When Leo looked at me for a second or so, he told me to do the job, he liked the way I was going to do it. "It's your baby, Steve," Leo told me.

Lenny dropped me off at my hotel early that afternoon.

I made sure I strapped my small gun to my ankle, and my other gun in my belt fully loaded. By five o'clock I picked Darlene up and went to dinner. We talked about what we had to do that night. I noticed she was a little edgy, but I didn't say anything. By seven-thirty I took her to where she had to meet her partners for some fur job. I waited for Lenny and Tom at the mansion smoking a cigar and talking to Sidney, the bartender at the bar. After a few minutes, they came in with worried looks on their faces.

"Something wrong?" I asked. "You guys worried about tonight? It will be okay," I told them as I smoked my cigar.

"It's not us I'm worried about, Steve; it's Darlene! We found out we got a stoolie at the police station, and the cops are waiting for Darlene and the others at the warehouse," he said, looking nervous and his face looking somewhat flushed.

I looked at them as I yelled out, moving toward the door, "Let's go! We can get her out of there!" I yelled out louder as I kept going for the door.

"Hold it!" Lenny yelled to me. "It's too late! The cops are already there, we have to wait it out. She went through this before, Steve. She knows what to do, and besides, we got a job to do. So, let's do it," he said nervously, showing a redness in his face.

"I can't let her get caught, Lenny, I'll go alone."

"I know Darlene, Steve; she's been through this before!" he yelled out.

"So let her do her thing. Come on, let us go do our thing tonight, okay, buddy?"

I gave in but reluctantly; she was more important to me than our damn job.

I worried all the time we drove to the gravel pit for our rendezvous with three cops that shot the bar up and almost killed Darlene and me. My heart was heavy, and I couldn't think straight on what we had to do that night.

We got to the gravel pit just as the sun was going down, with the darkness slowly coming on. Lenny hid in the tall grass to the right of an old shack. Tom was on the left side of the shack as I stayed behind, along the side of the road in the tall grass. It wasn't long before I heard a car coming toward me, and then it went by me. I wanted them to be in front of me, in case something went wrong, because I'd be behind them in case they tried to get away. I crawled slowly though the tall grass as they stopped their car. I was just getting close to them as the men got out of their car and looked around. That was when Lenny stepped out of his hiding place and fired at them while he was laughing like some crazy madman. Tom shot a man trying to get back into his car. When the third man ducked behind the car, he rolled under the car and shot Tom in the shoulder. Tom fell to his knees in front of the car, holding his hand to his shoulder, then Lenny ran to the side of the car looking for the third man, but he couldn't see him because of the tall grass. From where I was, I could see the man taking aim at Tom, then I quickly got up and ran closer to get a better shot at the man, and I shot him just before he had the chance to shoot again. The man never knew I was there behind him.

All this took only minutes to do that job. The men that shot us at the COACHMAN'S BAR were now dead! I was hoping they were the same men that killed Darlene's parents, but how would we know that? Maybe now she might consider quitting this and going home with me.

Lenny and I helped Tom to the car, then I put a towel that was in the back seat over his wound to stop it from bleeding. He would be okay until we got him to the doctor. Lenny handed me the bottle that was under the seat as he drove from there.

I took a drink and handed it to Tom. "Take a long drink, and relax now; you'll be okay, Tom," I told him.

I lit a cigar as my mind went crazy wondering about Darlene as I took a drink. I was thinking what if she got caught or maybe killed as I handed the bottle to Lenny. I noticed Lenny looking at me at times, and I supposed he knew I was worried also.

"It'll be okay, I know it will. You did a good job back there; we got rid of those bastards!" Lenny was telling me, but I wasn't listening; I was too worried and nervous about the woman I loved that was in danger.

Finally, we got to the mansion, and maybe now I'd find out some answers there. Maybe someone would know what was going on.

I got to the bar, where Leo and Sidney were waiting for word, but there wasn't any. Leo looked at me, nodding his head from side to side. It wasn't Darlene he was thinking of and being worried about; it was his deal for the contraband he was going to lose out on. I got a fresh cigar and a shot of scotch, then I walked out to where the yacht was tied to the dock. I walked alongside it, then I walked along the shore, where the waves came up over the sand. I looked out over the bay and beyond, where it went into the Atlantic Ocean. I was now looking out to the horizon, but I could see nothing; it was my mind going wild. I turned to see if she was with me, but I knew different; it was only me wishing. Then I thought I heard her voice, but it was only the wind and the waves I was hearing. I walked on as I smoked my cigar when I heard her voice again.

I turned to see her behind me when she ran to me and hugged me. I held her tightly, making sure it was really her I was holding in my arms.

We walked that night in the warm summer air, with the stars all across the sky. The moon was just coming out to show the beads of light upon the ocean waves as they came rolling in to shore. We held hands as we walked, bringing back the time we did this same thing before, when she left the hospital. That was when we really got to know each other, that also tied us together for all time to come.

She rubbed my hand to her cheek when she said, "Lenny told me you wanted to go after me, Steve. He said you almost ruined the job you went to do. I have to tell you something, I tell the police where to go and when, that's how I get them caught. They know I help them and so they won't ever expose me. Don't worry about me, okay, my dear?" She stopped and kissed me and went on, saying, "Tony got killed, Greg got it in the leg, and I helped him back to the mansion. Stan got shot by trying to shoot it out with the cops."

It was a surprise to me that she was telling the police about our jobs, then I stopped as I looked at her, saying, "I didn't know it was you giving the police the information. Lenny told me there was an informer at the police station, and I got worried. Another thing, Lenny said a guy was working at the police station for Leo. He tells Leo everything that happens there, so be careful he doesn't find you out," not only being concerned but very worried.

We walked back in silence until she stopped and looked at me.

"Worried, huh?"

"Thanks, Steve, I'm good at what I do. I trust you, so trust me too," she told me and hugged me.

"I love you, honey," she said in her soft way. She smiled as we got in the car and headed for the city.

I put the car in the garage when she asked if I'd like to go to a bar she knew. It was a friend of hers that she would like to see. She ran the place and it had been a while since she had seen her.

We walked two blocks to the place. I met Liz, her friend. She was a nice lady in her early thirties and had a good sense of humor, and I liked her. I watched them talking as I noticed they thought a lot of each other. We had a drink as I listened to them reminiscing about their old days.

Liz had to wait on some customers when Darlene looked at me and smiled. Liz had dark hair and was built like every line was in place. Her personality was on the quiet side, but she seemed to be happy and smiling. I liked the way she talked and listened; she was a lot like Darlene and every bit a lady.

Darlene asked, "Remember when you told me how it was when you're in love? You said it was wonderful, and at times it was hard. Well, it is, Steve," she said while looking at her glass. Then she took a drink when I told her she was getting drunk. She smiled and took another drink. "Yup! I'm getting drunk. I love you, Steve, and it's wonderful, but it's hard," she said again. "I worry about you, what if something happened to you?" She took another drink when I told her she was too young and beautiful to be drinking that rotten stuff. She looked at me, saying, "You're right, but I'm drinking it anyway," as she wavered unsteadily.

I had to laugh; she was funny. I told Liz to call us a cab, then Liz came to her, saying, "You're cut off. You've had enough."

That night I had to help her to bed. A few seconds later she asked me to love her. I was surprised to hear that. I waited a long time to hear those words.

"Love me, Steve. I don't want this to end until we leave this world," she said, hugging me.

The next morning I awoke with her kissing me, then she went in the bathroom, calling out in her usually soft voice. "You took advantage of me, Steve. I was defenseless and you did things to me."

I had to laugh as I got up, saying, "You told me to love you and I did, now you say I took advantage of you. That's not being fair," as she came out with a towel over her. "You naked under that?" I asked.

She looked at me and answered, "Yup!"

"Have you no shame?" I asked her.

"Nope! Not since I've been with you," she answered and sat down close to me and hugged me. Then in a serious tone of voice, she asked, "Why don't we get away from here? You wanted to before, why can't we go now? I want us to be like we are now, Steve. I don't ever want this to change, my love." Then in a low voice, she said, "Before something happens to us."

I wanted to say "Yes, let's go," but I couldn't. It was too late now; they would find us no matter where we went. "We're in too deep now, honey, and we know too much, you know that. We have to finish what we started, and then and only then we can leave this place."

She knew I was right, and as we got up to leave she patted my rear and laughed, getting red in the face. She looked me, saying, "I used to be innocent. It's your fault for taking advantage of me, Steve Mire; you corrupted me."

I looked at her. "Will I hear this all my life?" I asked as she laughed and answered.

"Yup! You probably will."

We sat in a restaurant that was close by, then I told her I had to use the bathroom and to order for us. I went out to the florist next door, telling the girl there to send flowers of different kinds to Darlene's apartment. I told her where to send them and I wanted them sent right away. In a short time later, we went back to her apartment. Inside were the flowers of all colors, in a big, beautiful vase on top her dresser, in front of her large mirror.

She looked at me, then hugged me. "I never know what you're going to do next, do I?" she asked. "Let's go to the shore and forget everything, Steve. It's Saturday and there's nothing else to do," she said

So, we drove toward Coney Island that rainy, cool morning. I stopped close to the water and just sat there in the car as the rain came down heavy at times. We talked about many things, like what we'd like to do after all this was over, if it ever got over. I told her about my place by the Adirondack Mountains, in the upper-northern part of New York State.

"I have some land I bought a long time ago I thought someday I would build a house there. It's a place of peace and serenity, where nature and beauty is everywhere, it's God's world. The place where my friend Ward and I go fishing and hunting. Where the birds and animals roam around freely. A land of beauty and tranquility, truly a land of paradise," I told her as I began to feel how much I was missing it.

Darlene looked at me and smiled just listening to me, then she asked, "Are you adding just a little to this?" She laughed and listened again about a place that seemed too good to be true.

I went on telling her about my place I was now longing for. I held her hand as I went on telling her about that place of mine. "There's a lake full of fish that at times jump out of the water, that's pure and clean, and how it glistens in the sun and the moon. There's this mountain just beyond the lake that towers over all. It looks down, making sure that all is as it should be, safe and protected. At times when you look up at it, you seem to feel within you, like it's saying 'You're safe now; I will watch over you for as long as you are here.'"

The rain stopped now as we got out, taking our shoes off and walking along the shore in the water, with the waves slowly hitting against our legs in the warm breeze. We talked about many things as time went by, being oblivious of anyone around us. It seemed like we were the only people there. It was a great day for the two of us, but it went by so quickly. By six that evening, we had a light dinner and ended up at the bar where her friend worked.

I noticed the name on the front windows that read "THE WALK-IN BAR." It was quiet there with a few people in the place. We had a drink when Miles and his wife came in.

Miles introduced his wife to me as Iris. She was an attractive blonde with a great shape and personality. We talked about the world as though we were old friends for many years. Miles got a call from the police department, so they said they would be back later. Darlene told me they liked me. I kind of liked that because I liked them too; they seemed to be nice people.

When Darlene left for the bathroom I thought about Miles, and what did he think of me? He must've wondered why I was still there, and I wondered how Darlene was giving information to the police without letting them know she was in the gang herself. Was she a stoolie? At times Miles made me feel uncomfortable by the way he looked at me. He must've known what I was doing there in the organization, but he said nothing. If he knew Darlene like he said he did, he must've known what in hell she did there.

Miles came back by himself. He looked at me and then at Darlene, announcing that the big brick building was raided. That was the place where Darlene and I got the dynamite and the new gun.

All the stuff that was there was sent to the military, where it was originally taken from in the first place. So, my wish was granted. I was hoping the police would close that place, and they finally did.

Miles left us when Liz asked if we would stay until she closed the bar at one o'clock the next morning. She hated to leave the bar alone at such a late hour. I told her we would stay, so by one o'clock we walked with her to her car that was parked in the back of the bar. It was very dark back there; I told Liz she should get someone to put some lights to show the parking area.

Just as we got to her car, two men came at us. They yelled for us to drop our money on the ground, wallets and handbags. I slowly put my hand to my gun I had in my belt and waited until the men got closer to us. The biggest man yelled out again, telling us to do what they told us before. That was when I saw one of the men pointing his gun at Liz while the other man was walking closer to me. That was when the man closer to me yelled out, telling his partner to shoot us or he would. At that time I fired, killing that man, to my surprise I saw Liz shooting the other man.

"Let's go!" Liz told us as we got into her car and drove away from there. She told us it was better not to get involved with telling the police about this, because it would expose us to those that were friends of those guys we shot and maybe they might try killing us later, when we didn't expect it.

Darlene agreed as I went along with it. Liz left us at the hotel and went on home like nothing happened.

In bed Darlene asked if I was nervous going to the Coachman's Bar again. I told her it was strange at first because of being shot there, but it was just an isolated incident and I doubted it would ever happen again. I was just going to sleep when a loud banging on our door made me jump.

I got up, opening the door, seeing Lenny there with eyes as big as saucers, looking like a train ran over him.

"Damn, Lenny! You drunk?" I asked him.

"Ya better come, Steve; Leo got hit a while ago and he's mad as hell. They sunk the yacht and killed three of our guys. It has to be that bastard Sam!" he yelled out excitedly.

"Okay, Lenny, be with you in a minute."

Darlene looked at me but said nothing. Soon we were on our way to Leo's when I lit a cigar thinking about all this. One good thing, three more rats were dead, I was thinking.

"Lenny, you think we should call Guns? We need some dynamite and some more ammo for our guns. I think you should get rid of Guns as soon as you can. But make sure he brings everything we need," I pressed upon him.

"Ya saying you want me to kill the bastard Steve?" he asked, looking at me.

"I mean just that! Think about it! He brings us dynamite and he hears that Sam's place gets blown to bits, huh? Think about it, Lenny, he'll tell anyone about it and it might be someone we don't want to hear."

I knew Lenny would think my way and besides, I wanted Guns put out of business. He sold to anyone that had the money to buy his deadly products of death and destruction.

Lenny looked at me again, blowing smoke from his mouth and in agreement of what I just said to him.

"Right, Steve, he'd blab his stupid head off. I'll take care of it."

We drove on for a few minutes, then he turned to me again, saying, "You know something, I found out the other day how Guns and his partner got all that ammo they got stored away. About a year ago, seven trucks loaded with that stuff was on the way to the Army Reserves warehouse. On the way Guns and his guys hijacked the trucks. After the trucks were unloaded, Guns had his men take the trucks into the woods and hide them. After that Guns told his men to shoot those truck drivers and buried them near the trucks. The trucks were found by some hunters just a month ago. Since then, they made a shitload of money. They had a good thing going, but like you said, Steve, we can't trust him."

I smiled hearing that. *Look who's saying something about trust,* I was thinking. Now there was one guy I'd never trust at any time.

It was two in the morning when we got to Leo's at the mansion. Lenny made the call to Gus for the ammo. I told Leo what Lenny and I planned for Gus and he agreed, then Leo turned to me saying I was in charge of making the hit on Sam. Lenny didn't care; it was okay with him. I told the men what to do, then Leo told us he would be out of town when we hit Sam's place. He'd be with friends until all this was over. He explained it would better because that way the police wouldn't think he wasn't involved with the hit. But that was his way of thinking. I was sure the police would have some idea of his involvement of some kind, anyway.

It wasn't long after when Gus came with the supplies we asked for. I watched Lenny take Gus to the office to pay him off when I heard a shot fired, then there was a yell and Gus hitting the floor with a thud, which all of us heard.

Another rat dead! Lenny came out telling the men to get rid of the body. I knew it was a job Lenny liked to do; he enjoyed killing. He never showed the sadistic side of him until he was actually doing a killing. He seemed to snap and become another person of cruelty of some kind.

I picked out four men to learn how to use the dynamite. I wanted one man on each side of Sam's house by a window so they could light the fuse, then break the window and throw the dynamite in and run like hell for their cars and go back to the mansion. But I told them to wait until it was five o'clock, then throw the dynamite in the windows.

Chapter Two

I figured Lenny, Tom and I should stay behind to make sure they were all dead. I had fishing gear put in Lenny's car so we could be fishing down the road after we got through with Sam. I figured after the blast from the dynamite we'd have just time enough to be fishing in case any police came around.

It was almost time now for the men to throw the dynamite into the windows, as I checked the gun I had in my belt, along with my small gun strapped to my ankle.

In the cool darkness, we waited by some trees close to the house in the silence of that early morning. We could see the sky just beginning to brighten.

That was when I sent the four men to do their jobs. A few minutes later, the house rocked and trembled as the shattering thunder echoed the terrible sound like bombs bursting, which ended the silence of a slumbering neighborhood that early morning. It was a loud, devastating blast that could be heard for miles around.

The men were gone now as we made our check of what was left of that house. As we looked around, we knew nothing could live through such an overwhelming, crushing and savage explosion. The three of us started for the car when a man came running from the direction of the water and shooting at us. He was shooting wildly as we hit the ground and fired back. He was hit a few times before falling backwards to the ground and still shooting, but then he lay there, looking up at the sky but not seeing anything. I recognized the man as I stood over him. He was no threat to anyone now; his days of killing and terrorizing were now over for Sam. The big man that Leo was worried about, Leo's biggest enemy, gone to meet the fires of hell. Another undesirable that our law enforcement could check off their list. How much better off we'd be without that scum and all of his kind!

But as far as the law was concerned, we'd be put in jail for doing what we just did. You'd think we'd get a medal for it. We were not supposed to kill murderers and drug pushers, no, they took them to jail, where they were living better than many people in our country could afford.

Killers that should be executed, but no, again they live for the rest of their lives being taken care of better than people that work and strive for a living, paying taxes and doing what's right. The sooner we got rid of those types of people, the better we all would be. Yes, we had some of our laws that stunk! Some of our lawyers made a lot of money on that kind of people, and in many cases the law protected those rats and the lawyers also. Now don't that make sense? The sooner we got rid of that kind of vermin, the sooner we could live without fear. But that was my outlook on that stupid subject, and maybe change some of our laws. Maybe it would save a lot of money that this county needed to save this country.

We drove down the road along the shore and set up our fishing poles to look like we had been there for some time fishing, then I got a beer and a cigar and sat down. Now we were ready if the police came by checking on the blast the dynamite made. In case the police were close by, we wouldn't have a chance to get away from there. But by making it look like we were fishing like being fishermen, we had a chance.

It was only minutes later when a police car stopped with cops asking, "You guys there! You been there long?"

"All night, sir!" I yelled back, when one of the cops got out of the cruiser, asking, "Didn't you guys hear that explosion up the road?"

"Yeah, we heard some noises, but we didn't think much about it, sir," Lenny told him.

The cops left as we fished for a while until things simmered down. It was an hour later when we figured it was time enough to get started, so we slowly drove by the house we blew up when a policeman stepped out, holding his hand up for us to stop. We noticed the police were stopping all cars and checking everyone. They asked many questions, but I told them we were fishing all night just up the road, then I asked, "What happened, Officer, they have a gas leak or something?" Like looking innocently and the good citizen I was.

"I don't really know but all inside are dead. Some poor guy over there got shot up like it was target practice," the cop explained.

I told the cop that some other cop stopped us where we were fishing just a while ago. The cop smiled and told us to go on.

We left there with the sigh of relief, then I took the bottle of scotch Lenny had under the seat and took a drink. I needed something to stop my heart from pounding; it felt like it was leaving my body.

I lit a cigar and relaxed for a minute or so before saying anything. "It went pretty well, didn't it?" I asked.

"Yeah, it did, Steve, we don't have to worry about Sam now, and someday we have to get rid of Leo! I want to take over," Lenny remarked before taking a drink of scotch.

It was now nine-thirty before we got to the mansion. Darlene was there sitting at the bar, waiting for me and looking worried. Tom told her Sam was killed, with bullets hitting him and he was still coming at us. Lenny told me he had to see me later because we had a job to do.

Darlene and I left in a car she rented for the day, and after we got down the road she asked, "Are you going to tell what happened?"

I lit my cigar and looked at her. "Oh! I didn't think you were interested. It was just some little thing we had to do."

She looked at me, being somewhat irritated. "One of these days, Steve Mire, I'm going to give you one of these." She showed me her fist.

I had to laugh at the way she was looking at me. "My dear lady, you know something? You are so sweet and so nice to me, you want to give me so many nice things."

She laughed, then told me I was crazy when she stopped at the restaurant for breakfast. While we ate, I told her about the job we did. I also told her about Guns and the supplies he brought to us. Then Darlene talked about Guns being a threat to people and how he sold guns to anyone and he should be taken care of like Sam was. She was so worried about it by the sound of her voice.

I looked at her, saying, "Honey, he's a nice man trying make a living, and he wouldn't do anything underhanded like that, Darlene." I waited for her reaction when she looked at me disgustedly.

"You are crazy! You're a lunatic! Why didn't I see that before!"

I took her hand before she said anything else; I could see she was getting upset. I quickly told her Guns was dead. "Yeah, honey, Lenny shot him before we went over to Sam's place. I was only kidding with you, my dear, calm down. I don't want you to blow up; it would mess up your nice red hair," I told her.

"I still say you are crazy, Steve."

We got up to leave when I put my arm around her. I told her, "It's okay, I still love her even though she says bad things to me."

She laughed as she drove to the mansion. I told her to meet me at midnight because I'd need a ride, she said I should walk.

I looked at her. "You bully, you."

She laughed and drove off.

Lenny drove in saying to get in the car and telling me he had to make another stop, to pick Aldo up along the way; he had a job he'd tell us about. He smiled talking about what we did that morning. He said, "Leo will be pleased to know what we did when he gets back from his meeting that evening."

We stopped as Aldo got in. I noticed how dirty he was and how he looked like a bum, and I could smell him too. The body odor was overwhelming. I lit a cigar quickly to helped me breathe easier. He was a big man with curly hair that wasn't combed or clean. His dark eyes were always looking like they were always staring. He was also a nervous man who always looked around as if someone was behind him. He started to tell us about the job when Lenny told him to hurry it up, we didn't have all day.

"Look, you son of a bitch! You got a rotten damn mouth!" he yelled at Lenny. "I don't like to get shit on, Lenny, you no-good bastard!" Aldo lit a cigar, then went on and looked at me while telling us about the job he had for that night.

"Now, Morty will be with us. We have to meet a guy on a yacht with the money for the cocaine. We row out to the yacht in a small boat to make the exchange, those guys on the yacht will watch every move we make, so my plan is to get rid of Morty and you take his place, Lenny. I made a deal with Leo for a hundred thousand for my take." Aldo puffed on his cigar as Lenny looked at him.

"You get well paid, don't you?" Lenny remarked coldly and changed the subject quickly when Aldo gave Lenny a nasty look of hate.

We talked about how we'd do that job and took Aldo back to where we picked him up.

We went back to that bay again, where the yacht was. Lenny was thinking on some other way to do this job. I knew he had something else in mind. He looked at me and asked if I could swim. I said I could swim and why? I asked. He pointed to the yacht, saying, "That far?" pointing at the yacht again.

"Okay, what you got on your mind, Lenny?" I asked.

Lenny threw his cigarette away, saying, "You swim to the back of the yacht and take those guys there by surprise, and we get it all. I take care of Aldo, Leo needs this stuff; he's low on money and drugs," Lenny explained.

We started back to the mansion as I thought about my gun in the water. I'd have to put it in a plastic bag to keep it dry. Also, I'd bring along a stick of dynamite just in case.

We got back to the mansion by the bay when Marie asked me if the job would go okay. I nodded it should go alright as I got a drink and walked out. She followed me out with a cigarette in her mouth and a drink in her hand. We walked along the shore in the soft breeze with the evening just getting dark. She was a great-looking woman all dressed up, and the perfume I could smell, that was special just for her; it also had a good smell to it.

She stopped taking a drink and a puff on her cigarette, then asked me a tough question. "I know you were going with Darlene, Steve, but is it serious? I mean, do you really want her? Or maybe you just go with her at times. You know what I mean," she stumbled on as she took a cigarette from her case when I held a light for her.

"As you know, Marie, we got shot in Lenny's place. That's how I got to know her; we go out now and then, but so far that's all we do. Why?" I asked.

"You know how I feel about you. I want you to go with me. Leo told me he wants you to climb in our organization; he thinks a lot of you and wants you to take over his place and very soon, and I personally want you to take his place also," she explained, looking at me.

"Sounds good to me, Marie, but as you know Lenny is looking forward to that position; he's looking to take over and he said so. He tells me all the time; in fact, every day he tells me."

"Forget it, he never will; the boss won't have it. Besides, the men will all quit, no, Lenny has no chance in the world." She puffed on her cigarette, then blew out the smoke. She smiled and kissed me and in a low, sexy voice she said, "We can go a long ways together, Steve, you and me." She took another puff on her cigarette, looking at me again. "I know what happens here and who to be careful of. I can show you things that will make big money for us, Steve. There's no telling how far we can go if only we work together."

I smiled as I looked at her, saying maybe when the time came I would think about it, but right now we were not sure of anything. We got back to the mansion, where Lenny was waiting for me.

I went in the bathroom and got a plastic bag. I put my gun and the dynamite in with my lighter. I then tied the bag inside my pants.

We drove to the bay, where the yacht was. I figured it was about two hundred yards away from the shore. I took my shoes off and dove into the water. It was cold at first but in a little while it didn't feel so bad. It was dark as I swam toward the lights from the yacht that was guiding me to it. I swam as quietly as I could so as not to attract any attention to anyone on the yacht. I was three-quarters of the way when I saw the rowboat with Lenny and Aldo making their way to the front of the yacht. I finally got to the rear of the yacht, and I climbed up slowly as the rowboat got to the front ladder of the yacht. I hurried to get the dynamite and my gun out of the plastic bag and waited for Lenny to make his move. He fired, killing one of the men that was standing there waiting for them to come on the yacht. I shot the other man, then Lenny turned to Aldo and shot him, then he pushed him into the water. Another man was coming up from inside the cabin below when I saw him just in time, before he could shoot Lenny.

It was then Lenny told me to run the yacht to shore. I waited for Lenny to get far enough at a safe distance before I threw the dynamite down below deck. I dove off the yacht and swam as fast as I could, but I was still too close for comfort when the yacht blew up into a fireball, with the debris falling all around me. I noticed some debris fell pretty close to Lenny in the rowboat. I took my time getting back to shore. I made it to shore, seeing Lenny there waiting for me, and I got out of the water acting like I was in a daze because of the explosion. Lenny helped me to the car as I tried making it look like I was hurt. I asked Lenny what in hell happened.

"I was just starting the motor when all of a sudden I was thrown from the yacht and found myself in the water." Lenny got me a cigar and a drink from the new bottle of scotch. I noticed Lenny was pretty nervous about the yacht being blown up.

All the drugs went up with it and I was happy about that; I wasn't going to let Leo have them. I looked at Lenny, trying to make him believe it was some kind of accident.

"It must have been a bullet that maybe hit the gas tank, or maybe some wires got shorted out, making the yacht blow up like it did. You know, Lenny, with all the shooting going on, it could have been a bullet that hit the motor somewhere, but who knows?"

"Ya! Damn, Steve, Leo will be mad as hell not getting the drugs, but anyway, we got the money," he said, looking like he was having a heart attack by worrying so much.

Darlene was waiting for me at the mansion. She drove back to her apartment as I told her what happened. She commented on the drugs that went into the water. She was happy about that. It wasn't long after we got to bed, she went to sleep almost as soon as she hit the pillow. I was tired but I couldn't sleep; I felt uneasy that night, so I sat by the window looking out at the big sky above. I was remembering the times Ward and I went fishing and hunting. I could see in my mind the lake and the mountain as I was now feeling the loneliness coming on. I wanted to go back there where I felt good, and thinking how great it would be to have Darlene see this wonderful place I had within the woods I called my paradise.

Darlene got up sometime later and sat by me. "Can't sleep, huh? You know, Steve, you've done a lot since you've been here. You got rid of many rotten people, and not to mention all the drugs you destroyed, it's remarkable. You got rid of Sam that the police could not; because of the smart people he knew in high places, he always got away with it for some reason or another. Now Leo is next and it has to be done, Steve. But not you, because you've done enough." She kissed me on the cheek and put her arm around me.

I pointed to the sky. "Look up there, honey. I wonder if God is looking down on us and seeing what's going on here in his world. He must cry seeing us hurting and killing one another, like we certainly and deliberately are doing, and we don't seem to care about it either. We don't care about anything or even the consequences of our actions that will come later. He sees us ruining and destroying the very land he created for us to live in, and the sad thing about it is that it isn't even ours. It's here for us to use and to take care of it. Yes, honey, I got rid of many rotten people, but was it right?

"I wanted so much to make it safer for people to live without fear, to live in a world like God meant it to be. What about me, am I the same as those I killed?

Will he forgive me for what I have done, and am still doing? But how in hell can I just let those rotten people go on and kill, or ruin the lives of so many?

"I can't do that, honey. I can't just turn away and let that kind of people do whatever they want to. I feel like I need to stop them wherever they are, right or wrong. We go to war to kill those that are killing innocent people, we get a medal for it, but isn't that wrong also? So where do we draw the line as when and why we kill? And where do our laws say we cannot kill those that kill others?"

I took a drink from the bottle I had in the dresser.

"I was sitting here thinking about my place up north of here, Darlene. How wonderful it would be to be there right now, for once in our lives to be able to say 'Thanks, God, for what you have given us.'"

Darlene sat close to me, listening to what I was saying.

"I guess with all I've done since I've been there in the city of New York, it was starting to get to me. I felt hurt and guilty by all this. I want us to have a home someday. I want you to live with me at my place. It's so beautiful there, honey. I never had anyone to share it with until now, my love, but by the way we're going we might never make it there," I told her.

Darlene leaned her head against my shoulder and said, in her usual soft voice, "It's me, Steve, being in the organization and wanting to find those guys that killed my parents I'm looking for, you wouldn't have done what you did. I'm sorry, dear, I'm very sorry. I love you so much. Don't let anything happen to us." Her voice was low and shaky as tears started to fall. I felt bad for her for feeling that way.

"It isn't because of you, honey; I wanted to be with you, wherever you went. I wanted to make sure you were safe, and besides, I wanted to be near you always. But being with Lenny and the gang and seeing what they were doing made me want to help in some way to get rid of them.

"It's when I'm with Lenny and saw the kind of animals that we have to contend with. The things our police have put up with. They're supposed to bring the rats in and are frustrated to see them back on the streets again. I see them taking in but the rats just laugh in the cops' faces when they get out, like it's all a joke. The police go out putting their lives on the line to get them locked up. Many are out in days after or even in an hour or so, they are out on the streets again. How in hell do you think our police feel seeing that happen after they work so hard to bring them in? No wonder some cops and even myself that go out being like vigilantes. I don't blame them a bit; we should have more of them. Our attorneys and judges are to blame, by letting the bad guys go free when they shouldn't. Some of our laws that protect the rats more than the innocent. Sometimes people don't attend meetings and vote the wrong people out when they should. It would stop a lot of things that go on are to blame. So, you see, it's not one group or certain ones; it's these things combined. So, I'm doing what I have to, no matter what. Soon we'll get Leo and then we can leave this rotten, miserable place."

I pointed out the window. It was starting to get light outside; the sun was just making its way up. It surprised us to know that we were there all night, how time flies by when we are together. We went to breakfast, seeing Lenny already there; he smiled seeing us going in the restaurant.

"You two are early. I couldn't sleep either. I got something to say. First, I want Steve by my side. I'm getting rid of Leo! I'll run the organization! I know I'll have to get rid of his loyal men, but I'll take care of that," he blurted out as he looked at both of us.

"What about the big boss, Lenny?" Darlene asked.

"There's no big boss! Leo is it! I know how to get him killed," he said like he really believed in what he was doing, and that was that; his mind was already made up.

I watched him talk, and the more I watched the more he looked like a maniac or a nut on the loose. Darlene said if there was a big boss it might not be the right thing to kill Leo, because the big boss might have other ideas, but Lenny wouldn't listen to that; his mind was already made up.

Darlene went back to her apartment as Lenny and I drove toward the mansion, but on the way there Lenny said we had to get rid of three cops that worked for Leo. He didn't want to have them around when he took over the organization.

We picked Tom up and drove to the place where the cops were supposed to be. Lenny stopped by a cottage, seeing a boathouse a hundred feet away from the cottage, when Lenny said there was an underground passageway from the cottage to the open bay. He told us about the drugs that were dropped in the bay with heavy weights tied to them. At night the bad cops would use their underwater gear and swim out to the drugs that were dropped by some ships. They had a line that went out to the drugs that they followed so they wouldn't get lost.

"What you think, Steve? We have to be in that tunnel by ten tomorrow night; that's when the men get the drugs from the bay to some unknown place."

We drove away from there as I thought about it. One thing I knew, they had to have a man inside watching while the three men were in the water getting the drugs. But we didn't know how many men they'd have there. I also knew we could not do that job alone, without more men.

"We need more men, Lenny, and another thing, we have to find a way in without being seen. If just one man there sees us, then it's all over, my friend. They must have men inside the tunnel, I would think, wouldn't you?" I asked.

"Yeah, you're right, Steve, okay. I have two men in mind, now how do we get inside?" he asked.

I looked at him and smiled; I had no idea how. "You had to ask, huh?" I remarked. "I don't really know, Lenny, but we'll see when the time comes."

We got back to the mansion and went over the plan such as it was, but it was the only one we had. We had a drink at the bar when I asked Lenny if he took care of Guns' partner.

"Glad you asked, Steve, son of bitch, I forgot. I'll take care of it. He must be wondering where Gus is, huh?"

"Yeah! I would guess so, Lenny. You know something, Lenny, don't you think we should go see him now, and at the same time take what we need for ammo, then blow that place up? I don't like kids buying guns. What do you think, Lenny?" I asked.

"Okay with me, Steve; we'll do that right now."

He drove to an old road going to the marshy area where a big brick building was built partly in the marsh backwater by a small inlet from the bay. The building was very old, made with brick and stones many years ago. Lenny greeted the man that was Guns' partner like they were old friends, but soon after Lenny hit him and held him up in case someone else was there in the building.

We pushed the man under a large counter, where he was hidden from sight. We quickly grabbed boxes of shells for our guns and some dynamite and put the stuff in the car when two men came to us from behind the building.

"Where's Sandy?" one of the men asked. "He was here a minute ago!"

"We didn't see anyone here, my friend. We needed some things and took what we wanted. Tell us how much and we'll pay you," Lenny told him.

When the men got closer we both fired, hitting them in the chest with our silencers. But not before Lenny got hit in the arm, but not enough to make it bleed. We made sure no one else was around and set fire to the paper and boxes and put some dynamite in one box, then we ran out of there before the place blew up. With all dynamite and bullets along with the gunpowder, we ran like hell.

The place went up in a big fireball and a minute later it blew up, sending all kinds of shit in the air. We didn't stay to see it fall to the ground completely destroyed. But I would think it would be completely destroyed because of all the ammo and dynamite that was there. I looked at Lenny, telling him we did a great job getting rid of that place. Lenny smiled as he lit his cigarette.

When I got back to Darlene's apartment, she was waiting for me to go to dinner. I told her about making sure that place Guns had wouldn't be in business anymore. Then I made the mistake we needed more help on the next job we had.

"I want to go, Steve, I want to be on this job," she insisted.

I looked at her, saying it was out of the question. She pouted and said she'd talk to Lenny about this. That got me a little irritated, but I took a deep breath and let it go. I was having a bad feeling on that job, and I certainly didn't want her to be in danger. I felt like she would be if she went with us.

We went to dinner and danced like we did before and thinking she'd bring it up again, to go with us, but she didn't. Instead, she was quiet and somewhat cool. It was now midnight before we got to her place. I shut off the lights and sat by the window looking out. I wanted to go over this job in my mind to see if I could minimize any of the dangers we were up against. Darlene sat beside me and put her head on my shoulder.

I turned to look at her, asking, "Did I hear something about bed? Or was it sex I heard?"

She laughed. "No, you didn't," she answered with a giggle. "I want to talk to you, and you are going to listen!" she said, sitting up.

"I always listen to you, but be careful now; I have tender ears, you know," I told her.

She giggled, saying, "That place of yours sounds so wonderful. I was thinking about it today; I hope we can go there. I can picture it in my mind and I want to see it, Steve." She put her head on my shoulder again, and in her soft voice she said, "I love you, always love me, Steve; don't be angry or upset with me," and hugged me.

Chapter Three

"You know, my dear, I had that in mind," I told her as we went to bed.

I stayed awake for quite some time that night. I worried about what was coming, and I wondered if I would be the one to get hurt or killed. For an hour or so I thought of many ways to get inside that cottage without being seen. But I'd see only a blind alley. I was thinking now, was I getting a warning or some omen? Whatever it was, it was scaring the hell out of me.

The next morning came with the rain coming down hard with the wind blowing in all directions. I could hear the rain hit the building and the windows. The thunder sounded very loud as the lightning hit close by, like a major storm was going on. Darlene looked out and then went in the bathroom. She came out saying she was going to ask Lenny about the job. She wanted to go with us; she felt that she could help us, and also she felt that I just didn't want her to go. I told her I was against it because something was wrong about this job, and I could feel it. I told her if Lenny said it was okay, then it was okay by me. She wasn't listening how I felt; she figured it was only that I didn't want her with us. She didn't say anything more.

We went to breakfast with Lenny and Tom. It was getting like they were there every morning waiting for us. It was then she asked Lenny. She got a surprise to hear his answer, and so was I. He told her it would be a mistake if she went along, because we didn't know what was there or what to expect. It could be, for all we knew, a death trap for us all. She showed some redness and irritation when I kissed her on the cheek. She just sat there when we left.

On the way I told Lenny I was happy he told her what he did. I told them both how I felt about that job, because I was worried about it, something was going to happen, when they looked at me but said nothing more about it.

"I have Marty and Greg with us, Steve. I respect your feelings, Steve. You know, at times I get those feelings. I know what you are saying." Lenny related he had the same feelings many times in the past.

At the mansion Leo called for Lenny and Tom to his office as I took a walk on the beach. The air was warm with the waves moving over the waters and slowly hitting upon the shore, pushing the soft sand. I sat there looking out at the horizon like I did at times when I was alone. I wondered what was over there beyond all that water, was it like it was here? Or was it a better place? It was good to be alone to try quieting my nerves. I tried to shake this feeling I had but I couldn't. I knew now something could and would happen.

I lit a cigar as I noticed the wind was picking up as the waves were becoming higher and splashing against the shore and pushing the sand. I wondered if Darlene was still angry with me. Actually, it didn't matter if she was or not, because at least she would be safe.

I started to walk, still in deep thought, then I noticed the bay was calm and smooth, and the air was getting warmer with hardly any breeze now. I changed like the bay just changed, calm one minute and turbulent the next. I looked up seeing the clouds move across the endless sky, and far off in the distance a sailboat was slowly going out of sight beyond the horizon. I walked on when I heard a car stop up ahead; it was Darlene looking for me. I watched her as she walked toward me. I could see the sunshine on her hair with the breeze brushing against her as she walked, with the posture and dignity she always had. She asked what I was doing here. I told her I was thinking as she slowly walked with me.

"Lenny told me you were worried about tonight. You have a bad feeling that something might happen. I thought it was me, but it isn't, is it?" she asked, looking at me with some apprehensiveness about her.

"No, it's something I know will happen, it always does. It happened in Viet Nam and now it's happening again. There might be more than we can handle there," I told her as I took her arm and looked over the water. "Leo needs this job, not that I really care, but we have to make it look good, don't we? He has to have the money and the drugs for his organization. Leo told me that place he always wanted."

She turned to look at me and kissed me, saying she'd be waiting for me until I got back, no matter how late it was. Then she smiled, saying, "Be careful, my dear. I don't care about the organization! It's you I care about! I'll be waiting." She smiled and kissed me, saying, "I'll always wait for you, Steve."

I hugged her, then I kissed her and I watched her as she left. What a beautiful lady I had that loved me, what else could I ever ask for? I felt so fortunate and blessed.

Leo was waiting for me as I got back to the bar. "What you think, Steve?" he asked with a worried look. He had that concerned look about him. I knew it was that place he wanted, but he didn't care about how I felt about it. But in the same time, he looked like he was thinking that I was putting on with what I was feeling. He didn't believe in what I felt to be true; he thought it was all in my mind.

"We'll make it, Leo; we had trouble before and we came through. We'll do the same now; I know you need this stuff," I told him.

It was now two that afternoon when Lenny came in with Tom. He said he had to make a hit on some guys that were trying to muzzle in on our territory. They already killed three of our men and took a big score that belonged to Leo.

"Steve! We'll take Greg with us. We have to settle this before we go on our next job tonight," he said, looking a little disturbed about it.

So we got in the car and drove on, as he went on to say that Leo wanted this job done right! Leo didn't want anyone to go against him and get away with it.

Lenny looked at me, smiling, saying, "It won't be long now, Steve. Soon all this will be mine! You and me will take over!"

Lenny turned to the back seat, looking at Tom and Greg, then took the bottle of scotch that was under the seat. I lit a cigar as I thought about the deal Lenny was thinking about. He wanted Leo out of the way so bad, he couldn't wait.

It was about a half-hour later when Lenny stopped by an old building on a side street. It was very narrow with a car parked on one side. Lenny told Tom and Greg to go to the back door of the building as Lenny and I went to the front door. I felt for my gun in my belt, making sure it was still there. I had a funny feeling about this; it seemed like we were walking right in the middle of a trap.

"Hold it," I said. "Let Tom and Greg get to the back before getting ourselves into a trap; it looks too quiet here for some reason."

Lenny looked at me and nodded with a serious look, then he took his gun out as Tom and Greg went around of the corner of the place.

It was a minute or two later when Lenny kicked the door in and went in shooting with me behind him. We shot two men when Tom and Greg came in the back, shooting two more men. We went through the rooms, making sure no one else was there. I saw a man run from a bedroom to the hallway and out the window. I ran after him and as I got to the window, I saw him hiding in the shrubs alongside the building. I fired and missed him as he ran for the street. I had to shoot three times before I finally got him, but he couldn't run any further. We took all the drugs and the money we could find and got back to the mansion, where Leo was waiting for us.

"Good! You got those bastards! That will tell them others to see me before they can operate! I say if they can or not!" he said, looking at us, and then he took a straight shot of whiskey, then lit a cigar when we took another drink from Sidney at the bar as Leo got up, saying, "You guys make sure you get that place tonight! I need that place, I've always wanted it, and now we got the chance to take it. I'll be away when you guys hit that tunnel, so good luck!" He smiled and left.

Lenny nodded and took a drink as he turned to look at me. I knew what he was thinking; I had the feeling that Leo wasn't going to be around much longer.

We had another drink and went to a place for something to eat before going to the next job, which was very important to Leo. All the time I was eating, I was feeling something I felt a long time ago; it was in the war with Viet Nam. I knew then something would happen to me and my men. The same feeling weighing heavily on me now, and I couldn't shake it.

It was time now for the five of us to get on our way to the to the beach cottage that had the tunnel to the bay. I made sure we all had our silencers and plenty of ammo. By the next hour, we parked the car and walked slowly toward the cottage as we stayed behind the trees trying not to make any noise. We then made our way to our new assignment.

It was dark out, making it hard for anyone to see us walking to the cottage. I could see the lights were on in the cottage, but no guards were in sight that we could see. Lenny and Tom went to the back as Marty and Greg stayed behind until we found a way in. I got to the front door and tried the doorknob, but it was locked. I went behind the cottage, where Lenny found a window opened with only a screen, letting the warm air inside.

I motioned to Marty and Greg to come on. After we cut the screen, we made our way inside, making sure that room was empty. Lenny found a guy on the toilet, motioning to him to be very quiet. When the man came out pulling his pants up, I could see he was very nervous seeing us with our guns out and going into that place like we did, especially when it should have been guarded. But it never was guarded like it should have been. I thought it was going to be a lot harder getting in, but it seemed much too easy, so I worried about that also. I was thinking we might run into a trap somewhere in that place before long.

Lenny went ahead first with the man in front of him as a shield. Lenny checked one room, seeing two men playing cards when one of the men fired, hitting the man Lenny had for a shield. The two men fell after Lenny and Tom shot them, but not before those men fired back. Their guns had no silencers, making a lot of noise from their guns going off, and I knew now whoever was in the place would certainly know we were there. We had to be careful making our way to the tunnel now. I told Marty and Greg to check out the last room and to meet with us back in the tunnel. We opened the door to the cellar and went down the stairs slowly and cautiously.

There was another door to the right side of us that moved. I motioned to Lenny to kick the door open while Tom and I got ready to fire into the room. Lenny stood to the side and pushed the door in when two men fell in a hail of bullets.

Tom and I fired as quick as we could but before we went any further, I quickly reloaded my gun to be ready before going on.

It was quiet now as we made our way toward the tunnel. I could hear the water ahead of us. We saw no one along the tunnel as we walked and, keeping watch at all openings about five feet apart, we noticed dim lights along the wall. Lenny and I went along together while Tom was watching our backs from behind us. We continued on as quietly as we possibly could. We could hear the water more as we got closer to the boathouse at the water's edge.

Just then I could see a man's head behind one of the boats to the left side of us. He didn't seem to notice us entering as we got closer, but he surprised us when he jumped up and fired at us, making us dive for cover behind some boxes and ropes by the row of boats while we shot back. I kept shooting at the man to give Lenny a chance to get him from behind. It took a few minutes for Lenny to finally shoot the man.

We got to the boathouse, seeing more boats tied up, but I couldn't see anyone else there. Then as I looked around looking for Tom, I heard a shot! Then I saw Tom fall to his knees when Lenny fired three times, killing the man that shot Tom in the back. I ran back to Tom as he held his stomach, but blood was starting to come from his mouth. I knew he didn't have much time left. I put my coat under his head after laying him down.

"We'll get you out, Tom, hang in there until we make sure no one else is here. I'm sorry, Tom," I said while seeing him slowly dying.

He looked at me, then closed his eyes. I felt bad for him. Why couldn't it have been Lenny instead? We checked the boats for anyone hiding in them, then we noticed three sets of clothing lying in a pile and we also knew that three men were picking up drugs somewhere out in the bay. We started back for Tom when a man from behind us told us to drop our guns and to turn around. I figured it was over for us too; we had no chance until we heard a shot behind us. The man fell as I turned around, seeing Tom drop his gun and go limp. It was over for him too, but he saved our lives with his last breath.

We went to see where Marty and Greg were; they should have been with us by now. We went back upstairs, going through the hallway to the bedrooms when we heard a groan like someone was in trouble. We took each side of the doorway as we put the lights on and quickly rolled on the floor to see anyone under the bed, but no one was there. We did the same routine for the last bedroom, seeing it was Marty lying on the floor trying to get up. He was shot in the shoulder and in the arm. We helped him up while he told us about Greg shooting him after he found a suitcase full of money, then he ran out with it. That surprised me because he did such a good job when he was with us that afternoon.

We took Marty to the car and went back for Tom, and as we got to the back of the cottage we saw someone running by the trees, so we followed and I noticed it was Greg trying to get away. We caught him and took him back to the car and tied him up. I laid him down in the back, where Marty held a gun on him.

We went back in the tunnel for Tom when we could hear someone talking at the far end of the tunnel. We got to the boats and watched the three men getting out of the water, taking their lung tanks off. They talked loudly, not knowing we were there. They were laughing and bragging how easy it was to take the money and drugs from the men out on the boats. They were the three cops that we came for. They took their air tanks off when one of the men ran for cover behind some coils of ropes. Lenny shot the man as he tried to run, then I shot at the man just standing there shooting as us wildly. Lenny looked around for the third man as the man stood up and shot me in the leg twice, making me fall as I tried to run around him. It felt like fire when I took my belt off and tied it around my leg to stop the bleeding, then I found a rag and tied it around the wound. The man was about to shoot me again, but I couldn't get under any cover quick enough, then Lenny shot him and yelled out to me if I was okay.

"Yeah! I'm okay!" I yelled back. "He got me in the leg! I'm over here, Lenny!"

He got to me, seeing me trying to get up. "You're hit! Come on, let me help you! Hell, man, use your other leg and help me," he laughed, looking at me and telling me what I told him before when he got shot in the leg.

"Very funny, get me out of here," I told him.

We got to the car when Marty yelled out, "Holy shit, Steve! Not you too! Let's get out of here! We'll all be killed! Tom was killed and I'm hurt, Steve's hurt and Greg is trying to get away with a suitcase full of damn money, what else will happen!" Marty went on, getting very excited.

"Steve, you can drive, huh? Go to the marches. I'll take the drugs in a boat and hide it until morning. You two need a doctor, get going, I'll see ya down the road!" Lenny yelled out as he ran back for the tunnel.

I lit a cigar and gave one to Marty. He tried to smile, saying he'd like to shoot Greg right then and there. I knew that and I couldn't blame him; he came close to being killed himself. Greg yelled out to let him go, he said, "Leo will kill him! He didn't mean to shoot Marty!" he yelled, almost crying, when Marty yelled back at him to shut up as Greg started to sob.

After picking Lenny up, Lenny asked Marty if he was doing okay, "and how is the cripple doing?" he asked, looking at me and laughing.

"Is this question-and-answering time?" I asked him.

He lit a cigarette and laughed again like he usually did.

I could feel my leg throb as I drove. I got to the mansion when Lenny called the guards to help us, then Leo looked at us as we got in, staring with a cigar in his mouth.

"What in hell happened?" he bellowed out at us. "And why is Greg all tied up?" he demanded as he stared at Greg.

Leo's face got red as his facial muscles could be seen.

Lenny pushed Greg to Leo, saying, "This son of a bitch tried to get away from us. He shot Marty because he found a suitcase full of money and tried to get away with it. He didn't care about us in the tunnel being shot at; he only thought about himself! He could have given us some help in the tunnel, but instead the bastard ran and left us. Tom got killed because he had no one to watch his back. Then Steve almost got killed by some guy who got behind us somehow, now if Greg done his job, all this shit would not have happened like it did!"

Leo looked at Greg as he took his gun out. Greg was too scared to say anything. Leo shot him without waiting for any reply or any excuses.

"I have no use for a lousy double-crosser," Leo remarked with a distorted face. "Steve, come to my office," he said, then told Lenny to give me a hand as Leo lit a cigar. He told Lenny to wait outside as I sat down in Leo's office. Leo looked at me, showing concern as he paced the floor.

"You knew something would happen." He puffed on his cigar, then went on. "You're hurt, Marty, hurt, and Tom is dead! I have a problem; Lenny is a good man to do small jobs, but to think things out or to plan things, no! He can't see beyond his ass. He's crazy, but he'll do what I tell him." Leo sat down and asked, "Could that job been done without all the bad luck?"

"Maybe, Leo; you know as well as I do things go wrong at times, even with the best planning. It was a simple job in a way, but I would have had more men, and the men I picked would have been the right men. Our backs would have been covered, as it was our backs were not covered. That's why Tom was killed, and it almost happened again to Lenny and me; our backs had no one to cover us. But although Greg did a good job when he was with us on the early job this afternoon, he surprised us both, Leo, I didn't think he was the greedy type."

Leo looked at me and commented on the feeling I had before we started that job. "I suppose you were right about that feeling you said you had. I never believed in such things before."

Leo puffed on his cigar again and let the smoke out and talked about Sam. "You planned that job, it went well, no problems. Lenny plans nothing and even if he did plan, he still bungles them. Okay, Steve, you get well, I'll talk to you later." Leo went out.

The doctor took care of me and got me some crutches. I went to the bar, where Lenny was waiting for me.

"Leo gave me hell, Steve," Lenny told me, looking very mad and disturbed.

"Well, don't feel so bad; he was mad at me for saying something bad might happen, and it did. You said you had those feelings yourself, Lenny. I can't help it if I feel things that won't go well."

"I know, Steve. I can't wait till I take over; I have to get rid of him," he went on. Then he took a drink and looked at me with wild eyes, saying, "I thought you were immortal! You never got hurt! I wondered who I was going around with, but you're human too. Now I can relax; you had me scared, ya know," he said, smiling, then he laughed and puffed on his cigarette, then said, "I thought you were supernatural or something."

Darlene came in when Lenny left. She asked if everything went well and before I could answer, she was looking at my leg and the crutches beside me.

"It's just a scratch," I told her.

"You were right, huh? Something did happen!"

The bartender handed her a drink as I told her that Tom got killed and Marty was shot. Leo shot Greg because he tried to get away with the money.

She looked at me and sat down. "You knew all this would happen?" she asked in wonder like Lenny was wondering. "I can't understand how," she remarked, looking at me again. She helped me up, saying, "Come on, old man, let me help you up," then she started to giggle.

I laughed at the look she gave me. She drove as I lit a cigar. I told her to stop by the marshes and to take out the can of gas she had in her trunk of her car and pour it over the boat Lenny hid in the bushes, then light it on fire so it would destroy all the drugs that boat was carrying.

We drove off slowly and watched the fire rising high into the night darkness. She looked at me, saying, "We're a great team. Another load of drugs that won't reach the streets. We got rid of a lot of drugs, Steve," she remarked, looking at me.

She drove as I smoked my cigar, and she'd look at me every now and then. I was about to take another puff when I thought about the cottage and the tunnel.

"Hold it, honey, we have to go back. We have to set fire to the cottage and the tunnel. Leo and Lenny will take over the place and buy and sell drugs there. I can still walk well enough to destroy that rotten cottage, as well as that tunnel."

Darlene turned the car around and in minutes we were back at the cottage. We then looked around, seeing no one was around the place, so we went into the tunnel and set fire to the boats and everything that was there. We set fire in the tunnel with a stick of dynamite close to the fire to give us time to get away before it went off. We went inside the cottage and set fire there, but before we left I threw my last stick of dynamite in the doorway and I tried to run from that place to the car, but it was hard to run with these crutches. So far there were no people around to see us leaving. We walked to the beach area, where we hid our car in the bushes. As we were leaving, we looked back toward the cottage, seeing it all in flames, then it blew up because of the dynamite I threw in the doorway, and the tunnel blew up, leaving an open trench.

As Darlene drove away, she lit a cigarette, saying, "That was exciting, Steve. I wish I could go along with you on more of these jobs; you know, we really do well together. Why don't you let me do this more often? I can help to watch your back like Tom did for you guys," she said, smiling as she drove on to her apartment.

"I'm not against it, honey; I just don't want you in any danger but like you said, maybe you can do more," I told her.

Back at Darlene's apartment, we took a shower and sat by the window and talked for a while, then she said, "I'm worried about you, Steve; you got hurt and almost killed," nervously taking my hand.

I told her we should go to my place in the woods; I had a week off and it was time to go. I wanted her to meet my friend Ward and his wife, Meggen. Darlene answered with excitement in her voice, saying she'd love to go.

We went to bed with a good feeling of leaving that big city; it would do us both good to get away for a while. She lay close to me, asking if my leg felt alright. I told her I felt great because I was with a lady I loved, and being close to her made me feel wonderful and the feeling I got just being close to her.

"Steve, remember you called me your queen? That was a nice thing to say."

"I remember, but why?" I asked.

"I remember things you say to me and things you do. I was thinking if anything happened to you, I'd have great memories. You gave me meaning to my life, someone to believe in and to love." She hugged me, saying, "Don't let anything happen, Steve, I couldn't take it. It was a terrible shock for me to see you with your leg all bandaged up; I thought it was a lot worse than it really was. It scared me."

"Go to sleep; we have a long trip to make tomorrow," I told her. I kissed her thinking how lucky I was finding such a lady like her.

It seemed we just went to sleep when we awoke with a loud banging at the door. I told Darlene to open the door as I held my gun ready. It was Lenny with a red face and eyes as big as saucers. I looked at the clock that said six o'clock that morning. He took the bottle of scotch I had on the dresser and swallowed two fast drinks from the bottle. I asked him if he ever went to bed.

"You won't believe what happened! Everything happens to me! The boat!" he said as he looked at Darlene. "I'm sorry, I'm so damn mad! Then Leo told me I couldn't do anything right!" Lenny took another drink as he staggered, putting the bottle back on the dresser. "Damn it, why does it all happen to me?" He bellowed out again, "The damn cottage and the tunnel destroyed! Someone saw us, Steve! We never saw anyone around except the ones we shot at!"

I got up, telling him to sit down and relax. "Now tell me, what in hell happened?" I asked him, trying to calm him down.

He lit a cigarette, saying someone torched the boat. "I hid the boat under some brush, no one could see it, that's all I know, Steve. Leo needed that boat, and he's so damn mad about it."

I looked at Lenny, saying as convincingly as I could, "Look, Lenny, if you think about it, I think it caught fire from a short in the motor or something like that. You said you covered the boat, so how can anyone see it? I think that's what happened. Tell Leo that and I think he'll believe you," I told him. "And Lenny, maybe someone saw us at the cottage, I don't know, but it's not our fault if anyone saw us, and what if someone did see you hide the boat and torch it? How can we help that, huh?"

Lenny left when Darlene looked at me, shaking her head.

"A short in the motor, how can you lie like that?" she asked when I just looked at her with a smile.

It was no use going back to bed so we got up, taking a few clothes in a suitcase for our trip north. We stopped at a restaurant and had something to eat before going on, and we got some coffee to take with us, then we were ready for our long ride to the country where I came from. I was excited myself as got in the car.

Chapter Four

Ever since I met Darlene, I wanted to take her home with me, and finally she would get to see my place and also my friends that she would meet.

I was also thinking now about my friend Ward. We were friends for many years. I worked for him in construction, and he always helped me any time I needed help. Ward was much older than I; he was in his late forties, with black hair and a good build about him. He was a good-looking guy and never let anything bother him. He took life as is and never complained. He went with the flow and did the best he could to dissolve whatever came along. He liked to kid around, taking life as it came, and he never complained about what was dished out to him through the years. He just went with the flow and did the best he could. Like I said before, he always did what he could to dissolve whatever crisis came along.

His wife, Meggen, was a pretty lady with black hair and very trim. She was attractive with a great personality of a saint. They always got along even through the bad times. They loved each other and made sure of each other's needs. Seeing them together gave me the feeling of what couples should do and how to act, or how to trust each other. I watched them show a love for each other that brought them through many trying times.

We headed north on the New York throughway, with Darlene driving as I watched her expressions. She was seeing animals along the way that she never saw before in real life. The beautiful scenery of lakes and ponds, the woods and open fields of hay piled in the fields. The white fences that stretched for a mile or two that gave the landscape the beauty all its own. When she saw cows and horses roaming the countryside, that made her smile in appreciation of what she was seeing. All that was new to her because she lived in a big city, where some animals didn't live.

We stopped for food and drinks at times, and also for her to get the rest that she needed. I knew she was getting tired, but she drove the long hours enjoying being free and away from the city she knew all her life.

We pulled into the driveway as Ward and his wife Meggen came out. Ward smiled with a happy tone in his voice.

"Look who's here! Meggen, about time, Steve!" He was surprised to see Darlene as she got out of the car. "Who's this lovely lady?"

"Yes, it is about time, Steve. Your lady is beautiful, and very lovely, I must say."

Darlene smiled at the way Ward looked at her. Meggen introduced herself to Darlene as they went into the house.

We talked until it was time for dinner. We went to a restaurant and enjoyed being with Ward and his wife. I could see Darlene was impressed with my friends; she talked with them like she knew them for years. We told them about the job we had at the organization and the lieutenant and all. They would ask many questions that were hard to answer or explain, so we managed to tell them it was a job we had to do for the police and we couldn't tell everything.

It was around midnight when we got to bed. Darlene and Meggen stayed in one room as Ward and I were in the other room. I went to sleep with my leg throbbing, making it hard to sleep. I kept waking up every once in a while, all night. I awoke the next morning with the smell of bacon and eggs. I got up, maneuvering my crutches toward the kitchen. Darlene asked if my leg was doing okay. She looked at me with a smile.

"It's doing okay, honey," I told her.

After breakfast we got in Ward's car and drove to the place I had in the woods.

Ward turned to me, saying, "I saw how Darlene helped you into the car; it was like a mother helping her son."

Darlene laughed when Meggen told him to stop. I had to laugh myself; it was funny the way he said it.

"He'll never change, will he, Meggen?" I asked.

"No, Steve; he's always the same, a nut as usual," she said, looking at Darlene.

They left us at my place while they went on to theirs just a short way farther up. I showed Darlene where I marked the place for the house, then I pointed to the mountain that stood beyond the lake that was visible from the tops of the trees, towering over all that seemed to be keeping its vigil over the animals and the land that God put there.

"See how it watches us?" I asked, looking at her.

She smiled as we walked toward it through a small path that went by the lake, and then the path turned toward the mountain.

As we walked she saw a squirrel run up a tree, and I watched her face as a deer drank some water from the lake and went back into the woods. She took my hand when she saw a woodchuck crossing over the path. There were other animals that paid no attention to us. They felt safe as we did.

As we got closer to the lake, we saw fish that at times jumped out of the water as we walked by. Then the sunrays were shining through the trees on the lake, and the breeze rippled along the water.

Darlene's eyes shined with wonder as we got closer to the mountain, as it got bigger as we got closer. Standing there looking up, she put her arm over my shoulder and stared at it, saying softly how beautiful it was. Then she would look at me, saying, "This is what you meant, isn't it? If you listen, you can almost hear it talking. I look around and it's so quiet and peaceful, it's like you told me, Steve, you said peace and tranquility. I thought you were making it all up. It's like another world here." She turned around looking at the trees with a light breeze that whistled through the trees, making the branches move the leaves and making their own sounds through the forest. "Living in a big city, I don't see the real country and I don't see the real beauty in our world like I see it now." As we started back, she said in a low voice, almost in a whisper, "It's more than I ever imagined, such an enchanting place. The scenery and the colors, the beauty, no one can really capture like I'm seeing it. They couldn't capture the feeling I have at this very moment, Steve, my dear."

I watched her as she talked, then she would look at me and she'd smile.

"I know I'm acting a schoolgirl, but it's so lovely here. I wish with all my heart we will be able to come back to this wonderful country. Now I know why you feel like you do about this place. I understand now why you are happy here; I know that by the way you talk about it."

When we got back close to the road, I lost my footing in some branches that fell from the tree close by. I tried to walk over them but I fell, twisting my ankle as I tried to get my foot out from under the branches. The pain was unbearable. It hurt so bad, I couldn't move enough to free myself. It must have shown on my face, because Darlene got panicky and nervous not knowing what to do.

"Oh, Steve! Your leg! I can't help you!" she cried out. She became afraid seeing me there in pain.

"It's okay, just go down the path and get Ward. Go ahead now, I'm alright, my dear," I told her, but I wasn't alright. It was really hurting, and I knew I made it worse by walking on it so much.

She went on and she'd look back at times. I lit a cigar as I saw a squirrel run by me. It was about fifteen minutes later when they all came back. I thought back when Ward told me I shouldn't come here without him.

When he tried to help me up, he looked at me, shaking his head. Ward smelled my cigar, then pulled the cigar out of my mouth and threw it away. "Now that's nasty! It looks like a dog's turd, if you what I mean."

Darlene laughed, agreeing with Ward.

"Will you two just help me up?" I asked.

Ward got hold of me and as he pulled me up, he complained how heavy I was. "Eating well too, I see. Less eating and no cigars will help you get well."

Meggen and Darlene had to hold their mouths closed so's not to laugh.

"Thanks for the help, not to mention the remarks," I told them, and they busted out laughing.

Darlene hugged me, saying how mistreated I was.

Back at the house they fixed my leg, making it feel a little better, but it didn't look that well. It was swelled up, but it did feel better after it was taken care of.

From that afternoon on, we talked and enjoyed our visit. I knew it would be some time before we got back there. I was also wondering if we would get back. So far we were very lucky.

At eight o'clock the next morning, we were ready to leave when I remembered about the suitcase I sent Ward from New York.

"Ward, the suitcase I sent to you, can I see it?" I asked.

"Sure, I'll get it, Steve."

Ward went to the bedroom and came back with the big suitcase, then Darlene looked at me. She was wondering what was going on. I opened the suitcase and took some money from it to show them. Ward and Meggen stared at all that money with wide eyes and not moving as they just stood there.

"There's over a half-million there. Half of it is yours. But spend it easy, that way the neighbors won't be the wiser. The money came from the drug pushers, so enloy it. The other half is for Darlene and me. Ward, I would like you to have your friend build our house, if you don't mind. You know what I want, we talked about it a long time ago; in fact, you have the plans in your garage."

Chapter Five

"Maybe the house will be built by the time we get back here," I told him and Meggen that morning with a lot of excitement.

"It'll be ready, Steve, I'll see to it. My friend is a good man; he will do the job," he told me.

We left him and Meggen.

Darlene drove for a mile or so when she smiled, saying how she approved what I did for Ward and his wife Meggen.

"It was a nice thing you did giving that money to them, Steve. You made them happy, and I'm happy too; that was nice of you. You know, there's so many people that would just keep all that money for themselves. Meggen told me how you felt and how you sounded over the telephone when you called them about me being hurt. Ward and Meggen think a lot of you, I think you know that, Steve. And so do I, my dear. When Meggen told me that, I knew you were hurting as much as I was hurting. At the time I couldn't understand why you felt like you did, because you were hurting too. But you weren't concerned about your wounds; it was my wounds that bothered you. That wasn't all I couldn't understand, Steve; it was the fact that we just met, so how could you feel like you did about me? How could you be in love with me when we were together for about one hour? We had never seen each other before. But then, when you came to see me in the hospital like you did, I was slowly falling in love with you. I didn't notice it right then, but as you came more and more I felt like I was alone whenever you left me. It was a wonderful feeling to be wanted, and to be loved, because it was something I wasn't used to. When you came for me at the hospital, we went to the shore and walked along the water. That was when I really got to know about you, and I tried hard not to give into my feelings because I had a lot to do before thinking about going with anyone. But as we walked and talked about many things, I was noticing just how much you cared for me, and the way you looked at me. Also, it was the way you held my hand so tightly, as if you were afraid I would run away or something.

Then you said things about caring and how you were feeling about me. Not really by words alone but by the way you acted, and it seemed as though I could feel what you were feeling. I knew you wanted me, Steve, but I didn't want to give in, but when you told me the things you said, and when we went to dinner, and we danced, I couldn't help but to give in because I wanted you too. As I sat there in the hospital room by myself, I'd think about what the doctor told me about you. He said you were always there at my room, seeing how I was doing, so you see why I love you as I do; it's because you were there making sure I was safe."

I sat listening to her telling me all that, and it made me feel great to know she really did love me. She knew now that I would do anything for her. She knew why I stayed with her at the mansion, to help to keep her safe. She also knew I would certainly go to any lengths to help and to watch over her as I had been.

She drove back, making a few stops, heading south now, going to a place we'd rather not go to. But we had our job to do, and we knew we had no choice until it was over. I knew Darlene wanted to stop and turn around and go back to my place and to forget about that damned mansion. But she knew she couldn't do that either. We got back to her apartment late that night and slept like a baby till morning.

It was eight o'clock the next morning when Lenny was at the door. We told him what we did and asked if anything bad or good happened while we were gone. He said nothing much except the things that had to be done each day. Lenny asked if my leg was doing okay.

"Not great, Lenny, but if you need me, I can make it," I told him, and asked him about his leg when he said it healed up and it was okay. I looked at him, asking if there was something for us to do.

"Well, since you asked, I met a guy with a high-powered rifle that will kill Leo," then he took a puff on his cigarette and looked at us with his eyes wide and staring. "You know I want him out, Steve; this guy I hired said he could shoot him from a tree that's close by. I'll pick you up around seven o'clock in the morning and we'll go over it."

"Wait, Lenny, you got this guy to kill him tonight?" I asked.

"No, Steve, he's gonna do it tomorrow night why?"

I told him, "We should be at the mansion so we'll be seen by whoever is there. We don't want anyone to think we had anything to do with it, Lenny, just in case there really is a big boss."

"Right, Steve, I had that in mind," he said and left.

Darlene looked at me with a worried look about her. She said if he got caught he'd implicate me. I knew she was upset about this, so to take her mind off of it I asked if she'd like to go shopping.

She agreed as we took off all day, going into stores. We looked more than we bought. It was good to just let go and do what other people did. We had a good time going around the big city. We went to many stores, and we also stopped at a bar for a drink or two and had lunch. That evening we had dinner at some other elegant restaurant. She wanted to dance but I couldn't by the way my leg was. It was too bad, because the song they were playing she liked the most was called "MAKE THE WORLD GO AWAY." It was really what she wanted, for the world to go away; no, she didn't like this world with all the violence and trouble. It was my world she fell in love with, my place in the woods up there in the northern state of New York.

It was now midnight when we sat by the window with the lights off in her apartment, looking up at the stars that lit up the heavens that we liked to see, like we did so many times before. She had her arm around my shoulder as I could see the outline of her face, then I had to kiss her, then she said almost in a whisper, "It is so wrong in what we are doing, but we are in too deep now; there's nothing we can do about it now."

I didn't answer her because I knew that. I knew we had to finish our job in helping the police to get rid of these bad people that we had right here at the mansion. It was too late to just run and forget and to try and live our lives like nothing happened. These rotten people needed to be caught or killed, and it didn't matter which as far as I was concerned. We had enough of these people and enough of this kind of living! We wanted to live in peace and to be able to love and to give each other a good life, but it wasn't possible by the way we were going.

I left with Lenny the next morning, and we stopped for coffee. I knew he needed it more than I did. He drank all night, and I knew that by the way he talked and couldn't walk straight. He slurred his words and talked like he owned the organization already. That was the way he was thinking; he was already the boss. He told me the guy he hired was ready to shoot Leo at eight o'clock sharp that night.

"It will be easy, Steve. It's you and me, buddy! We make money for us! I have to show ya something before we go see Leo," he said as we got up to leave the coffee shop.

But just before we could leave, a big man came in staring at Lenny.

"You were supposed to pay me my money! And I want it right now!" he yelled out again in a rough, angry voice.

Lenny started to laugh in his face, then looked at me, saying, "You get nothing! You get shit! That's what you get! Now get the hell out and stay out of my way, you rotten cop! I hate cops!" Lenny yelled out loudly, making himself clear.

The man went for his gun when Lenny already had his gun out and ready, then it was all over. The man fell backwards and fell, among the customers sitting at the table. We left there in a hurry as he drove to THE COACHMAN'S BAR. He said the cop worked for Leo and anyone that would pay him for information. He went on saying he hated cops that sold themselves! He hated cops anyway, he told me, puffing on his cigarette. He also told me he was the cop that told Leo about what was going on at the police station.

We got to his office in the back of the bar. He had a book in his desk that showed the names and places and all the people that he killed or had killed since he was in the organization. I could not believe what I was looking at! He must know it would incriminate him; if the police got hold of that book, it was dynamite!

He smiled as he showed it to me. "If ever I get killed or caught, use this book to keep the business going, Steve. You take over and this book will help ya, okay?" He then went to the closet and took out a big box full of papers and half a million dollars in it. He said it was for expenses. He told me to take ten grand; he thought I could use it, but I already had a lot of money. He forgot he gave me ten thousand before, so I figured why not? He handed me the money when he stumbled, trying to keep from falling. I put the money in my pocket, then a girl came in looking like she was around sixteen years old.

"Hey, Lorie, this is Steve! He's my friend, and don't forget him! If he needs anything, get it for him!"

She looked at me and smiled, she said she would. I told Lorie that by tonight he would be the boss. She smiled, looking at him, saying she knew he could handle it. She kissed him and got us a drink. She got a drink for herself and downed it like it was water. Yes, she was just like him; they deserved each other. Lorie made us another drink, and again Lorie downed it quickly as I had to smile at that.

Lenny took another drink and looked at me. "Steve, you think there's a bigger boss than Leo?" he asked, looking dumb standing there and staring at me.

"I don't know for sure, Lenny, but what if there is, and the big boss don't like you killing Leo, then you better be careful, Lenny. What about me if they kill you, I'd be out of a job." I thought I'd tell him that; it made him feel important that he was the big guy. "There's another thing, Lenny, I hope you get rid of that guy after he kills Leo. He can finger you after you pay him. He could also talk, you know, maybe to the wrong people."

Lenny looked at Lorie. "See! He thinks all the time, that's why I need him."

Lorie smiled and kissed him as we went out.

We headed for the mansion as he took a drink every now and then; I didn't know how he could still drive drinking like he was and raving on about Leo's loyal men he had to get rid of. He went on about many things as I sat there hearing and watching him drink, and I knew the scotch was getting to him because it was dribbling down his chin and his neck, making him look like a bum on skid row. He wasn't the Lenny I knew. The Lenny I knew was always clean and dressed well. Now he was a drunken killer that couldn't wait to kill again. I was now thinking about that book he showed me, how would that help me if anything happened to Lenny? I couldn't understand that; the book showed how he killed people. It was really a diary that Lenny himself was guilty of killing people.

It was noontime now as we parked by the mansion. He was already drunk and unsteady. Leo went to a big meeting for the day; he wouldn't be back until six or seven o'clock. The back room had a game going on and Lenny got into it. I sat and watched until Marie came in asking me to take a walk with her.

"I see Lenny is drunk and it's only a little afternoon," she commented, looking disgusted.

"Yeah, he's nuts, Marie; the man drank all night right up to until now."

"I know," she said, and she looked at me, then she smiled. "I have something to tell you, Steve. Leo is going up and you are taking his place. He told me that this very morning."

I looked at her. I asked if she was making a joke.

"No joke, Steve. I know what's going on here, and I'm here to help. I need you to help me, Steve; it is a big organization, and the two of us together, we can go a long way. I told you that before," she said, looking at me with staring eyes.

"What about Lenny, Marie? He's ahead of me; he's been here a long time."

"The men have no say in it; the big boss will say who he wants, and I also have a say in who will be boss here in this place."

I looked at her and smiled. "You know something! Lenny will go nuts if he doesn't get it! He tells me how he will run this place, and he raves about it all the time. It wouldn't surprise me if he tries to kill Leo himself. By the way he talks about, it wouldn't surprise me a bit," I told her because I wanted to see her reaction.

"He can try but he will lose. How about dinner tonight?" she asked.

"I thought you'd never ask."

We walked along the water, watching the waves coming in and splashing over the sand, and slowly went back out to the bay with the breeze being very calm and warm that late afternoon. We walked together sharing small talk, then she changed the subject, talking about working together. I could smell her perfume she always had on, maybe it was her trademark or something. She also told me she wanted me to live with her after I took over the place. Actually, she was a little demanding and very persuasive in the way she told me about it.

We got back in the mansion when I heard Lenny yell out for a drink. I thought by now he would be passed out and lying on the floor.

We left for an early dinner and talked more about what she wanted to do. It was almost eight o'clock by the time we got back. Lenny was still drinking heavily like it was his birthday, and still enjoying it. We sat down when an old guy came in telling everyone that Leo was killed at eight o'clock. Like Lenny said Leo would die at that time. Marie told the guy to come over and repeat what he said. He said it was on the news, and it was repeated over and over. Then, Marie had the bartender put the news on, and news was being repeated over and over. The news said an underworld figure was shot through a window of his home. I looked over at Lenny as he was listening to the news. I could see he was having a hard time holding in the laughter. He waited a long time for this to happen. He was thinking he was the new boss now. Yes, I knew he was waiting to take over, and by the look on his face he was having a hard time having to wait, because he wanted to start right now.

I got up, taking my drink with me outside by the water. I wondered, what now? What would happen now that Leo was gone?

Not that I cared, but I certainly didn't want Lenny to take over in spite of what Marie said.

"I see you're taking it rather badly. You liked Leo, didn't you, Steve?" Marie remarked as she walked closer to me. "Well, he liked you too, that's why he wanted you, Steve."

"I know one thing, Marie, if he takes over, we'll all be killed! He's crazy, I'm sure you know that yourself," I told her, trying to get things going that would get rid of Lenny and maybe a few more of that bunch.

"Yes, I know that, Steve. I will have to make some changes now and I will talk more in a day or so. Let things go until I arrange a few changes around here. In the meantime, Steve, go easy and let Lenny think he's the big man for now."

We went back in the bar, seeing Lenny having another drink and smiling like he won. Yes, he won this round, but what would happen for the next round? I was wondering about that now. Marie left me there at the bar when I got another drink. I watched Lenny looking around the place like he was already in command.

He smiled when he looked at me and puffed on his cigarette. He yelled out, "Steve! Let's get out of here! I had enough, I need some sleep," he told me as we got in the car.

It was something, and I still couldn't believe how he could still drive like he never had a drink. I couldn't tell if he was drunk or not, except when he tried to talk he'd slur his words or blink his eyes, or say the same thing over and over.

On the way back to his bar he lit a cigarette, then looked at me, saying, "I got an idea, Steve, why don't we have some fun tonight? I know three places where we can raid! Let's take the money from these guys that Leo lets operate in our territory. They pay him in drugs and sometimes in money, just for the privilege to sell drugs to anyone that wants to buy it." He puffed on his cigarette, then said he wanted it all. "I don't want anyone selling drugs or operating in my town!" he said in a nasty tone of voice. "Let's pay one of them a visit tonight and put them out of business. Tomorrow we can take over the other two places. I want to get rid of all the loose ends before I take over the organization. What do you say, Steve, you with me?"

"Okay with me. I'm with you, Lenny, you know that. I told you before, you're the boss."

He smiled and puffed away on his cigarette. "We're gonna make a lot of money together."

It was eleven o'clock that night when we stopped at a house close to the waterfront. It was being used as a warehouse for boat parts. We parked alongside an old boat that was being repaired, so I stayed behind him and followed Lenny to the back of the old house with a dim light over the back door. He knocked twice when a man opened the door, letting us in. The man seemed to be irritated that we intruded on him at that hour of the night. The man looked at Lenny, saying he gave Leo the money the other day and he couldn't give any more. He said he had to make a living. I knew Lenny wasn't listening by the way he was acting. I knew then we were going to have a fight.

"I want it all, Chuck! The money, the drugs, and get it now!" Lenny told him in a demanding tone.

The man's eyes widened as he moved backwards, looking scared, then he looked toward the back door.

I knew someone was back there as I took my gun out, taking cover behind a big chair, which was about twelve feet from the back door. I saw the back door open slowly, then two men fired at us from the dark room. Lenny grabbed the man by the neck, holding him as a shield while shooting in the darkened room, but he couldn't see anyone because it was too dark. I always carried one stick of dynamite just in cases like this. I lit the dynamite with my cigar and threw it in the room, and waited for the walls to come down on us. Lenny saw me throw the dynamite and quickly dove behind the sofa for cover.

After the blast and debris quieted down, we didn't bother to check the men in the dark room; it was destroyed. As for the man Lenny held for a shield, he had no chance; he was dead instantly. We searched the place, getting all the drugs and money, and we ran out and got away in minutes. Lenny drove as I took the bottle of scotch from under the seat, and we both had a drink to quiet our nerves.

Lenny smiled, saying we got more than he thought was there, and laughed, saying, "This stuff will give us a start in our own business, and in the morning we'll get rid of the other two places." He was happy about that and I was too, because we got rid of more trash, and besides, Lenny was helping me do just that.

I got back to Darlene's apartment around one o'clock. She was in bed reading a book as I went in. She smiled, looking at me, saying she heard the news on the radio about Leo getting killed. She looked at me, asking, "What will happen now?"

"I don't really know, honey. I'm sure we'll know in a day or so, according to what Marie told me. She said there will be a meeting and they will decide who the new boss will be, and when all this will take place."

I told her about what we did and what Lenny was thinking. I also told her Lenny would not be the one picked for the new boss, and that was final, according to Marie. I didn't say anything about Marie wanting me to be picked for the job, not just now.

I took a shower and got in bed, saying, "Lenny and I will hit two more groups of drug pushers tomorrow. You know, honey, when the news came on saying Leo was killed, I watched Lenny by the bar looking around, and I wanted so badly to yell out he was the new boss. He was almost bursting inside to let us all know he was the big chief in command, but he held it in and drank more. Now that he is so sure he's the one that will run this place. He's getting rid of the places that belonged to Leo.

"On top of that, he's getting rid of all the cops that worked for Leo on the side, and those that took bribes. Look what he's doing for us, he's getting rid of the trash for us, and he doesn't even know it. He's a nice guy, isn't he?" I asked her when she laughed.

So, for the next day as far as I knew that was what we'd be doing; it would be late by the time we got back to the mansion.

"Well, you were busy, huh? Be careful, Steve; you know how crazy he is, okay?" she asked, and kissed me goodnight.

I was up early the next morning having coffee when Lenny came in sitting next to me, with eyes red and looking like death warmed over by not having any sleep. He told me he drank most of the night. He couldn't sleep because of thinking about the business and what he would do to make it better.

"We make a hell of a good team together, Steve! We work great together, my friend. I know there's a lot of money to be made, and I want to get more ammo and dynamite; we might need it before we're through today. You know, Steve, it was a good thing you had that dynamite with you last night; I couldn't see anything in that damn dark room," he said, smiling.

"We got extra clips for the automatics and ammo along with dynamite in your car trunk, Lenny. Remember, we put it there from that place we blew up?"

He nodded, saying he forgot.

Lenny drove to a crowded street in the neighborhood, just inside a low-income section of the city. Lenny stopped in front of a small store that sold candy and soda, but it was a front to sell drugs; they sold to the younger group. I saw several young people going in buying that stuff. A big man sat at a desk handing out small envelopes to the those that bought them, and another man taking in the money at the door. By the back door were two men that seemed to be guards, watching the transactions going on. They stood up and stared at us as we went in the place.

"Hey, Lenny!" the big man yelled out. "What you doing here? Leo got paid yesterday, my man."

The big man took a cigar and was about to light it when Lenny told him his operation was being shut down. The big man looked at Lenny with narrowing eyes and getting red in the face as he started to get up from his chair.

"Are you telling me I can't operate from here, or are you taking over now that Leo is dead?"

The big man just stared as he waited for Lenny to answer. I could see others there getting ready for action as the place fell into silence that was beginning to be deafening. Three kids were coming in when I put my arm up, telling them to get lost. I then looked around the place, not really liking the odds because there were four against the two of us.

I waited for things to start happening when Lenny smiled, saying, "No, old buddy, I just wanted to see how you guys were doing. I don't care about you operating here; it's your baby," he said, still smiling and lighting his cigarette.

I could see the men there started to relax after Lenny's little speech, but I wasn't convinced because I knew Lenny better than that. He just relaxed the tension until he could react, before they knew what was going on.

And sure enough, he whirled around and fired at the big man and the two men by the back door while I shot the man taking the money. That was the fastest gun play I ever saw Lenny do.

The kids outside there watching us ran for cover in all directions. We picked up what money and drugs we saw and drove away before the police came.

It was now close to noontime when Lenny drove to the New Jersey side just over the bridge. He turned to a side street and stopped. He was silent until he shut the motor off. He lit a cigarette and took his gun out, saying, “We better reload our guns before we go in that tavern over there across the street. I need a drink and a sandwich, Steve, then we’ll wait until one o’clock before we blow that place up. There’s a lady that works there, she goes home at that time. I don’t want her to get hurt, Steve. She was always good to me.” He took out another cigarette.

I was surprised to hear that; I didn’t think he cared about anyone in his life. He took me completely unaware that he would care about some woman working as a waitress.

After the guns were loaded, we took one stick of dynamite each and walked to the tavern. Inside we sat in a booth close to the back door.

The waitress came to us with a smile, asking why Lenny was away for so long and telling Lenny she hadn’t seen him for some time.

“I’ve been busy, Milly, how’s everything here doing, baby, huh? The place still making money?” he asked with his usual smile and taking her hand.

“Oh, as you know, Lenny, it’s the same old crap. It’s making money but I don’t see any of it; I just do the work here. It’s sure good to see you, Lenny. Don’t be a stranger; I’d like to see you around once in a while.” She smiled, taking her pad out for our order.

We got a drink and a sandwich, taking our time eating and getting another drink. The waitress sat down next to Lenny, then Lenny handed her a handful of money and told her to leave there at one o’clock.

She gave him a smile seeing the money, then kissed him and said, “Thanks, Lenny. I understand, and please be careful, huh? Here’s my number, call me, okay?”

She left us to wait on customers. I noticed she disappeared at one o’clock.

We waited until the customers left, then a minute or so later three men came in that Lenny knew.

Lenny looked at me, saying in a low voice, “When we get to the door, we go out and turn around and throw the dynamite in and run like hell. I want them all dead!”

But as we got to the door, one of the men said he wanted to talk to Lenny, then Lenny told the man he'd be right back and kept walking, then Lenny and I quickly lit the sticks of dynamite with our cigars and threw them inside the tavern. It only took a few seconds before it went up in a terrible blast, scattering debris in all directions. I wondered what that was all about; he never told me who those guys were or why we did what we did.

After we got out of the area, he got the bottle and took a long drink, then handed the bottle to me, which was almost empty. He laughed like he always did after kills.

"Stop at that liquor store over there. We need another bottle; this one is empty," I told him. I took a drink out of the new bottle and lit a cigar, asking, "Why did we blow the tavern apart?"

"The owner that was in the kitchen doing the cooking was Leo's brother. He killed that waitress' husband, but she never knew that and I never told her. He got mad one night because Milly wouldn't go to bed with him, so he shot her husband while he sat there having a drink. He thought if he got rid of him and out of the way, then Milly would go with him, but she never would.

"Those three guys that came in as we left, well, they were the ones that got rid of the body, and besides that, they killed some of our men one night and took our drugs, but we couldn't prove that. I know they did it because I heard they did it by someone that saw them do it, so now I paid them back!

"Like I said before, Steve, I want to tie up the loose ends." He took a drink from the bottle and lit a cigarette and smiled, saying he had one more thing to do before this was over. "There's two guys Leo had for his bodyguards, and I want them dead, Steve! They will in time go against us, and I don't have the time to watch our backs every time they are around us. In about an hour from now, they will be at a bar on the other side of the city. We'll go there and wait until they show up; after that's over we'll go back to the mansion and see what's going on there."

Lenny had a smile on as he puffed on a cigarette. I sat back in my seat, smoking my cigar as he drove on. I watched Lenny at times, wondering what would happen next. He seemed to be in control now as he drove; he'd calmed down since the night before, when he was drunk. He was himself again and doing what he liked to do, killing people.

We came to a small bar on a side street. We went in, seeing only one guy sitting at the end of the bar. The bartender was a young guy that gave us a drink and smiled, saying he knew Lenny. But Lenny wasn't in the talking mood. The bartender went about his business until two men that we were waiting for just came in. Lenny hit my arm, telling me to get ready to shoot.

Lenny jumped up and fired three times, as I did the same. The men fell without the chance to fight back, or did they even know what was happening to them?

The bartender was standing there in a daze and not moving. Lenny gave him a hundred- dollar bill, telling him to forget what he saw. The bartender nodded, saying he saw nothing. We walked out and drove away from there.

It was a half-hour later when got back to the mansion, and nothing seemed to change. It was quiet as we sat down at the bar. Lenny looked around and asked for a drink. Sidney was the bartender that afternoon. He smiled, saying it was quiet all that day.

When Sidney left us, Lenny turned to me, saying in a low voice, "In the morning, Steve, I take over this place. I will tell them all what I want and if anyone don't like it, I'll kill them!" while taking a drink, like he was already the boss man now.

I looked at him and smiled; I was sure he would do just that, and at the same time I was wondering what in hell Marie was doing at this time. Was she having a meeting with the big guys, or was she just talking when she told me she would see that I would be the next boss?

I took a drink and called for another, then I told Lenny I was going to drink that night because I was celebrating him being the new boss. He looked at me and laughed, then he ordered another drink also.

"Yeah, Lenny, it's time for us to celebrate! Why not? You been here a long time, my friend; you deserve the position!" I told him as I put up my glass to his. "To you, Lenny, I hope it geos the way you want it."

He smiled and drank the drink in one gulp and got another drink for the next three hours.

I was starting to feel it when Marie came in, getting a drink herself. She motioned to me to go outside with her. I told Lenny to wait for me so I could try taking Marie for some loving. He smiled, telling me to go ahead.

We walked the sandy beach in the warm evening as the sun went down, with the night coming on. Marie sipped her drink, then looked at me, then she took my arm as we walked along under a beautiful sky full of stars. She stopped again and looked at me with a smile.

"Now that Leo is dead, you will take his place like I told you that before," she said in a tone of authority, like it was a done deal and that was that, whether I liked it or not.

I looked at her as she went on.

"I have a meeting with the big boss tonight at ten o'clock. Like I said, Steve, you take over. I will show you what there is to learn about our group." She looked at me, then asked, "I wonder what Lenny will do when he hears you're the new boss?" She took a drink and had a kind of stare while looking at me.

"I can answer that, beautiful. First, he'll go crazy and people will get killed, and probably I might just be one of those people!" I told her with a smile.

She nodded her head and agreed that might be true. "I'll have him removed for good," she said quickly, and then she looked at me again in a more serious way. "Do you think he had Leo killed?"

"I wouldn't be surprised; he's capable of it," I told her.

She stopped and took a puff on her cigarette and then she threw it away, then she turned to me, saying how she at times watched Lenny and me working together, working out the plans for a job. She knew it was the ones that I figured were the ones that went well.

"Look, Steve, I want you to take the job and don't worry, I can help you a lot. Will you take it?" she asked, looking at me.

Then we walked for a while as I thought about it, and it did sound good in a way, and in another way I was only there a short time, and no one there knew me enough to have that position, especially being a boss. But if they didn't care, then I'd take it. I thought maybe I'd be in a good position to know everyone there and what they did, and besides, it would be beneficial to me in every aspect. Like maybe Darlene and I could leave that city a lot sooner, because in many ways I could get rid of them every chance I get. So far Lenny got rid of many that I didn't have to do.

"Yeah, okay, I'll give it a try, but you'll have to help me get started," I told her when she laughed and hugged me at the same time.

"You won't regret it, Steve. You and I can go far. It has been my wish and my dream to have the money to get away from here. Together we can do that. Now is our chance, so let's take it." She smiled, showing her happiness.

"I'm with you, beautiful lady," I said when she kissed me, saying, "We are on our way."

We got back to the bar when Lenny told me we had to go. I told Marie I'd see her later.

Walking to the car, I noticed Lenny walking in a straight line. I could not imagine how, because like before he drank many drinks and drank them very fast. He drove like he never drank before, but like I said, before it showed if he talked.

He talked all the way home, bragging about his deals and what he was about to do next when he took over the organization. I called him boss now and he got a kick out of that; he felt more brazen now and laughed as he drank more from the bottle we had in the car.

Then I wondered about what he'd do or say when he found out it was me that would be the boss, and not him.

Darlene was sitting up against the pillow on the bed reading as I went in and patted her on the head like she was a dog or cat.

"Well, if it isn't the rover! I thought you'd be out all night," she remarked.

I told her I could have been, with the excitement we had today. I also told her what we did that day, how we got rid of the people Lenny wanted to get rid of. I looked at her after I sat down near her.

You know, we had a lot of drinks after we got to the mansion. I told Lenny he should be the new boss because he was there a long time and all that stuff. All the time I was talking to him, he drank one after the other for three hours, and it seemed like it never fazed him one bit. I couldn't understand how in the world he could drink that much and be able to stand up. And to be able to drive after all the drinking like he did.

Darlene looked at me, telling me as long as she had known him he was always a heavy drinker and he was used to it. Then she looked at me again, asking if he would be the next boss or if someone else would be.

I got up taking a drink from the bottle on the dresser and smiled. "Well, one thing I do know for sure, honey, he will not be the next boss, no, he won't get it. Marie told me that, she said the big boss would not hear of it. Now when Lenny finds out in the morning someone else will be the boss, he'll go insane with so much hate, and I know for sure he will kill anyone that gets in his way! I know that for sure, honey, his mind was set on being the boss for a long time now; that's all I heard from him every day."

Darlene smiled, saying she wondered who it would be then if it wasn't Lenny. I didn't answer that because I had to take a shower before going to bed. After my shower I put my pajamas on and got into bed, putting the covers over me, saying in a low voice, "I told her I was the new boss in the morning."

She looked at me and smiled, then she started to laugh. She got up and went in the bathroom and laughed all the more.

"It's not that funny, you know," I told her as she came out still laughing and putting her hand over her mouth, trying to stop laughing.

Then she even got her pillow over her mouth. After getting control of herself, she patted me on the head, saying, "My poor baby, he thinks he's the big cheese now. It's gone to his head and little brain. I haven't had so much fun in my whole life. Now go to sleep; you certainly need it," and she was still holding her hand to her mouth.

I looked at her and almost laughed myself. "It's not time yet; I have more to tell you since you are having such a great time. Lenny showed me a book with names and places, and all the people killed and by whom. That alone will hang him, whoever they are, and he has a big box with a suitcase full of money. There are lots of papers belonging to the organization and more. He even gave me ten thousand dollars. We have to find a way to give that stuff to the police."

Darlene asked if I drank too much.

"Yes," I told her, "but that has nothing to with it."

"Don't you know that's the most stupid and incriminating thing to do, to keep a book like that." She was so surprised and wondering if it were true what I was telling her.

"I know, but there it is," I told her.

"Lenny was there longer than you, Steve; he would have a better chance than you for that job. I don't care what Marie said. You were kidding me about being the new boss, huh?"

I looked at her, looking in her in the eyes and taking her hand. "Read my lips, honey child: Lenny is out, and I am in. I will have the job in the morning. I know he will try to kill me, I know that for sure. I took the job because it could make our job easier, to find the ones we want. We'll know what's going all the time. Now let's get some sleep."

She put her pillow over her mouth again and laughed all the more. I put the lights out as she lay close to me, and she'd giggle and shake her head, trying to stop laughing.

"Will you stop that? It's no laughing matter. For your information, it's a dangerous situation. You better have our suitcases ready at all times; we might have to make a run for it if anything goes wrong," I tried to explain.

I was up early the next morning and made sure I had my gun ready in my belt and the small gun on my ankle. Lenny picked me up by eight o'clock. He looked like hadn't slept in a week. His eyes were red with bags around them, making him look like he was ill for a long time. He was quiet until we got to the main road. I took out a cigar and asked him what he had in mind for our first job. He said he wanted to get the men out on their jobs first. Then we'd get rid of anyone that gave us trouble, and he went on saying who we would hit and what jobs we would keep. He had it all figured out in his mind. I was sure he did, because he was thinking about taking over for a long time now. For some time now, I could see how he reacted whenever Leo gave him an order.

I knew he hated to be told anything; that's why I always asked if he thought about this or that. It was just a matter of time that Lenny would have Leo killed.

I was surprised he didn't do it sooner, and more surprised, as much as Lenny hated Leo, why he didn't kill Leo himself. I firmly believed Lenny really believed he would be the next boss, but that was all in his own mind. Now I also believed he thought he could take over and the men would accept him happily, but I thought he had a great disappointment coming. I was afraid it would be too much for him to take, especially now that he'd planned this for so long and very carefully.

There was another thing that was bothering me; all the time he was thinking I was with him on this, I was not! It wasn't that I was trying to double-cross him, even though it might look like I really was, but in reality he was going to take it that way, no matter what, and I knew that for sure.

It was Marie that was making it very easy for me to take the position as boss. Being the boss of this organization could be very helpful to me getting them all caught or killed. That was the only reason I accepted the offer.

Chapter Six

Besides, I wanted Lenny out of the way because he was a very dangerous man. With him gone, it would be much easier for me to find ways to stop this organization.

As we got closer to the mansion, I reached under the seat for the bottle of scotch and took a drink. I handed it to Lenny, saying, "Here, have a drink to start our new adventure, boss. Let's drink to our making money."

He took the bottle and looked at me and laughed, then took a long drink as the liquid rolled down his chin and his shirt. I took the bottle and put it back as we drove up the driveway to the mansion. Lenny parked the car, then I noticed two guards were at the back door that I never saw before. I got nervous seeing more cars in the parking area that Lenny never noticed. I supposed his mind was being preoccupied with his own thoughts. Lenny couldn't see what I was seeing. I had the feeling in his mind he was going to be the next big boss, and there was nothing else to think about. Lenny was oblivious to everything else that was so noticeable to everyone else there.

Lenny never noticed all the men there sitting at the tables as we walked in when Lenny went to the bar. He couldn't wait to have that drink to get himself going. After all, in his mind he was the boss, and he couldn't believe anything else; there was nothing else as far as he was concerned.

I saw Marie in the back of the room motioning to me to come to her while I was looking around at all the unfamiliar faces sitting at our tables around the room. I was seeing men with stern and very serious looks on their faces as they observed everyone there while they smoked their cigars with drinks in their hands.

"You ready, Steve?" she asked, looking at me.

"Yes, I think I'm ready, if you are," I answered, being a little nervous about the whole affair.

"Come, it'll be over quickly," she said as she walked on with me behind her.

We sat down at the head of the table, then she stood up, looking around the room, and before she opened the meeting she said, "Men! I know you're all wondering what's happening here today. We have several men here from our main office and from the surrounding areas. They're here to see that no one will interfere with our new boss, who was already picked by our head office. He was picked by the head man for many reasons."

She looked around the room and Lenny looking in from the bar. She went on, saying, "The man was picked because he gets things done, and done right. You men that work here for Leo, you all know who I'm talking about. You all know he's fair and he expects you all to be the same. Now for those that don't know him, meet Steve Mire here! If there is any problem with that, then say so right now!" She said it out loud, being very distinct in every word she said.

The room got quiet for a few seconds, then yelling and cursing could be heard from the bar. Lenny threw his glass at the bar, then he came toward me with red bulging eyes filled with hate that could kill.

"Ya no-good rotten shit! You'll die for this, Steve!"

He went for his gun when three men grabbed him. He was subdued and handcuffed, all the while he screamed at everyone he'd get even with.

Marie told the men from the head office they could go, and she thanked them for their help; she told them everything was now under control. Leo's men were asked to wait. Marie and I went to the office, then she handed me a schedule to go by in assigning the men.

Then she looked at me, saying in a low voice, "Steve, we know Lenny had Leo killed. We also killed the man who did it, because he came to us asking for us to protect him from Lenny, but we had him killed because we couldn't trust him. We figured Lenny would try something like this, even I could see that, and I'm sure you did too, Steve. Now he's on his way to a one-way trip. He won't bother anyone from here on," she said with a cold look about her.

I looked at the schedule and kissed Marie before I went out to start my new job.

As I sat down with the men I knew, a loud cheer went up for me. They yelled out they were happy I got the job instead of Lenny.

I felt good about that. One of the men told me told me my gun was out first, but I didn't shoot Lenny, and he was glad I didn't because it showed I had control. I smiled about that also, but at the time I really wanted to shoot Lenny because it would have been over and done with, but was it really over with? I wasn't all that convinced just yet. I was thinking. I really wondered about the way Lenny was being taken away like he was. I was unsure and unsteady about watching my back from here on. Then I let go of the feeling I had because I figured Marie knew what she was doing. I also figured she had the right men to take him away and get rid of him for good.

I called for Bruce, Wayne and Timmy. "You men have the pickup today. You guys go on and remember one thing, all you men, do not take chances! We need the money, but we need you guys too!"

The men smiled when I said that, then they left with a wave of the hand.

"Johnny, Cal, and Mark and Allen, you men have an armored car to take. Get uniforms to look like theirs; it will be easier and safer. Remember, we need that money so make sure you all know what you are doing. You all went over and over on what to do, so go and do it! Manny and Trag and Darlene, your job is the warehouse for tonight, and again, you three worked together before; you know what to do. Okay, guys, but wait here before you go. I want to see that place first before you do anything; we'll go after I finish here.

"Fats, Boggie, Moore, Sims, Sam and Lou, you guys bring in all the bets from all points around the area; you all carry a lot of money from all parts. Now I will say it only once, bring in all the money to us. It belongs to us, not to you. You already make good money for the work you do. In the past some skimming of the money was taken out before we got it, just to let you know, I guess you call it skimming, like I know it is. So, don't let it happen again," I told them. "Mike, Walls and Gill, you guys are the guards of this building and parking lot. Make sure you guys know who comes here to these doors. It's your job to stop anyone you do not know, and no one parks on this parking lot! For all we know they might be someone that might try to kill us, I'm sure not all the people that like us. Just make sure of no surprises. If you need more help, tell me." I got up from my chair and went to see the bartender, Sidney, telling him, "Sidney, from now on, I want you to make sure you know who is coming in that door, you got that, Sidney? You got a gun, then use it. You never know when someone will try coming here to kill any one of us. Now you tell Jed and any other bartender we have here to do the same," I told him.

"I got it, Steve, I know what to do," he answered.

I went back to the office, where Marie was smiling and having coffee.

"You took over like a pro. You will do good here, Steve. The men like you, I see no problem. Here's the keys to Lenny's car; he won't be needing them anymore," she said without a care or any feeling for Lenny whatsoever.

Just the same, I got a chill when I heard that, like she told me Lenny went on a one-way trip. I knew one thing, if he got away from those men, then I better watch my back. Somehow I had the feeling he was taken away too easily. He was smarter than that. I figured he'd put up of a fight, yes, I figured I'd see him again, if he ever got away.

I took the keys from Marie, telling her to wait for me because I had to check on the warehouse heist. Darlene was on that list to take that place full of furs. I just had to see if it was safe enough for her, and another thing, I wanted make sure there was some kind of an escape in case of trouble. After looking around with Manny, he told me they knew what to do and how to escape. I told him I figured that but the furs we needed and how important it was.

I drove back to the mansion in Lenny's car and picked up Marie for lunch. It was two hours when we got back to the office. She told me she wanted to get rid of the organization when the time came and to leave with all the money. I had to smile at that, because it sounded just like Lenny again.

"You better go slow, beautiful. I hate to die so young. I'm with you in anything you want, but be careful," I told her.

"I'm always careful, Steve. Let's have a drink before we get started to work," she said.

She told Sidney to make us a drink, and before I could get the glass to my mouth I heard a familiar voice behind me. I knew only too well who it was. He had me cold! And I had no chance! I knew I was a dead man because I let my guard down and I knew it. Lenny was behind me with a gun in my back, and there was nothing I could do about it but to wait for the gun to go off.

I could see Sidney frozen as he watched Lenny, and Marie was scared to death as she wondered what was happening next and she didn't dare move. I turned slowly to see Lenny with the sunken eyes, glaring at me with such hate; there was no reasoning with him. It was too late for that; his face was distorted and saliva coming from his mouth resembled a mad dog on the prowl, ready to kill.

"Ya lousy bastard!" he yelled out. "You thought you could double-cross me and get away with it! You're dead, Steve!" He put his gun to my face, telling me to let my gun fall to the floor. "Don't try anything, you'll never make it, ya son of a bitchen rat!" he screamed out louder.

I knew that he was too fast to try anything. I had no idea what to do, so I took my gun out slowly and let it fall to the floor. Then he laughed out loud, because he was in command now. I was defenseless and I had no gun, he was thinking. He stepped backwards, waving his gun at me as he shouted.

"Get up!" he yelled with eyes that seemed to bulge outward and stare. "You're gonna take a trip, backstabber! Ya rotten shit! Ya thought ya could get rid of old Lenny, didn't ya? I was too smart for ya and your big deal! Those guys ya had were amateurs, and cowards! I killed them like rats! Now it's your turn, big man! You were wrong to cross me! Now get going! We're taking a ride, you and me!" he yelled out, shaking and breathing hard.

He yelled out to Marie he'd be back and he was going to kill all those that went against him. He said he was taking over and he was the boss. Then he looked at me, still yelling as loud as ever for me to get going; he was taking me for a ride!

I slowly walked toward the back door when Sidney went for his gun, but he wasn't fast enough. Lenny shot him as I ran for the side door that went to the office where they kept all their records. Lenny fired quickly, shooting over my head, and not missing by much. I got to the next room and hid behind an old desk as I quickly took out the small gun I had on my ankle that I never used before. I was thanking my lucky stars I had that gun on me. Now I had a fighting chance.

I could hear Lenny coming toward the room, yelling and cursing, "Come on out of there, ya bastard! Ya got no gun! I'm gonna kill ya anyway! Ya gonna die, Steve, ya can't get away from me!" He raved on like a crazy man gone out of control.

I never moved until he got right in front of the desk. It was then I stood up and fired three fast shots into his chest. He never knew what hit him. It took him by surprise because he never thought I had another gun on me. It was a good thing I never told him about the small gun, because that was my only chance to stay alive. Yes, it was my only chance and I thank my lucky stars I had that small gun with me.

He was on his knees staring at me as he tried to raise his gun to shoot me, but he didn't have the strength, and finally the gun slowly fell from his grip and hit the floor. "Ya had another gun. Ya had another gun," he repeated. Then slowly he was looking down at his own blood dripping from his chest on the floor. He looked up at me for a second and fell face down on the floor.

I stood there looking at a mad man, a killer many times over, and now he was dead! It was over, the fight I dreaded, and I knew it would happen and it did, but now it was all behind me. It was hard for me to believe Lenny was really dead; I had to look down at him again to make sure he was.

Marie came to me, staring at Lenny's body lying there on the floor, saying, "I'm so glad he's dead! My God! I'm so glad he's dead! You alright?" she asked as she shook with fear while looking at him lying there in pool of blood. "I never thought he'd get away from my men like he did. He could have killed us all, Steve," she remarked, still looking at Lenny on the floor.

Marie was shaken and very nervous as she tried to compose herself. I was more than shaken; I was lucky to be alive. It was the small gun I had on my ankle that saved me. I learned long ago to have an alternative, a way out, whenever possible.

"You saved my life, Sidney. I owe you one, my friend. You go home after the doctor sees you, and come back when you feel okay," I told him.

Sydney said he would call a friend of his to come and bartend for us until the regular bartender came on duty. After he called his friend, he left.

Walls, Mike and Gil came in saying they never saw Lenny come in the building like he did; they were surprised that he got in without anyone seeing him. I told them not to worry about it; Lenny was dead now and to leave it that. Lenny was a clever man that knew how to elude people any time he wanted to.

I had a drink to calm down, but it wasn't easy to just let it go, no, I made a bad mistake by not keeping myself more alert; it almost cost me my life. I told Marie I had things to do and I'd see her later. I needed to unwind; I was shaken and uneasy because I was almost killed, and it was my own damn fault not to be ready at all times. From now on, I'd make sure my back was covered. I couldn't leave things to chance because it could be deadly.

I got back and made a drink as I handed one to Marie, saying, "I'm putting another guard on the back door. We need more security. I don't need any more surprises like we just had."

Marie smiled and hugged me, agreeing to what I said. But that wasn't the only problem I had; it was the idea of me telling Darlene about staying with Marie, that was the next thing I didn't know how to handle. I drove back to the hotel, seeing Darlene just coming out of the shower. I told her we had to talk and it had to be right now. I told her about the takeover and it went smoothly. Before I could finish she cut in, asking about Lenny.

"Lenny didn't like it; in fact, he got downright nasty with the name-calling, so Marie's men took him away for a one-way trip. But he got away and we had a fight." I told her what happened next as she looked at me.

"I can't believe he's dead. I worried about him for a long time. Now he's gone, that's a relief," she said. "I can't believe you killed him, Steve! God! I'm glad he's gone."

I looked at her, saying in a low voice, "The next thing we, ahh, have to talk about is Marie."

She looked at me, wondering what was next coming up. I lit a cigar as I sat down. I didn't know how to say it but it had to be said.

"The next thing I have to do is to live with Marie for a while."

I tried to talk fast but it didn't work. She got up, glaring at me and very excited.

"You what? You worm! Your gonna live with her? No, you can't do that, Steve! Why?" she asked with her mouth open, waiting for an answer.

"Ahh, the flies, your mouth is open, you know," I quickly changed the subject.

"Never mind the damn flies, you rat, and other things you are!" she went on.

"Now wait a minute, she wants me to stay with her, and it's a good idea because I can get a lot of information from her. She'll think I'm with her all the way, and she'll let her guard down telling me what I need to know. It could save a lot of time for us, and I'm not there to make love to her, Darlene; it's just business and besides, she's a very cold person. All she cares about is money; she wants to take over the organization, just like Lenny wanted to do. All I want to do is to get this thing over with so we can leave this damn place. You got to help me with this, Darlene," I told her quickly as she stared at me.

"She's very good looking, and you won't make love to her? I don't buy that," she told me, looking rather mad at me, or maybe it was disgust, and shaking her head.

I got up and looked at her like I was hurt by the way she was feeling the way she was. "I'm surprised at your attitude. I really am. You don't trust me, do you? A nice way for us to start, honey. I'm hurt about this, I hope you know that."

She looked at me and started to laugh. "You're a rat, Steve Mire, and you're a fraud! I love you and I do trust you, but not with her," she said in a low voice. She put her head on my shoulder and muttered to herself.

"You're jealous, I like that, you sweet thing. How can I look at anyone else? I love you, beautiful," I told her.

"I love you too, but you are still a rat," she quickly retorted with a pout.

"Look, honey, let's get our job done so we can go north to our new home. Now, let's go out and have dinner later, but first I have to pick up the papers and that big box, along with the book at Lenny's bar. I need to have the police to get that stuff," I explained.

After she got dressed, we walked to Lenny's bar. We sat down at a table near his office. I asked Lorie, his young bartender and lover, if Lenny showed up yet.

"No, he's been gone since early this morning," she told us, looking very concerned.

"He'll be back soon, Lorie; he had things to take care of. He told me to pick up some things for him, okay? We'll have a drink first," I told her with a smile.

She said it was okay and left.

After we had our drinks, we got everything from Lenny's office and left in a hurry. We went directly to Darlene's apartment. Reading Lenny's book, Darlene couldn't believe what she was reading. She said she would get it all to Lieutenant Miles as quickly as she could.

We counted the money from the big box. It was five hundred thousand dollars, and Darlene couldn't believe that either. We got to bed late that night, as Darlene lay close to me, muttering her dislikes about me living with Marie.

Next morning, I kissed her goodbye for now. I told her not to worry; things would work out. I went to my hotel for my things and drove to the mansion. Marie was waiting for me with a smile and kissed me.

"You look lovely in that dress; it goes well with that shape you got there," I told her when she kissed me.

"Thank you, sir, I like to hear that." She hugged me and showed me a list she made out on the men. "Steve, Lou and Sam came in hour ago. Fats and Boggie came in a few minutes ago, but Moore and Sims haven't shown up yet."

"I think it's time we replace them, Marie; they've been taking money out every time they went out and they're always late coming back. That was the way ever since I've been here. Don't you think it's time we got rid of them?" I asked, looking concerned.

"I will have two men here tomorrow, Steve," she quickly let me know.

I went to the bar for coffee. In the same time I told Jed, the new bartender to have Walls and GILL come to the office. As I turned to leave the bar, Moore and Sims came in.

"You guys wait here until we count the money," I told them. I told Walls and Gill to hold them until I got back.

Marie counted ten thousand dollars short, like before. I went back to the bar telling Walls and Gill to take those two out of here and get the money back that they took. When I said that, Moore went for his gun when Walls quickly shot him. Sims ran for the door when Jed the bartender fired and shot Sims.

"That was pretty fast shooting there, Jed," I told him as he smiled, putting his gun back in his belt.

Walls just looked at me when Marie came in seeing the two men dead on the floor. She then ordered Walls and Gill to get rid of the bodies.

Johnny and Sid came with the uniforms; they looked real for the armored car heist. They left saying the job was going to be easy, then Marie asked about the warehouse job. I said it should go smoothly. Mike, our back door guard, came in saying Shags wanted to see Marie.

"Let him in!" she called out.

"Hi doll, I got another deal for you and it can't wait," he said, smiling. He was a big man with reddish hair that was uncombed and not a bad-looking man in a way. He talked like he was from Australia and seemed to never waste any time; he was always in a hurry.

"Good to see you, Shags. Tell it to Steve, he's the new boss here," she told Shags.

"Okay, Steve, nice to know ya. I got time if you do. It's not far from here," he said with a serious look and lighting a cigarette.

"Okay, let's go," I told him when Walls came in saying that Mark was here and it was important.

I told him to send him in. Mark and Allen came in with red faces and shaken. Mark started to talk when Allen butted in.

"The damned police! They were there waiting for us! Cops all around the damned place!"

Just as we got there, Mark and me saw the stinking cops shooting it out with Tommy, Sid and Johnny; they got shot and we saw them fall.

"Phil got hit but got away, but it's only a matter of time, he'll get caught too. We took off and it's lucky we got away at all, damn it! We could have made it," he said disgustedly.

Allen was a skinny man with very little hair on his head; he was half bald and always worried about something. Mark was a bigger man who always had to take care of Allen, it seemed. Wherever Allen was you were sure to see Mark there too. For some reason he always watched Allen like they were brothers.

"Okay, go home and be here in the morning. I see we got a stool pigeon here," I remarked like I was mad that armored truck deal fell through.

"Yes, we have. I tried to find the guy, but I haven't the slightest idea who the hell it is," Marie answered and lit a cigarette, then looked at me.

"He has to be caught, Marie; he'll ruin our plans, we lost already a hell of lot! The armored truck job, Marie. Maybe Shags got something for us; he usually does, Steve," she told me.

"Okay, see you later. I'm going with him right now," I told her.

I drove as Shags bragged about his escapades. The more he talked, the more disgusted I was getting.

We drove along the Queen's highway and off where houses were being torn down and rebuilt. We parked in some messed-up parking lot that was abandoned for some time. Shags told me at seven-thirty that night he was to meet with two guys in a truck from Florida. They had three million in drugs and three million in cash.

"What you think, Steve? Can we take it?" he asked, puffing on his cigarette.

"Why not? I think we can handle that," I told him.

He had a smoke every minute he sat in the car and smiled that I approved of his deal.

"What's your take in this, Shags?" I asked.

"Like it's always been, Steve, I get the deals and I take my part and Marie gets hers. We do pretty well that way, Steve, okay?" he asked, looking at me.

"Okay with me." I lit my cigar again that went out, then drove back to the office. I told Marie what we had; it looked good to me, and I had to meet Shags by seven that night.

"I have a surprise for you, Steve. As soon as your job is over, we have a date and it's important."

"Oh, I thought all dates were important," I told Marie.

"Steve, we have a meeting with the people that want to meet you, that's our head office. You'll be meting them all. We're supposed to be there by nine o'clock, can you make it?" she asked while taking a cigarette from her pocket.

"We'll have to make it," I told her.

By seven that night I met with Shags, then we headed for the meeting place. The truck was parked there in the abandoned parking lot, waiting for us as we drove close to the front of the truck so they could see us.

They watched us get out with our suitcase of money, they thought it was money, but instead it was all paper with hundred-dollar bills tied to each bundle to make it seem like stacks of money. It looked real in the suitcase. Shags had the suitcase and opened it to show them the money.

They got out and walked to the back of the truck as we followed them, then Shags pulled his gun out. One of the men waited for such a move; his gun was already out. He fired, hitting Shags in the arm, but Shags managed to fire back and shoot the man as I shot the other man.

I had to act quickly; I wasn't prepared for this. Shags should have told me what he was going to do. But again, I should have known and been more alert. I was lucky I only got hit in the shoulder, but too bad.

Shags quickly drove off in the truck as I drove away, leaving the two men dead in the parking lot. Marie fixed my shoulder after I took a shower and dressed. I remarked how well we looked in our new clothes.

"We certainly do," Marie answered, smiling. She handed me a new set of keys. "These are for your new Lincoln. Lenny's car has to go; it's in his name," she explained.

I opened the door of my new Lincoln, with Marie getting in, smiling and saying how great everything was going. Now we'd both get everything we wanted. She was happy but for how long, I was wondering, and where would all this end? She was smoking her cigarette as I wondered about tonight. We were on our way to meet the big guys of the organization.

Chapter Seven

We went up the long driveway, just across the street from the big open bay to a big, beautiful building. We parked as three guards watched us. We walked by many parked cars that were lined up. We entered a large foyer that was big enough to put another house in that led us through double doors, into a large room that held many people. The mansion was nothing more than beauty and elegance. Everything in the greatest taste, built by the old master craftsmen. I don't know why but I always seemed to notice houses I went into, what kind and what they were made of.

As we walked in among the people sitting at the tables, I noticed Marie was well known, seeing all the people greeting her. I had the feeling I was being watched by all there as I was asked many questions, like who was I or where did I come from? I just smiled and made off I didn't hear them, or I'd just walk on.

A waiter came by carrying a tray of drinks so I took one, and as I turned around I bumped into a young lady.

"Sorry, are you okay?" I asked her.

"Yes, I'm okay. I know you, and I think everyone here does too. You're the talk of the town. I'm the boss's daughter. I'm Gloria, I'll talk to you later," she said as she walked off. She was twenty years old, I found out later, with black hair, and a very pretty young lady with a good personality. She also had a nice smile.

I saw a man in a wheelchair coming my way with a cigar in his mouth, smiling as he came to me. He put his hand out to me as we shook hands. He said he'd know me anywhere.

"Marie told me so much about you, Steve. I'm impressed in what I hear, and now I know why Marie cares for you. She does, you know; I see it in her eyes every time she talks about you. Come with me to the porch so we can talk."

I followed behind as he made his way through the crowd. On the porch he lit his cigar and went on telling me many things.

"I own this place and everyone in it."

Just like Leo told me when I first met him. I guessed Leo and this man I just met liked to hear themselves say how big and important they were.

"A long time ago I was in love with Marie, Steve, then sometime later I got into an accident. What can I do, being like this?" he asked, looking sadly and making a gesture with his hands.

I felt badly for him. I knew he still loved Marie by the way he talked about her, and after about an hour of talking he said he had to take a nap because he was tired. He started to leave when he smiled.

"I been talking and never told you my name. I'm Ted Belini, Steve. I like you, my boy, I feel like I knew you for a long time. If you need me for anything, you call me. A deal?" he asked.

I had to smile when he said that. "Yes, it's a deal. I'd be honored to talk with you, sir," I told him.

He wheeled himself out as I watched him go. He seemed to be so fragile, but he couldn't get to where he was now without some pushing and killing. Ted was a big man with black hair and dark eyes that looked right through you. He always had a cigar in his mouth and talked like he had good schooling and a proper bringing-up. What he said was gospel, and he was rough enough to back it up, especially with all the men he had around him.

I got to the bar when Marie came with some creep, hanging on to her arm like he had no energy to walk by himself.

"Steve! I'd like you to meet Kendall Owens; he's our attorney."

I shook hands with him that felt like a wet fish. "Nice to meet you, sir," I acknowledged.

"My pleasure, Steve. I heard many good things about you, my boy. I must say you're quite a man. You have done well with us, and I like that. We'll talk soon; I have things that need my attention, forgive me," he said in a sickening girlish way.

I watched him smile; it seemed like he was afraid to show his teeth, and his hand grip was like holding nothing.

Marie said he was big in the organization. He ran things for Ted. "Where you been for so long?" she asked.

"With Ted; he talked to me like a father," I told her.

"Don't let him fool you; he's a very powerful man. He'll have you killed anytime he wants to. He sits in that wheelchair like it was his throne. Have you seen Gloria yet?" she asked.

"Yeah, nice young lady," I remarked.

"Think so? She's trouble; she'll have you in bed with her if you don't watch yourself," Marie announced with some animosity in her tone of voice.

I looked at her. "That's terrible, Marie. Of course she can try, but her daddy and I are good friends," I told her.

Marie looked at me with a grin on her face, saying she had to go to a meeting.

After she left, I went to the bar for a drink. I lit a cigar as I walked out to the garden for a smoke. I walked around looking at the flowers and the statues that were all around, like being in Italy. It was so beautiful and picturesque.

"Steve!" Gloria called out. "Like our garden, Steve?" she asked.

I looked at Gloria, and at the same time I could see seeing Ted and Marie up on the second-story balcony. I made off I didn't see them there as Gloria came to me, saying, "I like older men, Steve, do you like me?" she asked.

"Yes, Gloria, I like you, you're a good-looking lady, and you have everything going for yourself. You're a very pretty young lady, Gloria, and you have a father that can give you anything you want," I told her.

"That's true, Steve, but I don't want it! I want a man to love me. Will you love me, Steve?"

I looked at her, wondering what to say. "I'm too old for you, Gloria. You're young; there are many men your age that will be happy to give their right arm for you. If I was a younger man, I'd be chasing you right now. But I have a lady friend, and she's beautiful and I love her. I couldn't hurt her by going with you, now could I? I want to be your friend, that means a lot because friends are hard to find. Would you be my friend, Gloria?" I asked with a smile.

Gloria looked at me, then she took my arm as we walked to the other end of the garden. I could see Ted and Marie smiling, while Gloria was talking fast like she was in a hurry or something.

"I didn't think you would turn me down, Steve, but I understand. I know you go with Marie, but I can't find a man to go with; he finds out who I am and meets my father, then he runs away."

"I'm sure that will happen, but you can't really blame them, Gloria; they're afraid of your father. Now I know for sure you will find a man when the time comes, that will be the man that won't run. I'm sure that will happen for you, that will be the man that will want only you, and your father won't scare him off."

Gloria smiled and kissed me on the cheek, then she disappeared into the crowd.

I walked around meeting people for the next few minutes until Marie came back. She said she wanted to leave, so we waved and said goodbye to those that were close to us, and Kendall was waving also. I told her to look at the snake waving to us.

"Be careful of him! He's a dangerous man! The people you just met are people from other organizations. Now they all know you. If you need any help from them, they will help you and vice versa," she explained.

While we drove home, Marie told me about her and Ted watching Gloria and me. Ted was pleased in the way I handled his daughter Gloria. Also, Ted wanted me to go higher up in the organization, because he liked me.

We were up early the next morning having coffee when we heard on the radio that a warehouse was being robbed. The police stormed in and killed one man, and the other man was taken into custody.

I looked at Marie with a disgusted look. "We better find the one that's ratting on us to the cops. If they know about that job, then they must know about all of us here. That worries me! Marie!" I told her, making my voice sound worried.

We got to the office and Marie tried to call Kendall, but she couldn't reach him.

Marie said, "Kendall knows somebody in the police station that lets us know what's going on. He'll find out for us."

Just then Kendall came walking in, sounding and acting like some sissified old woman.

"Good morning, you two. I thought I'd come by to see you two at work."

I almost laughed out loud in his face, seeing him standing there by the door. He sat down, wiping his glasses, looking stupid. I got ill watching him, I didn't really know why, but it was the way he acted, like an old lady.

"Marie told me you know someone at the police station, Kendall. Maybe you can find out who it is that's tipping the police about the jobs we send our men to do," I said to Kendall.

He looked at me, then he smiled. "Yes, I do know such a person, my boy. I know this has been going on for the last three years now. I also know who it is; I expected it all along." Then Kendall looked at me with a blank expression, then he went on. "You of all people, Steve, you must have known, or you should have known. Yes! I mean Darlene! She's been telling the police everything, my boy. She's a cop! An undercover cop! My source told me he knows her well. He saw her shaking hands with the lieutenant, and she was giving him other information, about us and other places as well."

Kendall lit a cigarette as he watched us, and I felt very uneasy and stupid. Darlene was a cop! She had me fooled completely. I thought she was looking for the ones that killed her parents. But to be a cop, it was too hard for me to believe that.

As I took a drink of whiskey, I said, "How stupid can I be? How could she fool me like that? How could I be fooled in thinking she was okay?" I then looked at Marie and Kendall, asking them, "How could she do this, and me not knowing? I must be utterly stupid. I'm completely taken by surprise hearing Darlene is a cop."

Kendall smiled looking at both of us and, taking another cigarette out, he held it, saying, "Women can turn a man's head very easy, Steve. You got taken, but so did a lot of men. Stay with Marie, Steve; she's a lovely woman," he said in his girlish way.

I tried looking angry and in the same time I felt relieved Darlene was safe, at least for the time being. Kendall got up saying Marie had to go with him to a meeting and would be gone until the next day.

Marie looked at me and then at Kendall. "I want to put a hit on Darlene!" She said it looking tough and very demanding.

Kendall looked at her, nodding his head; he answered quickly and very abruptly.

"No! This is not the time, my dear, maybe later," Kendall answered, giving her a look that seemed odd.

"Steve, I wouldn't do that to you," Marie remarked.

I watched them go out as I sat there wondering what in hell was going to happen next, I went to the bar for a cigar, then Jed asked if he could come on some jobs with us. I told him I would think about it, then he looked at me, saying okay.

I did the work all that day until Shags came in with the money for Marie. I put it in the safe and went to an early dinner. It was kind of hard for me to comprehend; it bothered me all that day, and I had no idea what would happen now because of Darlene being caught as an undercover cop. And what about Miles? He knew Darlene was there for that purpose, and what about me? He knew I was here doing what Darlene was doing, and I was still here doing the same thing. Darlene must have told him about me being here working with her and going out with her.

My head was spinning as I was thinking about Darlene again. I loved her, but what should I do now? I didn't even know where she was so I could talk to her. Should I go on with this bunch of misfits? Or should I get out of here? But how could I? I just couldn't leave here without knowing where Darlene was. I couldn't leave this place without her being with me.

At seven that night, I went to the WALK-IN BAR and sat down with my head still going around. I thought maybe Liz could tell me more about Darlene because she knew her for a long time, and the way they got along she must know more than I did about her.

Liz brought me a drink, telling me to stay put and don't move; she had to make a call, she told me. I waited for a few minutes until she got back.

"Miles needs to talk to you, Steve. I told him you would wait, okay?" she asked.

I nodded my head yes, and I took a drink. Liz came back saying it was a shame Darlene got caught; now she couldn't go back to do her job.

"Yeah, she had me fooled, didn't she? I almost had a heart attack when I heard she was a cop. I don't know you either, do I? I guess you women are good at making fools of men." I took another drink as Liz glared at me, seeing how worked up I was about all this.

"I guess I better go and get the hell out of here; at least I can handle a drink."

"Now wait a minute, Darlene had a job to do, and she did it well. It's not her fault she got caught. She loves you and she didn't want it to happen, but it did.

She needs you more now than ever. She went through hell trying to get rid of the trash and the shit there at that place. She told me since you were there you got things going and got rid of a lot of drugs and many rotten people. So, you both did a good job."

Miles came in as Liz gave me a hard look. She brought Miles a drink, then we went in the back room, sitting in the dim light away from the customers.

"I noticed Liz lecturing you. She's a great girl, but sometimes she's a mother, if you know what I mean." He smiled and took a drink, then lit his cigar as he watched me. "I know you never knew about Darlene's job at that place, Steve, well, we didn't know about you either, right? You could have been a plant to catch an uncover agent. We couldn't know that, now could we? I'm happy to know that you're a man who wants justice, like we do. You can do what you're good at, what you're doing there right now. We cannot, my friend. We have to take them in, and as you know they walk out on the streets again. I was informed by Darlene about the things you have done there at that place. She was very taken by you, Steve, and she loves you more than anything. I want you to stay put, stay right there, and do the job as an American, as a man with principles that I know you have. I need you there, my friend. Now how can you keep me informed?" he asked, puffing on his cigar.

"I don't know. I'll find a way, Miles. How is she doing, Miles, I miss her," I asked.

"She's okay, Steve; I'll tell her you asked. You know, Steve, all the time she talked about you, she lights up like a Christmas tree. Something I never thought I'd ever see," Miles told me.

"Miles, I met the big guys the other night, Kendall Owens, you know him?" I asked and took a drink.

"Everybody knows him; he's a snake and he's trouble. He's in the wrong profession; he gets the rats out almost every time we get them in jail," Miles complained and puffed on his cigar, then he looked angry when he said, "Kendall is a brilliant lawyer, but for the wrong purpose. He defends the rats, the killers, and you name it. Yes, he gets them off, but I have to say he's a great lawyer, and it's too bad he's on the wrong side of the fence."

"Yeah, I know, Miles." I took a drink and asked Liz to bring another drink for us. I lit a cigar, then I asked Miles, "Did you know that Kendall knows a guy in your department that tells him what goes on there? He's the one that fingered Darlene; Kendall told Marie and me about it himself this very morning. Marie is big there; she has a lot of authority there. She also told me and Kendall she wants a hit on Darlene. I hope you keep her safe, Miles; I'm worried because they have a lot of men that might go looking for her. Ted Belini is the top man there. I only stayed to keep an eye on Darlene, Miles. She told me she wanted to catch the killers that killed her parents, and I wanted to help if I could. I had no idea what her real job was. Actually, maybe it was better I didn't know, huh?"

"That's right, Steve. Liz is a cop too, you can call on her if you need to, and Steve, maybe you're right about not knowing about Darlene, because you might have made a slip to the wrong people. Or maybe some unforeseen thing that might point to Darlene. Now as far as the guy in my department giving out information, I'll find him, you can bet on that." Miles left, leaving me feeling a little better.

I liked Miles for some reason; he was upfront with everything.

I sat with Liz for a drink when she told me about herself and how she lost her man and would like to find another to go with. I knew she was a lonely woman by the way she talked.

I left her around eleven o'clock that night and went to Marie's place. After a shower I sat on the porch, looking out over the bay, seeing the waves slowly coming into shore. I stood there for some time, until Marie came in.

"Miss me?" she asked.

"I certainly did, honey. I thought you were staying until tomorrow. How'd the meeting go?" I asked.

"We finished the meeting sooner than we thought we would. It was a big meeting, Steve; our plans will have to wait, I'm afraid." She took out a cigarette with a disappointed look on her face. "Ted said it was better for us to be one. In other words, he ordered us to close our place here and to move to his place. Now, the men he doesn't want, he'll have them killed. That means we can't make the money we wanted, damn him! That ruins all my plans," she said angrily as she looked at me, disappointed and very hurt that her plans were on hold now. All she kept saying again was "We can't make the money like we want to." She was so intent on making money, it was hurting her judgment.

I handed her a drink and held my lighter to her cigarette, then I asked, "When will all this take place?" I took a drink of my scotch, looking at her.

"Right now, Steve. He wants Shags to take Bruce, Timmy and Wayne on a job with him, then he's supposed to kill all three of them, and also, Ted wants you to work with him, at his place."

I got up, taking her arm and pulled her to me. "What do you want?" I asked in a low voice, looking at her straight in her eyes.

She looked at me and smiled. "You know what I want. What are you thinking of?" she asked, still smiling, then the look on her changed and she asked again, "What are you thinking of, Steve?"

"Well, for one thing, I'm thinking if we let Ted do what he wants, then what about us? What do we want? Now you said you want to make money so we can leave this place. You want us to stop him or just let him go on telling us what to do, Marie? It's up to you; I'll do whatever you want. You know I'm with you, my dear, so you tell me." I took a drink and watched her at the same time.

She laughed out loud, looking at me, then she took a drink and looked at me again. "You must be joking. You can't just go there and stop him; he's got too many men, and he's too powerful in the organization. You must be crazy, Steve, to even think of this." Marie sat down and puffed on her cigarette for a second or two, and she took another drink and looked at me with wonder in her eyes. "It really does sound good, but that's a terrible big chance to take, Steve," she said to me.

"I know, Marie. You said many times before you want to have money enough to get away from here. Right now, it's your chance to do just that," I told her, and besides, it was my chance to get rid of more rats, with her help.

She took a drink when she got up, then looked at me with that look about her. If I really could get rid of Ted, it would maybe get her wish back again, about making money. That was all she had on her mind, money.

Marie took out another cigarette, still wondering if all this we were talking about would really work. I could see it was making her think about getting rid of Ted. I knew she would do anything to get her hands on money. I knew she was still thinking if I could accomplish this.

She was now looking out over the bay, then she nodded her head, saying, "Do you really think you can pull this off? Can you take Ted and his men? If you fail, you know what will happen, don't you?" she said very nervously, and making sure I knew what she was talking about.

"You for it? If you are, I can do it!" I told her as I lit a cigar.

She asked with her full attention on me how I was going to do it.

"I haven't the slightest idea how, but I'll find a way," I told her, seeing her eyes getting bigger as she thought about it.

Then she came to me, looking at me. "Okay, Steve, I'll go along with it," she finally agreed. I knew she would, because she was greedy just like Lenny was; they were two of a kind, and besides, I knew she was thinking if Ted was out of the way, she would take his place as top dog in the organization.

I kissed her, then we had a drink and went to bed.

The next morning came with rain and high winds. It was a lousy day, but it was a beautiful day for Marie, as far as she was concerned, because things were still going her way, she was thinking. As we drove to the office that morning, Marie talked about what she'd do after she took over.

It was like hearing Lenny all over again. She was just like him in many ways, but she wasn't as crazy as Lenny was, although her attitude and her manner and what was in her heart was just as ruthless as Lenny was.

We got the men out on their jobs and started working on the books when Shags came in. Marie told Shags to do the job that Ted wanted done. She told him to take Bruce, Wayne and Timmy along, and we didn't want them back! She told him this in a chilling and uncaring tone of voice.

"I understand, doll, leave it to me," he said, as I watched her when she told Shags it was the way she looked; she wasn't the Marie I knew before. No, she was some other woman filled with greed and cruelty.

Things were going her way now, and she was changing right along with it. I wondered if I wasn't needed anymore, would I be taken out and executed in the same manner? Yes, I wondered about that. She was the woman in charge now, and the woman that wanted a lot of money to be able to live in luxury. I knew I had her pegged right from the start. I also knew she cared for no one, or anything, except money for number one, and that number one was herself.

I lit a cigar as I was thinking about the job ahead of us for that night. Marie would look at me every once in a while. She knew my mind was on Ted and his men. I called for Jed the bartender as he came in asking me if I wanted a drink.

"No, Jed, get Walls, and I want to talk to both of you."

He nodded and went out.

Marie smiled as she lit her cigarette. "I knew I could count on you, and if it goes okay tonight we'll make the big time," she said, smiling.

It was a few minutes later when Jed and Walls came in.

"I want you two here at ten o'clock tonight sharp! We have a job to do."

They agreed and went out.

I watched Marie working ever so busily on the books. I could imagine what she was thinking at this particular time. What if this job went wrong, or badly? She would have to think up some kind of an excuse or reason to save her own skin. Knowing her, I was sure she had already worked that out in that scheming head of hers for some way out.

"Steve, one thing I want to impress on you, Ted is an important man! He has people in high places, and he uses them. He killed many to get to where he is now. If he gets away from you, he'll kill us without a blink of an eye," she said, looking very concerned and also very worried.

I could see it in her eyes, and by the way she was telling me and in the tone in her voice, she was really uncertain about the whole thing. I looked at her and wondered what she just said, yes, I knew Ted must have killed, and many other things he had to do, to be where he was now.

"We'll do what we have to do, Marie. I have Walls and Jed, I know I can trust. There's Sam and Lou, and maybe Fats and Boggie."

Kendall came for Marie for a meeting they had to go to in Boston. It would be midnight before they got back from Boston. That would give me time to do what was needed to be done. I made sure I had enough dynamite for each of the men. I hated to destroy such a lovely mansion, but it was more important to get rid of a bunch of rotten people that cared nothing about other people; it was just themselves they cared for. They cared nothing about killing and robbing, and not to mention ruining people's lives. Tonight, with some luck, I wanted to destroy Ted's place forever.

Chapter Eight

We all met at ten o'clock. I wanted to talk to the men before we did anything; I wanted to explain tonight's job.

"Men, we have a tough job for tonight. First, Ted, the big man of the organization, wants us all go to his place and to close this place up for good. But he wants to kill some of you guys off! Now that's why I'm telling you guys about this. I don't want to go to his place, and I don't want any one of you here to be killed. So, I'm asking you men. I am not telling you that you have to do anything. But I am asking you for your help. I want to destroy Ted and his mansion. I want them all dead in that place, that's why I have dynamite to do the job. Now the job we're going to do will be risky," I told Walls and Jed. "If we fail, we're dead, that's all I can tell you right now. You will all get paid well for this, and make sure you never say a word about this, because it might get you killed."

I briefed them as we rode to Ted's place. We parked the cars on the bayside and walked just a short way to the trees and brush close to Ted's mansion. The men had their regular guns except for Walls, Jed, and me; we had silencers.

I had Boggie and Fats go to the front of the mansion, Lou and Sam went to the side door. Walls, Jed and I went to the back door.

The night was warm and dark, with no moon or stars, with fastmoving dark clouds that made it better for us. Our clothes were also dark, which made it hard for anyone to see us. At least that much was in our favor. I pointed out that a guard was sitting by the back door and as Walls and I fired together, the man fell without a sound. I tried the door but it was looked, so I checked the guard's pockets, finding the key, and got the door opened.

We went inside a hallway, seeing no one, then continuing further. We made our way to a room that had a coffee pot on for the guards that was still hot. I stayed behind Walls as we walked slowly toward the next room, then we heard shots from the front of the mansion. Then we heard a few more shots from the side entrance of the mansion.

We stayed still until it quieted down. We then continued toward an open door, but it was too dark to see in that room and I wondered about that, then I jumped as a dog ran by me and went in the dark room, then two more shots rang out, making my heart skip a beat. Then we heard the dog moan and it went silent.

I threw a chair into the dark room, then again two more shots rang out. Then I thought about the room where the coffee was. I saw some paper bags and newspapers. I put the newspapers in the bag and lit it on fire, and threw it in the dark room. A minute or so later some guy ran to put the fire out, then I shot him. I stood to the side of the doorway and reached in with my arm, feeling for the light switch. I snapped it on as Walls went in shooting. I saw one man I recalled, seeing him at the meeting at Ted's place when Marie and I went there, was lying there on the floor face down.

We could hear shooting from all parts of the mansion as we went on searching the first floor, seeing four of Ted's men dead. Then we saw Boggie and Sam were dead in one room, and two rooms down Lou and Fats lay dead a few feet apart from each other. It was now that I got nervous; I didn't see Ted or his bodyguard, who stayed with him at all times. I motioned to Walls to take the left side of the stairway, going up to the second floor. Jed took the other side with me behind them, protecting their backs. It was quiet now as the three of us slowly went on, making our way to the next room.

Walls and Jed each got to the side of the doorway as I got to the doorway like before. I snapped the switch on for the light as Walls and Jed fired into the room from each side of the doorway. We left the lights on as we went on to the next room. We did this to each room as we went through, but we still had three more rooms to go through. I happened to look farther down the hallway, seeing a closet door almost to the end of the hallway move. When I quickly touched Walls' back, he turned to look at me, then I pointed to the closet door, letting him know someone was in there.

Walls stopped Jed and pointed to the closet door, then they fired into the door, seeing a man slowly fall to the floor.

I felt for another ammo clip when I felt the dynamite I had for an emergency. I forgot all about it when I quickly motioned to Walls and Jed to hold up. I gave them each a stick of dynamite, telling them to throw one to the rooms that was on each side of the hallway. They quickly lit the sticks of dynamite and let them fly, and in seconds the rooms blew apart with a shattering roar that hurt my ears. It also made the mansion rumble like an earthquake that shook violently.

We had one more room to go to, but first we checked the two we just blew up. Ted and his bodyguard were dead. We looked around, finding a suitcase full of money, which we took. The other room had more money and a dead body face down with two guns beside him.

The last room was dark, so I picked up some clothes and threw them inside the room, then two shots were fired, keeping us at bay. Then I remembered Gloria, maybe it was her in there.

I called out, "Gloria! Are you in there?" A second or so later, I yelled out again, "Gloria! It's me, Steve! We came to help! It's okay, Gloria, we're here to help!" I told her. "It's okay, you're safe now," I said again.

A few seconds later or so, she called out, saying and almost crying, "It's me! What's happening? The shooting and the explosions! What's going on, Steve?"

"I'm coming in, Gloria; you're safe now, we were too late for your father," I told her as I went in.

She was scared and shaking, then she showed herself from behind the bed.

"Come, we have to get out of here before the police get here; it'll be hard to explain us being here."

I helped her to the hall when Walls took her hand and helped her down the stairs. I told Jed not to say a word to Gloria about this whole thing.

After they went downstairs, I set fire to each room as I went down the stairs. I wanted to destroy the drugs that were there hidden everywhere in that mansion.

We walked to the cars, seeing some people looking toward the burning mansion. They never noticed us leaving there. I gave Gloria the suitcase full of money in it, and I told her to go where she had friends. Jed asked if he could go with her, and I knew he took a liking to her so I told him to go if he wanted to.

I noticed Walls looking at me and shaking his head and showing his disapproval. I left those two off at the bus station, and Walls and I headed for the first bar as we came to down the road.

After we got a drink, Walls looked at me, saying, "I can't figure you out, Steve. We killed Ted, the big boss, and his men. Then you let Jed go, and you know he's one of them. He might hurt you someday, you know. You had the other men come with us, knowing they would get themselves killed, but why?" he asked, looking at me, looking for an answer.

I took a drink and lit a cigar from my pocket. I smiled by the way he was looking at me.

"Is it so strange to let two people live and be happy? Gloria never had the chance to be happy. She had a father that was a rat, and she couldn't do what she really wanted to do, because people hated her father. Now maybe Gloria and Jed can find a new life, my friend. At least I hope they do," I tried to explain to Walls.

He smiled, saying, "I have to say one thing, Steve. You certainly have a big heart. I just hope it doesn't backfire on you, and maybe get you killed."

I lit my cigar as I looked at Walls. He was a decent man I got to know in a short time. He was fair and honest, a good-looking man in his thirties, and had black hair and a mild manner about him. I thought it was time to talk to him now. I felt it was now safe enough to bring something out in the open.

I took a drink and ordered another round for us. "I want to tell you something, Walls. I took this job to find those that shot Darlene and me. I also wanted to find the ones that killed Darlene's parents. My only concern was to destroy drugs and killers that I actually knew. In other words, Walls, I wanted to get rid of those that prey and threaten the innocent and the young people. I found out that Ted was ready to kill off some of my men. Because he wanted me to work with him at his place. It was Lenny that killed Leo, in case you didn't know that.

"Then Maire wanted me to live with her, so I pretended to be her man. I really did it to be able to find out whatever I could, to get the information back to the police. It's Darlene Walls that I love, and that's another reason why I stayed here, to be near her and to protect her."

I took a drink, then smoked my cigar for a few seconds and went on, saying, "I came here from Upper New York for a vacation, and I stopped at THE COACHMAN'S BAR. That was when I met Darlene, and at that time we both got shot. I fell in love with her the first time I saw her. So, I found myself wanting her more and more, that's why I'm still here. She's the best thing that's ever happened to me. I vowed to stay with her no matter what happened, even if it killed me, but without her it wouldn't have mattered anyway."

I took a drink and looked at Walls sitting across from me, watching me and listening.

"I suppose you're wondering why I'm telling you all of this, huh? I just want to let you know what's going on here. I was helping Darlene, but I never knew she was a cop, now she was found out by someone at the police station. She's hiding somewhere. Miles is the only one that knows where she is and is watching out for her. But Marie wants a hit put on her. Now, this guy Kendall is supposed to be the organization's attorney, and he told Marie this wasn't the time for that. So, I hope she's safe for now. The time she was found out, I went to see Miles because I didn't know what else to do. He told me to go on like I was until this was over. Something else you should know, I know you're an undercover cop too. It was very obvious; your actions gave you away. It was how you looked before doing a job, you had to make sure first if you wanted to do that job or not. You were too cautious to be just any other drug pusher or some killer. You see, I know my men and what they are capable of. I know who should be killed or saved. I want you to know something else, Walls. I never killed anyone myself, unless someone tried to kill me. Lenny done most of the killings, and like I said before, I killed only if someone tried to kill me. Now if I put killers and drug guys in harm's way, then I can't really help it if they get themselves killed." I took a drink and lit my cigar again.

Walls smiled, saying, "Hell! I think you said it all. That's why you had me with you all the time, huh?" he asked, smiling.

"Yes, that's one reason, Walls. I also knew you to be honest and trustworthy. I knew I could trust you not to shoot me in the back. I couldn't do that with any of the men we have here; I had you for my own safety and my welfare.

"I'll tell you something else, Walls. Marie will pay you well for what you've done this night. Take it for your retirement. We got three suitcases from Ted's place. I gave one to Gloria, one for yourself, and put that money away where no one will know about it. You deserve it. I'll take the other one for myself. I'm going to send it to my friend to hold for me. We'll tell Marie that Gloria was not at Ted's place and Jed was killed along with the other men."

I left Walls off at his car with his suitcase of money and drove to Marie's place. She was waiting impatiently for me as I went in. She handed me a drink as she watched my reaction. Her eyes told me the suspense was killing her. But she was also very worried about the whole thing.

"Well! Tell me before I go crazy," she pleaded.

I had to smile as I said, "It went okay, my dear. Ted is dead and all his men are gone to the happy hunting ground, or to the fires in hell! Gloria wasn't around. We lost five of our men. Walls and I are the only witnesses. I would like it if you paid Walls a little extra. He's a man we can trust and we need him."

She came to me and kissed me, then she hugged me tightly, saying, "We should celebrate! I have to let out the feeling I have within me, Steve. You're the man I waited for, we have to celebrate, Steve, okay?" she asked while hugging me tightly. "I have some friends in Manhattan, and they have a party going on there right now. Let's go and enjoy it; we're on our way up, Steve," she laughed and hugged me again.

"Isn't it a little late to be going out?" I asked.

"We won't be long. I want you to meet some old friends of mine," she pleaded.

I agreed, and by one-thirty in the morning we arrived there. The place was jumping with many people there dancing and drinking.

I met Louie and Manda, but Louie looked like a big dummy. I met his kind before, and I certainly would never trust him.

He was a bragger with black hair that looked like some hairpiece. By his actions, he couldn't care less for anyone but himself. He was the type that never looked at you whenever you talked. Manda was an attractive lady, with dignity; she had a pretty face and long black hair. But I noticed she never smiled. She was very unhappy and I could tell by just looking at her, sitting by herself. She couldn't care less about the party and the people that were there. They were Louie's kind of people, drug pushers and killers like he was, and God knew what else.

Marie danced with Louie as I danced with Manda for a few minutes. Manda pointed to the stairway. "There they go! Every time they get together," she said in an angry tone.

I looked at her, wondering just where they were going. And what was up there beyond those stairs?

I turned to look at Manda. "What's going on, Manda?" I asked.

She looked at me in a nervous way and took me by the hand and motioned to me to follow her upstairs. In one of the bedrooms, she pushed a large picture to the side, revealing a small hole in the wall to see through. Manda stood to the side and motioned for me to look. When I did, I got the surprise of my life! It shocked me to see what that little hole in the wall was revealing to me, something I would never think possible, but there they were, in bed having a great time. What was she doing with Louie? A big dummy like him! I couldn't understand that. I got angry, and then I got mad! What in hell was she up to? The woman that told me she never went with anyone.

Manda put the picture back the way it was, then I told her to leave that piece of shit.

"I did once before and he found me. He beat me up so bad, I couldn't go anywhere for a month, until my arms and legs were healed. I'm afraid of him, and I know now someday soon he'll kill me. I know he will, Steve."

I looked at her with her pleading eyes, then she looked away, saying with fear in her voice, "Louie leaves in the morning on a drug deal. He'll kill the man for the drugs and keep them for himself; he's done that many times and gets away with it. He's a killer, and he'll kill me, I know he will," she told me.

I could see the fear in her eyes as she told me this, then she asked, "Will you help me get away from him? Please, I'm begging you. I can tell you where he'll be, and I can meet you there. I just need some money to go somewhere to be safe. That's all I ask." She was looking at me with a frightened and nervous expression on her face.

"What time and what place?" I asked her.

She told me as we got back to the dance floor. I told her I'd help her, and for her not to return to this place. I told her to be ready to travel.

It was a little later when I saw the happy couple coming down the stairs. They started to dance when I looked over at Louie as my blood started to boil.

"You two have fun upstairs?" I asked.

Marie looked at me when Louie came at me like a mad bull, and just as he got to me I hit him as hard as I could, sending him against the wall, and then he fell against a table and never moved; he was out cold.

As I turned to go out, one of the men there came at me, then he stopped when he saw my hand in my belt. The man's eyes were staring at me with hate and ready to kill.

"I'll be happy to oblige you by blowing your stupid head off, you ugly piece of shit!" I told him while his eyes were glaring at me when I was going out the door.

Marie couldn't wait to ask me what was that all about, with her face showing red as she followed me out.

"What in hell was that about in there?" I looked at her disgustedly, saying, "I don't like being made a fool of! You came here only for one reason, to be with that stupid-looking, fatheaded jerk. The idiot with shit for brains. If you wanted sex, then go get it! Don't ever drag me along! I remember what Ted told me, he would give you the world because he loved you, but your love wasn't there, was it? Now you are doing the same thing, with me!"

She sat there in silence smoking her cigarette. She was wrong and she knew it.

"Okay, I didn't think, that's all, I didn't think. I'm sorry, Steve, let's forget it and start over. Don't be mad, let's not spoil what we have," she said nervously.

I looked at her and smiled; I was surprised she even apologized. "Okay, let's forget it; I can't stay mad at you anyway," I told her.

She got close to me as we rode in silence until we got to her place.

The morning came quickly since it was after three in the morning before we got to sleep. We had breakfast when I asked if she was okay.

"Yes, are you?" she replied.

"I'm okay, it's just that I trust you; I think a lot of you."

She smiled, liking what I said.

Just as we got to work on the books, Kendall came storming in.

"You people know what happened last night? No! I guess not! Ted got hit! He's dead! His men are dead! His mansion is in shambles! It's in ruins!" He raved on and walked around like an idiot.

Marie told him to calm down and tell us what the damn hell was going on.

"Well, for one thing, Gloria is gone! She was taken away, or maybe she's dead! No one knows what happened there. We have to have a meeting now, to see who the next boss will be. We need to rebuild,' he said excitingly.

"You can be the next boss, Kendall, and why not? You know the work and the people," Marie told him, then she glanced over at me.

"Oh, no, I have no time to play boss, but I thank you for asking, my dear."

I watched him looking at Marie with undressing eyes and drooling like a pig. I was getting ill again; there was something about him that made me feel sick just looking at him.

"You two will be at my place at eight o'clock sharp tonight, remember, eight o'clock sharp!" he repeated like a father to his kids. He left with a tata, like an old woman would say.

We almost laughed in his face. I told Marie I'd like to hit him just once. It would maybe help me to feel a lot better.

She laughed, looking at me. "He's guarded more than Ted was. You said Ted would give me the world. Ted owned me like I was his possession. I was afraid of him, and he would kill for no reason and I knew that. Kendall never said he was sorry Ted was dead, did he? That's because he never like Ted. They fought many times," she explained.

I took some coffee to quiet my head from pounding because of all the drinks I had the night before. As I sat there, I got the notion about Marie making a play for Kendall.

"Why don't you make a play for Kendall? He'd give you the organization by the way he looks at you. He'd give you anything you want. You'd be very wealthy, Marie," I told her, then she looked at me with a disgusted look that made me laugh.

"You are joking," she said with her mouth open and that disgusted look about her.

"No, I thought you two would make a beautiful couple, the beauty and the idiot."

She started to laugh and went for a cup of coffee. "You're crazy," she said and laughed again.

Shags came in, telling us he had the money for us and he took care of the three men. He said they were surprised when he shot them and left.

I got some coffee and went to work on the books. A few minutes later I said, in a low voice, "If I were you, I'd go after Kendall. Do you know Kendall would give you the whole organization? Do you know what that means, Marie? You would control the whole area, giving you the chance to have more money than you can imagine, just think about this, Marie. I know you don't care for him, but think of the rewards you'll have."

Marie put her head on the table and moaned. I had to hold in from laughing by the way she was feeling.

"Okay, my dear, now think about this. Once you think you have enough money, then we can get rid of Kendall like we did with Ted."

"Will you stop it! I'd vomit on him just getting close to him," she said, looking sick again.

"That's terrible! He wouldn't like that. Marie, no, you can't ruin his suits," I told her, almost laughing.

She laughed also, shaking her head and giving me a disgusting look.

A while later the phone rang, telling her she had some meeting to go to. It was good timing, because I had a date to meet Manda. After she left, I called Walls to meet me. I told him what we had to do as we drove to the bar, where Manda was to meet us. I almost forgot about meeting with Manda.

In minutes we were at the bar, where Manda was waiting for us. The bartender brought us drinks that we just let sit there, then a man came in and went to the restroom with a suitcase that seemed to be full and heavy. Soon after, Louie came in and went into the restroom, not noticing me at the bar. Walls was watching my back as I got my gun out, and I rushed in after Louie shot the man. Then, I shot Louie before he could shoot again, and as he fell he had a very surprised look on his face when he saw it was me that shot him. I opened the bags of cocaine and dumped them in the toilet. Walls and I ran out to Manda, who was waiting in her car. I gave her the money, she said thanks and drove off.

We drove away from there, then Walls laughed, saying I was a regular Robin Hood. I had to laugh about that, because it did go well. Two more rats bit the dust, and drugs destroyed that people wouldn't hurt themselves with. In the same time, I had the chance to free a lady that deserved to be free.

I got back just as Marie came in, saying that Kendall had a deal for the next day at noon. He wanted two men to do the job. It was a frozen-food truck that was supposed to have a box of cocaine worth two million dollars on the streets. So again, I tried to put the bug into Marie's head about being with Kendall.

"Now, if you were the top boss, all that would be yours," I told her.

She laughed, then she slowly nodded her head as she got a cigarette. "You never stop, do you? You're right, you know; if I could only stand him, I could do it. But he's so repulsive!" She was thinking now, and I knew if I kept it up she'd go for it.

I left her there, saying I had to buy a new suit, I'd be about an hour or so. I had to call Liz to warn Miles about the frozen-food truck. Miles had to get the message.

By the time I got back to Marie, she was already dressed and looked very beautiful. I took a shower and put my new suit on. We went to an early dinner, and as we ate I asked Marie if she could act. She looked at me, wondering what I meant.

"You know, to be an actress. You could play up to Kendall and be the boss over all," I told her.

"You trying to get rid of me?" she asked, giving me that sly look.

"Now why would I do that? You know, I'm hurt to think you would even give that a thought!" I had to hurry and take a drink because I was about to choke on what I said. Then I went on, saying, "We could be doing a lot better after you took over. Just think, honey, after we get rid of the idiot, who knows? The whole northeast territory," I told her, smiling.

She looked at me, then she got a cigarette out and before she lit it, she said, "I think you want something, come on now, I know you want something. You are not pushing me for nothing, so what is it?" she asked with a grin on her face.

"Well, yes, I do," I said slowly, and before I could say anything else she butted in.

"I knew it! You do want something! You fraud, you!"

I had to laugh by the way she looked at me.

"Sure, I want something, but not what you think. All I want is this little old mansion here we've been operating from. That's all, Marie, now you didn't think I'd want anything else, did you? How could you think such a thing, you sweet thing, you."

She laughed, saying I was still a fraud. "I can't do it, Steve! I just can't do it. I'd be sick all the time I'm with him, I can't," she pleaded, looking sick already.

"Okay, you'd have that big mansion that Kendall has, and I would only have this little old mansion here and nothing more," I told her as we walked out to the car, with Marie laughing. I had to chuckle myself thinking about it.

As we drove to Kendall's place, I'd look at her and smile, saying in a low voice how well off she'd be if she could just play up to him. She just sat there and shook her head and then she'd bust out laughing.

We drove up the long, beautiful driveway and stopped by a four-car garage, seeing several guards watching us. Kendall's mansion, it was beautiful overlooking the bay.

I said to her in a low voice, "See all this, it's all yours, my dear."

Marie told me to stop because somebody might hear me.

Actually, as I looked again at the mansion, it seemed to me it was nothing more than a small castle. All the windows around the house went from ceiling to the floor. The mansion was just as big as Ted Belini's mansion. But one thing about it, it was more exquisite, in every detail. I was astonished to see such a place. Everything there was nothing more than perfection. It seemed to me these guys tried to outdo each other, or maybe that was how they showed their strength and who they really were, or just maybe who had the most money.

Kendall took Marie's hand and kissed it. I thought he was going to eat it by the way he held it.

"You look lovely, my dear, but don't you always?" he said in his sickening voice as he showed her to her seat, with me following behind.

The table was enormous, with nine other men sitting there watching and drinking scotch and smoking big cigars.

Kendall was watching Marie like he wanted to chew her up. It was like he was hypnotized, or maybe he was so taken with Marie he couldn't take his eyes off her.

He sat down and then he got up, saying, "This meeting will come to order."

I almost busted out laughing, and Marie was looking sick from his girlish voice, trying to look important. I took a drink from the waiter that held a tray before each of us.

"My friends! We all will take a vote for the next new boss. The one voted in will run this place here, and the other mansion will be closed for good. You will notice there's a pencil and paper at each place, except for Marie and Steve. They will not vote. I must bring to your attention to Steve and Marie; these men are bosses from other areas. They will decide our new boss for this area. Now you will begin," he announced as he watched Marie with staring eyes.

I watched the men as they voted, then I looked at Kendall as his eyes were glued on Marie. He then picked up the papers and looked very surprised.

"I'm bewildered, yes, I'm quite surprised it's a tie. That means I must vote, but first I have a question."

Kendall looked at Marie and each one of us with a curious look about him, then his face changed to some kind of blank expression. Kendall took a drink, and that was when I started to get worried! Yes, I was worried. Because maybe he got wind of our getting rid of Ted.

Somehow he found out it was Marie and I that did it. I also thought it was we who caused this meeting.

Kendall took another drink, then he looked at Marie and smiled. "As you know, my dear, I have adored you for so very long." He got a little red in the face when he went on, saying, "Would you consider being my wife?"

Marie sat there, not moving. I thought she'd quickly drink all the drinks that were there, in one gulp, or maybe just pass out! I know I would have if it were me. Marie was red in the face, not knowing what to say or do. Then Kendall told her not to answer now, but he wanted to know within the next two hours when the meeting was over. I could see the men wondering what her answer would be, and so was I with great interest.

We went through the worksheets for the organization for the next two hours. I knew Kendall couldn't wait to hear Marie's answer. I watched Marie, wondering how she would get out of this predicament. Kendall would look at her and drool like a sick puppy. He also looked like he was ready to die right there if she refused his request.

We were told to take our places as Kendall played God at the head of the table. Now was the time for the big answer, would she? Or would she not?

Marie got up and emptied her glass. Then she took another drink from the tray and held it up. "Gentlemen! I hope you all will drink to our wedding!"

I looked at her as I got up with the others and added my cheers. I couldn't believe what I just heard. I could see Kendall was overwhelmed; it surprised him as it did me. Now he would give her his vote, she won, I was thinking as I watched them both.

Kendall stood standing as we all sat down. "Well! I must say I'm astonished, and very happy with your decision, my dear. I will now give my vote to Steve."

When he announced that, Marie looked at me with a surprised look.

Then Kendall went on to say, "My new bride will work with me in the main office. She will be giving you all orders at times, gentlemen, and I would take it most seriously, if any of you to refuse those orders. I will expect your utmost courtesy."

Marie's expression quickly changed. She was smiling now because she really won. She agreed to marry Kendall the idiot just to get that position.

Kendall announced that day they would be going to the Islands for their honeymoon, and the rest of us would carry on until they returned next week, which would be on Saturday. "Steve, I want you to carry on at your mansion until we return. Then it will be no more, my boy. I also know you took liberties with Marie. I would take it most regrettable if you continue to do so. Now please help Marie from her apartment with her things. Bring them here if you will, Steve," he said with a staring look.

Marie met me at the car and as we drove on, I told her I couldn't take liberties with her now because Kendall told me not to. She laughed and kissed me on the cheek.

"How in the world are you going to get close to him? You cringe just looking at him," I said to her, and at the same time I was watching her reaction.

She looked at me with that sickening look on her face. "I don't know, but I have to live with it for now. At least I'll have control of this area, but I'll need your help, Steve. I hope in a short time we'll get rid of him," she said, looking at me.

I saw how she was almost pleading for me to help her. I told her to take one day at a time. I would try to make it as soon as I could; it wouldn't be long, I told her.

We got her things and got back to Kendall's place, then I looked at her before she went in, I couldn't take liberties anymore. She smiled and went in the house.

Driving back down the driveway, I stopped to look at the flowers that grew along the roadway to the garage. Even in the darkness the landscape was so beautiful. Looking out over the bay that opened to the open sea far beyond was wonderful to see. I marveled at such beauty; it was hard to comprehend. Why did people of Kendall's kind and Ted's caliber have such masterpieces as the mansions they lived in? They had everything they wanted, and why not? They killed and robbed people for the money so they could enjoy themselves. All that they had really didn't belong to them.

I was overpowered by the enchantment of Kendall's place. The moonlight was now shining over the waves in the bay, making them shine like tiny little beads as they rolled toward the shore. I was still there at Kendall's place, admiring his breathtaking magnificent home of his. It should have been built for a king and queen instead of the trash that now lived there. But all in all, it made me feel good just to be there to see something like this.

I didn't sleep well that night; I had many thoughts that crowded my mind. I wondered how Marie was going to make Kendall happy by playing the role as his wife. Then my mind changed to Darlene. I was feeling kind of low and lonely. I sure missed her, and I had no idea where she was or what she was doing. I was worried for her safety and hoping she was well secured, like Miles told me. He said he was making sure of her safety.

But there was something in my favor; I had free reign now. I didn't have Marie looking over my shoulder all the time. I felt good for that, because now I could get things going to undermine their organization.

The next morning, I got the men out on their jobs. I told Walls I called Liz to get in touch with Miles to stop a frozen-food truck with drugs. "You know Liz Walls, she works at the WALK-IN BAR," I explained to him.

"Ya, I know her, she's a pretty good-looking woman, married to a cop."

"Yes, she used to be; he was killed two years ago. I think it's time you meet this woman; she's okay in my book. Tonight is a good time to get acquainted. We'll be there at seven o'clock at her bar. I'm still the boss, Walls," I told him, smiling.

Walls kind of chuckled as he left.

I got Mark and Allen to do the drug job, then I called Liz asking if she got a hold of Miles, but he was out and she would try again. I told her about going to dinner with me and a friend that I would like her to meet. I could tell she was delighted and excited; she said yes.

It went well that day and that evening we had our dinner, then I left Walls and Liz; they didn't need me around. It was the same thing the next day; the routine didn't change that much.

By three o'clock, I went to my car when a new Cadillac came and stopped alongside me.

"Steve! You know me, I was one of the men that voted for you. I voted for you because I heard you done many good things about you."

"Yes, I remember you, you're Curtis, right?" I asked. He was one of the guys that drank heavy all through the meeting.

"That's me. I need a favor and I'll pay well for it. I lost three men last week, and I know who they are that killed them."

Curtis went through the whole thing. I told Curtis I'd see what I could do about it. I told him it would not cost him anything. He smiled and handed me an envelope with fifty thousand dollars in it. I figured I'd give it to Walls. He could use it to take Liz out. Curtis wouldn't take the money back, and he wouldn't leave until I kept the money. He gave me pictures of the men he wanted killed and told me where they would be found.

I was wondering why Curtis asked me to handle his problem, because he had men; he knew the men that killed his men. I watched him leave as I stood there for a minute or so, thinking about that. Was he playing games with me? Or was it because he wanted to know if I could handle this job, or maybe he had something else in mind for something later.

Chapter Nine

I went back in the office, telling Sidney I'd be out for a while. I went out the back door to talk to Walls, telling him we had something to do tomorrow morning at seven o'clock. I told him I would like to have Liz with us for added protection. He didn't like the idea having her in any danger, but I told him I just wanted her to do the driving for us. I assured him she wouldn't be in any danger. I went to see Liz after I left Walls at the back door he was guarding.

I told Liz what I had in mind, and she was very happy to help. From that day on I had many things to do, going over the books and seeing that the jobs were completed. I worked all that day without going to lunch. It was now around eight o'clock that night when I went to dinner at some place by the bay, then I went to bed.

It was warm and sunny the next morning as Liz drove Walls and me to New Jersey. We parked on a side street in a quiet development of small houses being built in a row. There were trees that grew as fences around each house. I handed Walls a cigar and a stick of dynamite, then he looked at me with that look of his because he didn't like dynamite; it made him nervous just to be around the stuff.

We walked to the house that was hidden by the row of trees as Liz stayed in the car, keeping it running just to be ready if we had to get out fast. Walls went around to the back as I went to the side of the house to throw the sticks of dynamite though the windows, but we had to throw them at the same time. Looking as our watches, as soon as it said nine o'clock that morning we threw the dynamite through both the windows.

The two dynamite sticks blew the house apart.

Just after the blast I ran inside the open doorway, finding two men dead. One under a pile of rubbish, one thrown against the wall. I was about to leave the house when Walls came in the back as I looked up, seeing a man bleeding and shooting at me. I fell backwards from the force of the bullet; that had to be a big caliber to be able to push me backwards and make me fall like I did. Walls got him from behind before he could shoot again. I got up slowly and went outside. Walls helped me to the car and drove away quickly as we could as Liz drove.

Walls looked at me, seeing me holding my arm, and asked me if I was alright. "Your arm is bleeding," he told me.

"I know, and it hurts like hell," I told him when he took his handkerchief and put it over the wound to stop the blood from coming out like it was.

Liz drove to the bar so she could get back to work. Walls drove to the mansion quickly so the doctor could fix my arm. It was just an hour later when Curtis came in smiling. He was carrying an expensive bottle of scotch.

"I'm pleased you're with us, Steve; you sure get things done. Now I'd like to have a drink with you," he said, smiling and pouring drinks in three glasses. "To us, Steve." We drank as Curtis went on, saying, "I have things to do, but first come to my car; I've got something for you."

We followed him to his car, and under the seat he took out a package.

"This, my friend, is for you. I'd be very offended if you didn't accept it. Someday I'll do you a favor." He got in his car and drove off.

In the bar Sidney and Walls watched me unwrap the package, a pile of hundred-dollar bills and a new thirty-eight automatic with two clips and a silencer. I gave my gun to Sidney, and I put the new gun under my belt.

Sidney made us a drink, then he looked at us, saying, "I met a girl last night, she's beautiful." He went on, telling us all about it.

It felt good to hear that. As we listened to him about his new love, it reminded me when I met Darlene. Walls smiled, telling Sidney to be good to her and to treat her right.

Sidney went back to work, then I told Walls we only had one more day to be free because after tomorrow, which was Saturday, Kendall and Marie would be back from their honeymoon.

Walls went back, guarding the back door of the mansion, and I went to work in the office. By five o'clock that afternoon, I went for a walk by the bay. I was missing Darlene more now and more each day, and it was bothering me. I just wanted to see her, but I knew I couldn't because of her safety.

I could see her in my mind, such a lovely lady I was thinking, in the warm afternoon sun. I could see her smile and her expressions as I teased her. Her red hair and shining eyes that brought out her natural beauty. Yes, I was missing her very much. I was also missing my place in the woods and longing for the day when Darlene and I would be leaving the city of New York. I knew I had to make some kind of move to get all this over with.

I went back to the office to finish what I had to do, and as I sat there in the office I was thinking I had to figure a way to stop Kendall now. Maybe with him out of the way, I could take Darlene out of this place in a shorter time.

It was almost seven o'clock when I locked the door to the office and sat down at the bar, telling Sidney I'd have one drink and go home. Sidney started to make the drink when one of our men came in, saying he was robbed and almost killed. He sat down, telling us he was just getting in his car to bring the money from all the betting places he collected from around the city when two men jumped him and knifed him in the arm and shoulder. I could see where he was bleeding, and he seemed to be getting weak from bleeding so much. His shirt was all bloodied on the side where he was knifed.

"You know who they were, Johnny?" I asked him when he fell over and hit the floor. He was out like a light.

I called for the doctor, who came within minutes and was there taking care of Johnny. The doctor said Johnny would have died if he wasn't taken care of when he was. I then called for Walls to meet me here at the office. I wanted to find those two guys that robbed Johnny. When Walls came, I told him what happened to Johnny and I wanted to go and find those guys. We had to go to the Harlem part of town, where Walls was a little reluctant to go. Hector and Sam just came in to play cards and have a drink. I asked them if they wanted to make an extra thousand dollars. They said they would like to, so I told them what Johnny told us and where those two guys would be. We went in two cars and parked under a streetlight right on the main street.

Walls and I walked about a hundred feet ahead of Hector and Sam. As we walked along, we watched for the ones we wanted and to make sure by the time we got to the other end of the street we would know everything and anything that was there on that street, and also the other streets. We were not letting anything go by us. We walked the streets for over an hour before we saw one of the men we were looking for. I motioned to Hector and Sam, letting them know who I was after and to surround him.

As they made their way, slowly going behind the man standing in front of a liquor store, Walls and I walked to the front of the man.

I asked him, "Hey, man! The place open or what?"

The man looked at me and started to run when Hector grabbed him as Sam took hold of his arm and pushed him into the alleyway.

They held him there as I said to him, "You and your friend robbed one of my men this evening. I want you to tell me where your friend is, and right now! Or my men here will cut you up so bad, your insides will just fall out! Do I make myself clear?" I stared at him, trying to look mad as hell.

The man was middle age and frightened while I was still staring at him. He said the other man was home and he had the money with him. He told us not to hurt him; it wasn't his idea to rob our man, it was his friend's idea.

I lit a cigar as I looked at the man. "Let's go see your friend, and you better be right about this or these guys will carve you up right now. I know you don't want that. Do you?"

"Take it easy, man! I'll bring you to him, okay?" The man was very nervous and shaking, looking like he was ready to faint.

He brought us to an apartment on the second floor of an old building that needed repairs badly or to be rebuilt. We got to the door when I told the middle-aged man to call out to his friend and tell him he had to see him right away.

The man knocked on the door, then we heard a voice inside. The man inside yelled out, "Yeah! Who is it?"

"It's me, Ben! I need to talk to you, Larry! It's important, man!"

The man inside said, "Okay to come in, the door is open," and he was in the kitchen eating.

We all had our guns out as Ben opened the door and went in the living room with Ben in front of me for a shield and for safety's sake. We then went in the kitchen, not seeing anyone there we quickly looked around, then I saw the kitchen window was open. All of a sudden, a man from the bathroom shot Sam, then Walls turned and shot that man, whoever he was, we didn't know. But at the same time, shooting came from the window. Ben fell after he was shot twice, and I fired at the window.

I quickly ran to it, seeing Ben's friend Larry running down the fire escape. I went out the window with Hector behind me while Walls ran down the stairs to head off Larry. I couldn't get a good enough shot at Larry because he was fast and staying close to the trees. Just as I got to the bottom of the fire escape, Walls was running by me, going to the trees. When Walls fired, he got Larry in the leg, making him fall, but Larry lying on the ground was still shooting at Walls but missed when Walls quickly shot back, killing Larry.

I told Hector to go back up to the apartment and look for the money Larry took from our man. While he went back up, Walls went for the car and drove it close to the building, then I went back up the fire escape with Hector. We found the money and ran back down the fire escape, and drove off before anyone came looking around. After we got back to the office, I gave Hector his money and thanked him for his help. I also told Hector I was sorry that Sam was killed; he was an okay guy. Hector said he would miss him.

We sat at the bar with our bartender Sidney having a drink when Hector said, "It got a little scary there at that kitchen, didn't it?"

Walls laughed at the way Hector said that; he looked like he was ready to faint.

"Yeah, it did, Hector, but we got our money back and we also got rid of two guys that won't rob people anymore," I told him. "I'm sure Johnny will also thank you, Hector, for helping us catch those guys. You know, Johnny was cut up and in pretty bad shape."

We had another drink and then I went back to Marie's place to get some sleep.

The next morning, I was at work early to make sure I had everything done that I was to do. But I dreaded the next day, which was Saturday, because Marie and Kendall would be back. The men were all out doing their jobs while I was counting money and finishing up what I had to do on the books. When I looked toward the door, to my surprise Marie and Kendall came in. They had a tan and were smiling.

"Well, you two are back early, how were the Islands?" I asked, looking at Marie.

"Lovely, my boy," Kendall answered in his girlish kind of way.

Marie smiled and nodded, looking at me.

"We had a wonderful time, didn't we, my dear?" Kendall went on saying. "I'm impressed at the way you are at work, Steve, I like that. We came back to take care of business. We have to eliminate someone from our organization, Steve!

The organization tolerates no wrongs done against it! There will be a meeting at my place this very night! Be there at eight o'clock sharp! I detest anyone that's tardy. Come, my dear," he said as Marie gave me a look.

I watched them go, seeing Kendall hold her arm like a child afraid to let go. It disgusted me to see two first-class rats that really deserved each other. They would probably end up hurting or maybe try killing each other.

Walls came in as I was lighting my cigar, then I was about to say something when we heard on the radio that a policewoman was found dead in her apartment. The woman who found her was another policewoman. It was said she was shot in the back as she was entering her apartment that day. Her name was Darlene Preston.

I put my cigar down, wondering if I heard it right. It couldn't be Darlene! Not my Darlene! It had to be someone else! Then it was repeated again. I knew then it was no mistake. I heard it right.

Walls looked at me like he was as much in shock as I was. I got up and walked outside to the back porch, looking out at the bay. I was looking but I couldn't see anything. I just felt like I was dead. Walls was talking to me but I couldn't hear him, all I was hearing was the radio saying Darlene was dead. She was gone! I wiped the tears that fell almost out of control.

I sat down as my body started to weaken. I got up again and slowly walked back to the office, with Walls following me in. Walls told me we had to think this thing out, and he was right, I had to calm down. I had to get control of myself, but how could I?

All I could understand was I lost the woman I loved, and for some reason I couldn't think straight. All I knew was she was taken away from me. Who in hell killed her? I really had no idea who.

Right then I couldn't hear Walls trying talk to me, because I could hear Darlene's soft voice and laughter. I couldn't see anything but her red hair that hung down to her to shoulders, her shining eyes when she would look at me.

Almost in a whisper, I said, "It couldn't be, it can't be, Walls!" But then, a penetrating realization of what I heard was stabbing me like a bolt of lightning going right through me. She was gone and I would never see her again.

I felt cold shills going through me, making it hard for me to breathe. I felt weak and unsteady as I tried to get hold of myself. I took hold of the bottle of scotch I had on the desk and took a long drink from it.

Walls sat down looking at me, wondering what I was thinking about, but he also knew I was planning to fight back because he knew how I felt about those people, and he also knew I was trying to get rid of them every chance I had. Then it came to me. I looked at Walls as I remembered what was said when Marie and Kendall came back early.

"That bastard! Kendall said Marie and him came back early because they had to eliminate someone that's in the organization. I should have realized it then, I should have known he meant that someone was Darlene!" I took another drink from my special bottle, looking at Walls again. "You know, Walls, Kendall said to be at his place at eight o'clock sharp, and he said not to be tardy. Yeah, I'll be there! Walls! I'll be there right on time!" I told Walls with a stare.

Walls looked at me, seeing how I was thinking now.

"Wait, Steve, I'm going with you; Darlene was my friend too! What's on your mind?" he asked, knowing only too well what I had on my mind.

"We're going to do something we should have done a long time ago. We're going to get rid of Kendall! That girlish-talking piece of shit! Yeah, Walls, we'll be there at his house. It'll be the only kind of meeting he will understand," I said, taking another drink.

I lit a cigar as I tried to think and to calm down.

"Eight o'clock was the meeting with his men and Marie; they will be there and waiting for our surprise. I have four sticks of dynamite left. We will use them all! But first I have to get my things from Marie's place. I have to bring my things back to my hotel room that I never used until now. You know, Walls, I asked Miles to watch Darlene; he told me he would make sure she was safe, but she wasn't safe, Walls. He didn't do his job like he said he would. I wonder what part he has in the organization," I said as I lit my cigar with Walls looking at me with a look of concern about him. He didn't like the remark I just made about his lieutenant.

"Now wait just a damn minute, Steve!" He jumped up. "I know Miles! He's one man I trust! You're way off base, Steve; now let's take care of Kendall tonight. We'll go from there when this is over," he said, staring at me.

I didn't say anything more at that time, but I felt that Darlene was betrayed, and not only her, I was also betrayed because Miles told me himself he would see to it that she'd be safe. I still say he didn't do his job. We took my things back to my hotel room that I hadn't used much.

Chapter Ten

Walls and I got our guns and dynamite, and we had drinks before going to the job we had to do.

The time came to make the twenty-minute drive to Kendall's place. We both wore dark clothes to make it harder for anyone to see us. The night was warm and getting darker, and looking more like a storm was coming as the clouds were beginning to form, making it that much better for us because with the darkness and the rain people wouldn't be out walking around to see us.

We parked just a few minutes away from Kendall's house, then we walked, keeping low among the trees and the brush. We got to the side of the house, with the big windows that faced the bay, that was where the meeting room was, and I could hear them inside talking. So far, no one saw us and I wanted to look in but I didn't chance it, because if anyone saw me it would give us away and ruin our chance to do what I wanted to do, and that needed to be done.

It was starting to rain lightly as it got much darker. We looked around to the back of the house, seeing a guard there smoking. I shot him with the silencer on my gun. We went to the other corner and shot the guard that was there. Walls and I each lit a cigar, then Walls went to the other side of the house as I waited for one minute for him to get there. I lit my two sticks of dynamite and broke the window, and threw them inside. Like Walls did the same on his side. We then ran for cover behind some trees and lay on the ground. It wasn't more than a few seconds before all the dynamite went off. The blast blew the walls and windows flying everywhere, the debris flew in every direction, almost hitting us. After the shattering blast was over we ran inside, making our way around the rooms to make sure all were dead.

Six men dead that I met earlier were scattered around the meeting room. They were the top men from the other states.

We couldn't find Kendall or Marie, and somehow they were not there. We went through the rooms that were broken up and badly destroyed. We checked all the rooms. But some of them were so broken up, it made it hard to get around in there. Then Walls went to check the basement as I went to check the back of the house. So far all were dead that we checked. But we never saw Marie or Kendall, the ones we wanted the most.

I was checking the kitchen and the back pantry area when I heard a shot from somewhere in the house. Just then I saw a closet door move. I was just ready to shoot when some damn cat came running by me, scaring me half to death. It took some time for me to compose myself after that.

I forgot the closet and started to go down to the basement to help Walls when the closet door opened and a gun was in my back. I knew then I made a bad mistake. I also knew I was a dead man when the gun pushed harder against my back. I turned around slowly, knowing only too well who it was. Kendall was standing there with his two red eyes bulged out like two baseballs, staring at me with such hate and calling me so many names I never even heard of before. He was breathing hard and was wounded, with cuts and bruises about his face, with some blood running down his arm.

"Drop that gun, Steve! And don't you even move!" he said in an unsteady voice. "You did a terrible thing, Steve! My house is in ruins! Why would you ruin your position with us? How could you do this to me?" He went on as his gun was wavering about and pointing at my chest. I thought it would go off any second by the way Kendall was looking at me.

"You shouldn't have killed Darlene!" I yelled at him. "You had her killed, Kendall, you rat, you!" I shouted again.

"What are you talking about? I know nothing about your Darlene! You raving, insane maniac! You did me great harm and I cannot let this pass! My house! It's ruined! Look at my house!" he yelled out again. 'No! I have to kill you!" he yelled out as I just stood there.

I knew my time was up, and I knew I wasn't going to get any mercy! Then I heard a shot, knowing I was dead, but then as I stood there I saw Kendall falling slowly as he grabbed for my shirt with eyes staring at me. Then the gun slowly dropped from his hand. I was still looking at him as he fell to the floor. I was still thinking it was me that got shot and was falling to the floor.

It was Walls that shot him from the cellar doorway as I just stood there like in a trance. I couldn't move.

"Well, you going to stand there?" Walls yelled out.

I looked at him, hardly believing I was still alive. "Yeah, yeah, I'm coming, Walls!" I yelled out to him as we ran for the car.

I sat there in his car thinking how lucky I was. Yes, I certainly was thinking how lucky I was that Walls was with me. I gave a sigh of relief as I took a cigar from my pocket.

"I could feel that bullet, Walls. You saved my life back there, you know."

He smiled as he drove on.

It was sometime later when we stopped at a bar for a drink. I mentioned to him I didn't see Marie at Kendall's place. Walls agreed that he didn't see her either. He said maybe she was on her way there, or maybe she wasn't supposed to be there at the meeting for some reason.

"You know something, Walls? Kendall was about to shoot me when I thought he had Darlene killed, but he just looked at me surprised like, and he denied it. If he was really guilty and was about to shoot me, then why would he deny it?" I lit my cigar as I sat there thinking about it.

"I don't know. Maybe he didn't, Steve. It could be that Marie did it," he said as he smoked his cigar, then looked at me, asking, "Did you tell me that Marie put a hit on Darlene? I think you did, Steve. I'm wondering about that now, if she did have her killed."

"Yeah, you're right, Walls; Marie really did say she wanted to put a hit on Darlene in the first place. It has to be Marie; we have to find her, Walls. Let's go to the mansion; she might be there," I said and hoped she would be there.

We drove for the mansion as I reloaded my gun and Walls' gun for him also. It wasn't long after we drove up the driveway, seeing it was quiet and not many cars there either. I was wondering about the men there, if they heard anything about Kendall being killed or maybe his house being blown up or not.

We went in seeing the men playing cards and having a drink. It seemed like it was always the same as before. It also looked like they had no idea of what happened. But we were ready just in case for whatever action would take place if it did. Sidney smiled, getting us a drink and asking what we were doing there at that time. I told him we were looking for Marie and we thought we'd have drink as well.

"It's quiet tonight; the guys are just getting some booze in them for the night," Sidney told me when Marie came in, telling Sidney to bring a drink to her at the office.

I looked at Walls, motioning him to stay there and keep watch while I went in the office.

"I came from Kendall's place! You really did it," she repeated again. "You got rid of him, Steve. Now it's all ours. I didn't think you would do it so soon, though. What made you do it tonight?" she asked.

I looked at her, wondering if she really knew what this was all about. Was Marie really unaware that I was after her, as well as Kendall?

Sidney came in with a drink for Marie as I sat down, watching her. She took a drink and looked at me, waiting for an answer.

"Yeah, Walls and me took care of Kendall, Marie. But it wasn't that I did it for us! It was because when you and Kendall left me this afternoon, Kendall told me that you both came back early from your honeymoon for one reason, that was because you had to eliminate someone that was against the organization. Then, just minutes later, after you two left me, Walls and I heard on the radio that Darlene was dead! She was shot in the back! I got mad as hell, Marie! I went out of control; he shouldn't have had her killed like that. She didn't deserve that! So, she was a cop, and she fooled me too, but to be shot her in the back! No, that got me mad as hell," I told her in a low voice as Marie stood there looking at me with her mouth open. I got up, taking a cigar from my pocket while she just stood there watching me.

She took a drink and sat down, then looked at me again. "I guess you really liked her, didn't you? Why else would you feel like this? Here I thought you killed Kendall because of me, and for us," she said with a low tone in her voice that sounded hurt and disappointed.

I lit my cigar, which had gone out, and I watched for any unusual look or some gesture from Marie. I needed some kind of answer who it was that killed Darlene. I was giving another dig at Marie.

"The truth is, it wasn't Kendall that killed Darlene, was it, Marie?"

She looked at me with wonder as her face got a little red. "Wait a minute! You don't think I had anything to do with her death. You heard Kendall, he said no to any hit on her. At the time I thought about it, but I would never go against Kendall, as powerful as he was. No, Steve, I did not have her killed. And besides, Kendall told me to forget Darlene, because she could not hurt us in any way because he knew the police captain was putting her to work at the station from now on."

Marie lit a cigarette, then she said, "Steve, we came back early because we had to stop one of our top men in New Jersey; he was taking all the money from that section. My God, Steve, you killed Kendall for that? Here I thought you killed him for us, but it wasn't, huh?" Her voice took a higher tone as her face got red. "You really liked Darlene, didn't you? I'm sorry as hell about that, Steve, I really am. I'm sorry it wasn't me you liked. Here all the time you made me feel like you cared for me," she said in a kind of a hurt way that showed in her voice again.

I puffed on my cigar as I looked at her, wondering if I made a mistake, maybe a bad mistake. Maybe Marie wasn't the one that killed Darlene; by the way she talked, I seemed to believe she didn't have anything to do with it after all.

"Okay, I made a mistake about you and Kendall. Now you got it all, Marie, the whole damn area; that's what you wanted in the first place. Now you do whatever you want with it," I told her as I was going for the door.

Marie got up very solemnly as she said, "I need you, Steve; we can be bigger than ever now that Kendall is gone." She took a drink and sat back down like she was thinking about it. "Well, you know I can't do it alone; I need you. I know now you liked Darlene more than you did me, but I still like you, Steve; I always did, because you got things done," she said, looking down, then taking a drink.

At that moment, I felt kind of bad for her; she felt very down and it made me feel the same way, but someone killed Darlene, or had her killed. I had to find the bastard! I wouldn't rest until I did find that rat, right now. Nothing else meant anything to me. With Darlene gone, I was at a loss. I was feeling weak like the strength and the will just left me completely. But there was something else I had to do. I had to get back and be myself again, and to go on and act like I was in charge and ready to fight again. I had to fight these low-class people. I had to finish them off one way or the other, before I went back home.

"I'm sorry I accused you, Marie. You said you wanted to put a hit on Darlene, and I thought you actually did. Yes! I did like Darlene, but she's gone now. It's over, let's forget it," I told her, trying make her believe it wasn't bothering me, but it was bothering me; it was making me sick just remembering about Darlene being shot in the back. A beautiful lady I loved and lost.

I sat down again, saying in a low voice, "You know, Marie, whatever I did here while I was with you, I did it for you. You told me you wanted money to leave this damn place, well, so do I. For your information, I do like you, more than you think, Marie. I was doing everything for you as well as for myself. I always made sure that you were safe. I knew how much you wanted to get from the organization. Also, you knew I would get rid of Kendall someday anyway, so it was sooner. Okay, now it's up to you. We can do it together or you can do it by yourself. I don't care about it one way or the other. Actually, I'd rather go home, Marie; I'll leave that up to you. Right now, you have it all. Take over this whole damn area, and make all the money you desire.

"Another thing, Marie, I never knew Darlene was a cop. For all I know, maybe you're a cop. But that's a chance I have to take, and maybe I'm in trouble anyway. Darlene must have told the police what I was doing here. I'm glad that Kendall is gone; I couldn't take him much longer."

"Okay, Steve," She smiled, saying she'd like to go somewhere for a few drinks and talk.

I agreed and we went out to the bar, where Walls was waiting for me, ready for action he thought might come. I told him it was okay and I didn't think Marie did the killing. I told Walls I'd see him in the morning.

We went to a bar just a mile from the mansion. We sat in the back of the room and talked about the next day. It wasn't going to be easy now, because we lost many men and we needed to find more. She told me she knew a guy in Chicago; he was big in the mob there and parts of Canada. Marie said she'd give him a call in the morning for a talk. Meanwhile, she wanted the men we still had to continue with the work that had to be done.

We went to her apartment that she still had before, on the second floor overlooking the bay. We had a quiet evening going over what we had to do. She seemed to be quite happy by the way it was going. I didn't sleep too well that night because my mind was on the lady I loved, and knowing she was gone now and I wasn't handling it very well. I was going wild, and inside my head was hurting, and the pounding seemed to never stop. But at least so far, I was getting back to feeling better little by little. I knew I had to keep alert and do my job, and in the same time I had to find ways to let Liz know what was going on here.

I got up and stood by the rail of the porch, looking down at the bay below. The stars and the full moon were lighting up the heavens, with just a slight breeze that showed a ripple over the waters below. It was so quiet, and I saw how beautiful it was while looking out at the bay. My mind was quieting down now; I felt a lot better being alone for a while. I guessed being out here just looking around and seeing how wonderful and beautiful the scenery was in our world, we don't take the time to look around. I believed now I could sleep; my head and nerves seemed to be quieting down now.

I was up early the next morning feeling a little tired, but at least I felt somewhat better. I washed my face, trying to look and act like my old self again. Because for one thing, I didn't want Marie to think I was grieving over Darlene. Even if I was, I didn't want to show it. I was looking in the mirror now, and I wondered why I was still there.

I wondered why I didn't just get them all killed. Even if I happened to get killed myself, who would care anyway? I had nothing to go home for anyway.

I heard Marie coming as I wiped my face with the towel, trying to compose myself.

"You got up early, Steve. I hated to wake up," she said, smiling.

"Yeah, I really couldn't sleep. I only tossed and turned, so I got up. I didn't want to bother you, seeing you there out like a light."

Marie kissed me on the cheek, then smiled and went out to get dressed.

In a short time, we went to breakfast. She told me about the first guy she went out with a few years ago. He got so involved in the underworld that he forgot about her. She said he even treated her rough like all thugs usually do. Like they own you and can do whatever they want.

She told me his name was Antone Agustis, a man with no feelings for anyone or anything. He was hard core with a heart of stone.

I looked at her, asking, "You want someone like him to come here and help us? Why? He sounds like trouble to me."

She looked at me, looking a little surprised. "Well, for one thing he knows where to get men, and we need them right now, Steve. He also knows the top people that can help us even more."

"Okay, but be careful; he could get rid of us and take over this entire territory. Or, he could try to take you away from me," I told her as I watched her reaction.

She smiled as her face got a little flushed with redness showing when she got up, saying, "He can try. Antone is a bully and a killer, but one thing about him, he gets things done. He's like you, Steve, well, in a way he is. He does it by force, you do it by using your head," she explained.

We got the men out on their jobs, then Marie was on the phone making a call to Chicago. While she talked to Antone, I went out to the bar, seeing Walls coming in. He motioned to me to go outside with him.

"Steve. Liz got word to me to tell you to meet with her tonight. It's very important." Walls looked around like he was worried someone was looking or listening. "Okay. There's a guy Marie is calling on the phone, he's called Antone Agustis. She's trying to get him to come here to help us. Get the news to Liz, maybe Miles can set up a welcome committee for him."

Walls left as I went back to the office

Marie was still on the phone. She smiled, then hung up. "He'll be here in a few days. He said he can get me as many men I want, Steve, so that takes care of that. He also told me he wants to meet me in Lake Placid for a meeting before coming here; he wants to talk to me first. So, I'll leave this evening, Steve," she told me with a smile, looking more relieved that she was getting herself back together again. "We'll be bigger than ever; we'll make big money now," she said, smiling more now.

By seven that evening, Marie had left for Lake Placid, which was situated in Upper New York State. So now I'd be alone with Walls to carry on here until she got back. Walls picked me up at Marie's place just as Marie left. I lit a cigar as we rode to his apartment so I could take a shower and change clothes. He looked at me and started to tell me what happened to him some time ago. Walls said he was a good friend to me, and it was fortunate for him that I had him with me in all this mess.

I watched Walls light a cigar, then he said, "I know what you are going through, my friend. I know only too well, Steve." Then he puffed on his cigar and looked around, and he went on, saying, "I had a girl, a beautiful girl, that meant more to me than my own life. That was over six years ago, Steve. I haven't been with any women since. You helped me to forget my past by getting me to go with Liz. That's what you have to do, Steve, forget the past," he said in a low voice. He looked at me, saying, "I never told this to anyone before, Steve, it bothered me too much to talk about it, but I can now. One night six years ago, I was out walking with my girl when a shot came out of nowhere. My girl fell and died in my arms as I held her. She never had a chance, Steve. It also killed me.

"It was a long time before I could think straight. But a friend told me to get away and forget. I'm your friend, Steve; I'm telling you to do the same, to get away from here. You need to forget and to see different people and different places.

"I know what you are feeling right now, and I did what you did; I went out and found the killer, and I killed him for what he did to my girl and to my life. I found him like we found Kendall and others. And we both know they had nothing to do with Darlene's death. They said so in their dying breath. Well, the man I killed didn't either. The man I killed robbed a store that we walked by, and as the man ran out the store owner shot at him and said it was the robber that fired that shot that killed my girl. But the robber had no gun, all he had was a knife. I later found that out, but it was too late.

"After you've rested for a while and you need my help, we'll find the one that killed Darlene. Knowing you, I'm sure you will be out there looking for the killer anyway." Walls smiled, looking at me.

I turned to look outside the car window, knowing Walls was right. "Yes, Walls, I need to rest for two days or so, then I will find him!"

I sat there and lit my cigar again. I was tired and sick; I just couldn't find the energy to really care now that Darlene was gone from my life. As I sat there smoking, Walls went on telling me what I should do, and so on. After a few minutes, I asked him about Miles, the lieutenant. The way I put it to him, he didn't like it; in fact, he got very irritated.

"It seems kind of odd that Miles was supposed to watch for Darlene's safety, but she was shot! You think Miles had her killed because he needed some extra money for his retirement? He was the only one that knew where she was. What do you think about that?" I asked him while watching his reaction, also for some kind of answer.

Walls gave me a look showing he was totally upset with me. He was also upset with my lack of confidence and the mistrust I had for his lieutenant.

Walls took a puff on his cigar, and I could see some redness showing on his face and showing a little anger along with it. "You're way off base! Damn it, Steve!

I've known Miles for years! He's a damn good cop! He's not the guy you're looking for, so take that out of your head!" he said sharply. "Now take a shower and change clothes. I have some things to do. I'll pick you up in one hour, so be ready, will you?" He went out, leaving me there with my thoughts.

It wasn't easy, being alone now. I was thinking of Darlene as a tear or two filled my eyes. I took the shower as my mind was looking for some answers to her death. I still had no idea as to who could have killed her. Then I started thinking differently; maybe it was some guy trying to rob Darlene, or maybe it was someone she knew. I couldn't think anymore; my mind and my body were tied in knots.

I changed clothes that Walls had in his closet, then I stretched out on the bed and went to sleep instantly. I slept until Walls woke me up, feeling numb and a little weak. He said we had to leave; we were supposed to meet with Liz at the WALK-IN BAR. Then he told me he had to pay some bills and other things that had to be attended to.

We got to the WALK-IN BAR, then Liz looked at us like we were ghosts or something.

"Where in hell were you guys?" she almost yelled out. "I was so worried about you two! I heard on the radio and the TV about gangs and the underworld fighting each other and all were killed. God! I thought you both were killed," she said with a sigh.

I looked at her, seeing how worried she was, so I told her what we did. "Look, Liz, when I heard Darlene was killed, I thought Kendall and Marie had her killed. I went crazy, Liz. Walls and I went after them and killed them, all that we know of except for Marie. At the time we blew up Kendall's mansion, Marie wasn't there. Actually, I don't think she had anything to do with it. Anyway, I told her while Walls was listening to me."

Liz made drinks for us, then said she had something to tell us. "I tried to get a hold of you guys, and no one at the station knew anything either. Where in hell were you guys, Steve?" she asked as she looked at me. "Darlene isn't dead! Miles put out that report because he thought maybe somebody would try again. She's alive but not expected to live. The doctor said there was no hope! He's done all he could to save her." Liz laid her head in her hands and cried. She went on, saying through her sobs, "I don't want her to die; she's my best friend!"

Walls tried to console her as she said again she didn't want Darlene to die and cried all the more.

I was trying to comprehend what I just heard as I stared at Liz. "Did you say she's alive? She's alive, Liz?" I asked again.

Then Liz came from around the corner of the bar and hugged me all while still crying. She wiped her eyes, saying, "She's dying, Steve! Oh, God. She's dying! They can't do anything for her, and she's my best friend. The doctor said it's up to God now." Liz wiped her eyes and sat down, but tears came down her face again.

"When can I see her, Liz? I have to see her, Liz!" I told her, not realizing I was demanding, then I told her I was sorry to be acting like I was.

"I'll call the doctor in the morning, Steve. I'll let you know around nine o'clock, or maybe you should call me," Liz told me with tears starting to fall again.

I left them. I needed to be alone; I needed to take a walk to be able to think. I walked for blocks as the tightness was slowly losing the tight grip it had on me. At least Darlene was alive; there might still be some kind of hope that she'd make it.

I got to my hotel and sat on the bed as I thought about the times we talked and made plans for our future. But now it was a future that might not be. All the planning and the hopes we had were now slowly dying away, like they never existed. Tears were now falling, and I couldn't stop them. I had to wipe them away and try to rest.

I lay down, closing my eyes, only to see her in my mind, reminding me she was alive, but then I had that feeling again that she might not make it. I got up and washed my face, then I went to a bar for a drink. By nine that night I went to dinner. It was eleven o'clock when I was back at my hotel. I made a drink and sat by the window. Then, I was looking up at the stars, like Darlene and I did many times before. The night sky was covered with stars; some of them would blink, and some were bright and lit up the heavens. Every once in a while I saw a star falling.

I went back to the time I first met Darlene. I remember what we said and what we did. The dreams, the hopes, and all the wishes we shared that night as we sat at that very window. All that was putting more pressure with in me.

I sat there for hours, wondering what to do or where I should go. At that time, I had no idea; I was at a loss and confused seeing my world changing ahead of me, and I didn't like what I was seeing. I had a hard time coping with it.

The next morning, I awoke still sitting there by the window, in the chair all night. I called for Liz to hear for some kind of word, but Darlene was still the same. And Liz was waiting for some word from the doctor.

All that day I waited, then at five that afternoon Liz called me. She said I could see Darlene at seven o'clock that next evening, and not before. But I had to see the doctor first, but at least I knew I'd be seeing her soon. That kind of news made me feel so much better. I went to dinner feeling I could eat now that I would be able to see the lady I loved. I got to bed by ten that night, and I slept more soundly than I had for some time.

I was up early the next day, with a new hope and a new start and outlook. The sun was coming up, warming the air, which felt pleasant. After I had breakfast, I drove toward the shore for the day, just to be alone and to think. I sat by the water, looking out over the bay. Just beyond the bay was the open sea. It was quiet there as I was remembering the two of us sitting at that same spot. Memories now were coming back to me as I got up and walked along the beach. It was right there that Darlene and I spent time talking and making plans for our future. Every now and then I seemed to hear her voice, but it was only my mind wishing it were true.

As I walked along, I thought about the wonderful times we had right there at that spot where we sat after I took her from the hospital and drove her here. And it was here we got to know each other. All this was now hurting me more, as I could see her face and her smile, her soft voice talking to me. These memories I would have and would be a constant reminder for my entire life if she didn't make it.

As I drove along the shoreline, my memory brought back the many things Darlene and I did, then as I drove on I didn't realize how close to Ted's mansion I was. I stopped to look at a house of beauty. Of course, the beauty was only on the outside appearance that graced the shoreline. But it was a house of evil on the inside.

It was a house that was everything against the people. And what was far worse, it was against God! In every possible way!

I stopped the car as my eyes looked at the house that Ted said he had built. It was truly a magnificent mansion, but now it was in ruins. It was built with blood money from those that were murdered and robbed by Ted and his crew of killers and people killed that got in his way. Built from all the dead bodies he created for his mansion. And it was too bad to destroy such a masterpiece. A beautiful structure that loomed with the aura of evil, destruction, suffering and anguish. It stood there high and mighty, with the violence it portrayed and practiced. But that same violence came back and destroyed it and all those that dwelled in it.

I drove farther up the coastline to the next mansion, or should I say the castle! The place was far more magnificent than Ted's masterpiece. That was a structure that was built by the master of all builders. But did that builder really know why he built that beautiful building? And for whom that building was being constructed? I wouldn't think so, because if he did know that, then I doubt very much if he would have built it with all his expertise, his technical knowledge of find craftsmanship. No, in his heart he would not put together, with such precision like he did, that was so well planned and executed.

Yes, when I first entered that exquisite mansion, I couldn't but noticed the architecture, the flawless workmanship, and whoever built it made themselves proud. Again, it was a place where someone used his every means for everything for the wrong purposes. For the underworld to spread its murderous deeds on unsuspecting innocent people. They unleashed violence and murder wherever they pleased. Yes, another masterpiece that fell in ruins and rubble. It too fell by the same violence it portrayed, and it stood no more.

These places stood only in ruins now, to show all the world that in time that was what would happen to all those that went against the law of man and, most of all, against the law of God!

I left that place knowing I had a hand in destroying it, even though it took us too long to do just that. Because including myself and my men, we should have acted quicker and a lot sooner. But at least all those that lived in that place are now gone. Maybe God will find a place for them.

I drove farther down the shore. I took my shoes and socks off and walked on the sand in my bare feet. It was what my beautiful woman that I loved had done before. Just letting the waves go over my feet. As I looked around, I could see a few people doing the same as I was. I had to smile, noticing they were laughing and having a great time. I was thinking how terrible it would be if Darlene didn't make it, if she left this world. It certainly wasn't the world that I was worried about, no! It was me I was worrying about. It was me that needed her and loved her. It was me! who cared, not the world; they couldn't care less about my feelings or for the love I had for my lady. No, it was not the world.

After all we did and went through together, and to be no more and gone from my life would be hard to bear. I left there with the hope maybe something would happen to change things.

I stopped at a bar not far away for a drink when I heard a voice that I knew before. I turned around, seeing Shags coming in and sitting next to me.

"I thought you were dead!" he told me.

"You know I was on a job, Steve, when I heard about Ted and his men. Someone did him in but who cares? I never had dealings with him. He wanted it all, but he wouldn't come to terms with me on anything. I figured you got it yourself, Steve. We worked good together, care to do it again?" he asked as he ordered another drink.

We had a few drinks and talked about the jobs he wanted me to do with him. I told him to give me a call at the hotel. I gave him the number to call whenever he was ready for me.

It was now three in the afternoon as I went to see Liz at the WALK-IN BAR. A few minutes later, Walls came walking in as I got a drink. He said he checked everyone at the police station but found nothing yet.

I told him about Shags and how he wanted me to go do some jobs with him like we did before. I told him I would because maybe I might just find something that would lead me to Darlene being shot like she was. Who knew, I might just turn up something.

After a while I left there and went to wash and change clothes for my visit with the doctor at seven o'clock that night. I was anxious and excited to see Darlene. I met the doctor in his office, and he told me she wasn't responding.

"I've done all I could for her, my friend. It's up to her now. But I doubt if she wants to live. I believe she wants to let go. Anyway, that's the way it looks like to me. It's also up to God; he's the one who will have the say if she lives or not!" the doctor told me sadly. The doctor took me to her room and left me at the door.

I went in slowly, seeing her lying there with her eyes closed. She was very still like she was already dead. But even as she lay there, she looked like a beautiful princess. She was as beautiful as ever. I could feel tears coming now, as I was now feeling her pain. How I was wishing it was me lying there instead of her. As I looked at her, I was seeing all my hopes and wishes slowly fading away. I could do nothing but stand there like a damn dummy, and I felt so helpless and was getting so frustrated.

If she would only open her eyes, she would see I was there for her. She would see I was there to help her. How I wanted to shout it out loud, for her to know I was there with her now. But what good would that have done? She wouldn't think she would hear me anyway.

I went to the window, looking out over the big city and the crowded streets, seeing people coming and going in all different directions. I found myself praying to God, to save her life and to please let her live. But how could I do that? I didn't even know how! It was something I wasn't familiar with. I didn't even know what to say or how to say it. I wiped my eyes as the doctor walked in.

"See how hopeless we can be? That's how I feel at times like this," he said as he nodded his head and went back to his office.

I turned from the window and went closer to Darlene, seeing her there looking like she already passed away and had gone to the other world. I pulled a chair close to the bed and sat down. I took her hand and, without realizing it, I was talking to her out loud. I was saying in a low voice that was broken up, between wiping my eyes and the hurt that was in my heart. It was very hard for me to say the words I wanted to say. I tried to find the right words that would comfort her. But how could I comfort her when I was slowly dying myself? As I sat there, I was talking to her as though she was hearing what I was saying to her.

"I don't blame you for not wanting to come back here to this place, and to this world of ours. I don't like it here either, my dear. With all that goes on in this damn world, I can't blame you. But you know, Darlene, my love, it isn't the world or what's in it. I'm thinking about no, my dearest. It's you and me! You're the best thing that ever happened to me, and also the only thing that matters to me. I only hope you know that, my love. If you only could hear me, you would know I'm trying hard to ask you to stay here with me because I need you, honey, and I love you more than anything in this world. Please come back to me, so we can both live," I was almost begging.

I wiped the tears that were in my eyes as I turned to see the doctor behind me.

"You love her, that's good! She'll need that, and what's more, she will need your patience as well. Come, if she heard you at all, she'll come around. Go home or go somewhere so you can rest. You'll be sick if you stay here like you've been. It's up to God now, so go and rest. If something happens, I will call you," he said with a smile and being very sympathetic.

The doctor was a middle-aged man, about fifty years old. He had white hair and looked tired. He was kind and considerate by the way he talked. I knew him to be a man that took pride in his work and profession. That made me feel like Darlene had a chance now, as long as he was there for her. I gave him my phone number at the hotel and also at my friend Ward's house.

I was thinking I'd go north to visit my good friend Ward and the place I had in the woods. Maybe I'd be able to rest. The doctor was right; I was tired and weak. I could feel it as I walked back to my hotel. I had trouble breathing, as my chest was heavy and seemed to be weighing me down. But instead of going to my hotel, I went to the bar to see Liz. I told her what the doctor told me and how Darlene was doing.

I gave Liz my number and told her Marie wouldn't be back from Lake Placid for a few days. It would give me a chance to leave for a while.

We talked for a while, and every once in a while Liz would have to wipe her eyes. She was a very emotional lady. She told me she knew Darlene for a long time and they were like sisters. Then we talked about Walls and how she loved him. She thanked me for having Walls go to meet her. I told Liz to tell Walls to watch the mansion while I was away.

It was around eleven o'clock that night when I left there and went to my hotel. I was very tired, not physically but mentally.

I kept thinking if I would have been with Darlene, maybe she wouldn't be where she was now. If only I knew where she was supposed to be hiding, maybe I could have saved her. I thought so many things that night as I tossed and turned before going to sleep with exhaustion.

It was warm and sunny the next morning as I got up and on the road by six o'clock. I was tired, but I also felt with the new day that somehow things would change, at least I was hoping they would. But I was also hoping for the doctor not to forget to call me soon, or at least by the end of the week.

I drove until I got tired, then I'd stop for coffee and a sandwich. It was a long drive from the city to my place up North. I drove at normal speed and, smoking my cigar, I had the radio on, listening and enjoying some soft music that seemed to calm me. It helped me to drive those long, lonesome hours.

I was thinking about the doctor now, about the way he looked at me as he told me about Darlene. He was very professional in his work and, from what I saw about him, his concern and ability as a doctor. I knew he had done his best for the woman I loved. He even prayed for her to live, giving me the feeling that in some way, if there was any chance at all, he would bring her back.

When I arrived at my place, Ward and the men were working on my house. Ward smiled, asking me about my beautiful redhead. I told him what happened as he looked at me so surprised when he had the look of hurt and sadness that showed on his face. He felt so badly to hear that kind of news. Ward and Meggen loved Darlene, as though she was their own daughter and part of the family.

Later he showed me where the rooms were to be and what was going on with the house he was building for me. We talked for the next hour, then I left him to walk the path to the lake; I needed to be alone for a while. I had no idea of what to do. I was in some kind of trance as I walked along the path in deep thought. I was startled by a rabbit that ran in front of me, then it ran across the path and into the woods. A few minutes later a deer stood by the lake, looking at me as I watched it, then it took a drink and went back into the woods. I sat there by the lake, taking a cigar out of my pocket and looking around.

This was the place I longed to be. I missed being here; I was hoping it wouldn't be too long before I got back. I sat there a while trying to think things out, seeing Mother Nature all around me, seeing the beauty that I wanted to share with Darlene. I tried not to think negatively but I couldn't help it. My mind went back to what the doctor told me; it was up to Darlene now if she wanted to come back or not. It was also up to God if she was able to come back here. It would be a terrible shame to lose her now. Like the doctor said, she might not make it, and that sent a chill through my body that alarmed me.

I heard Ward calling for me as I watched him making his way toward me.

"You okay? It's getting late, my friend, let's go have a drink."

"Yeah, I can use one right now. I'm having a hard time, Ward. It's killing me not knowing what's happening. It's tearing me apart. What will I do if she doesn't make it, Ward?"

"Come, let's have a drink and talk; we used to do that many times, Steve. It helped then, and I'm sure it will now," he said, patting me on the back.

We talked until late that night. He felt so badly for Darlene, but in the same time it was me he was feeling mostly for. He knew what I was going through. We'd been friends for many years, and he knew six years ago since my wife was killed. That was how long it was that I hadn't been with any women because I didn't trust women, on account of my wife playing around with any man she took a liking to all the time I was in Viet Nam. Now I found a lady that I wanted, but she might not be around much longer.

The next day I watched the men working on my house, and as I sat there I was wondering if all this was for nothing. I watched them for the next two days, letting time just pass by. Waiting for some word, or maybe a phone call, but neither one ever came. I waited for something to just let me know if everything would be okay or not. There was nothing but agonizing fear and the uncertainty of what was to come.

That night I walked along the path with enough moonlight to see my way into the woods. The stars were out all over the sky, with a slight breeze that rustled through the trees in the warm night air. Walking slowly, I could hear the frogs over by the lake, and the beetles were also making themselves heard. I walked along the edge of the lake, seeing the cool water glisten under the moonlight. As I looked up over the trees, I could see the mountaintop just beyond the lake, standing there like a watchtower silhouetted against the sky. As I stood there staring at the top, I seemed to hear Darlene's voice in the passing breeze. I never realized by standing there I was asking the mountain for help. I was praying, but not in words. I was praying with the feeling I had in my heart and my soul. Then, I was trying to find the words, the right words, and to say those words like I should say them, but I knew nothing about talking to God because I never did before, and I wondered if I should now. I also wondered if he would hear me if I did talk to him, or would he turn away? Why would he bother to listen to someone that never recognized him before? Or even gave a thought that he even existed?

As I looked high above the trees at this mountain, my eyes got watery as I asked, "Make her well, God! You have that power to give life, or to take life." I stood there as if the mountain would answer my plea, and somehow I was hoping it would. I was so much in need of help from the highest source. Like the phone calls I waited for that never came. The torture I was going through, waiting for just some kind of news that never found its way back to me. I had never asked for help from anyone in my entire life. But this night as I stood before this great creation that only God himself could put together, I was asking in my own stupid way for his help that I so desperately needed. As I turned to leave that place, I thanked him for whatever help he could grant me, no matter how little. I would always have him in my heart.

It was late before I got to sleep that night. With the worry and the agony of the uncertainty, it was impossible to rest my mind and my body.

I left the next morning for the long drive back to the big city of New York. I had to get back. I hadn't rested or relaxed since I'd been away. How could I? Not knowing if Darlene was alive or maybe passed away while I was at my place. And God knew I was slowly dying myself. I certainly wasn't really alive.

It was very late that night before I got to my hotel. I had to make many stops for coffee and to control myself enough to go on. Like Darlene, she didn't want to go back to the city any more than I did after she saw my place in the woods. We had no choice, like right now I had to go back to that city where she was fighting for her life, or at least I was hoping she was fighting hard to come back to me.

The next morning, I went back to the hospital. I bought a small radio with a cassette tape. She liked the song "MAKE THE WORLD GO AWAY." So many times, she told me as we danced, she didn't like this world.

I went to see the doctor before seeing Darlene.

"You certainly don't look any better, Steve. You didn't rest, did you?" he asked. "Have a seat; I have something to tell you." He looked at me and smiled. "Your lady is slowly responding. She will make it, my friend. When you talked to her before you left, she must have heard you. You know, my friend, sometimes when people talk to those they love, they at times will hear and that will bring them back. She will become stronger little by little, but it will be slow, and I hope you will have the patience because that you will need, my friend," the doctor explained to me with a smile that showed how happy he was to give me that good news.

I sat there listening to his words, but I needed more time to let all that he told me sink in. Now as I sat there, I started to feel the strength coming back to me, with that heavy weight starting to leave my body. For the longest while I was feeling like I didn't care what happened to me. Now I felt like I was alive again and ready to go on with my new life that was just given back to me.

I tried to find the words of some kind to adequately express my thanks for taking care of someone who was letting me live once again. For someone that I so desperately needed, but somehow I didn't have to, the doctor knew how I felt. He knew what was in my heart. I shook his hand like he was God himself, and to me he certainly was!

I went in to see Darlene, and like before she was lying there not moving. I put the radio on low and sat down near her, holding the hand of the one I was so in love with, the one I adored since I first met her. She opened her eyes and then slowly closed them. My heart jumped, and I knew now she would live; she was coming back to me. She knew I was there with her, but most of all she knew I would be waiting for her. She also knew I would do anything for her. I was excited now with this new hope and the new strength I was now feeling within me.

I went to the window, looking up at the sky, knowing my prayer was heard. I was granted what I asked for, and I wanted to say thanks but it seemed so little for what God had done for me. He answered my prayer and I could ask for no more. My lady would live now. I would never forget this gift that was granted to me for as long as I lived.

It was noontime when I left there. I went to a small bar not far from the hospital, where I had a beer and a sandwich. I noticed our waiter from the New Yorker Restaurant that Darlene liked. He was sitting there looking at me, asking how Darlene was doing. I told him the story up to now. He looked at me and was about to leave, saying, "You found the away, my boy," then he turned to me, saying, "You received a gift. I would hope you'll never forget that!" Ben smiled and he left.

He left me as I thought about it, yes, he was right about that. I found out there was someone we could always turn to. But sometimes we forget that. I know I have. I also know now that there's always someone that hears and will help if we seek him out, if we only take the time.

I went to my hotel and lay down for a nap. I didn't wake up until midnight. It seemed so good to feel rested.

Chapter Eleven

I washed and was about to go out when the phone rang. It was Shags. He wanted me to meet him; he needed me to help him on some job he had two hours from now.

I met Shags on Fifth Street. We had a drink, then he told me about the job he had. We were supposed to intercept two men with the money they took in from all the bets throughout the big city. Shags said it was about two hundred thousand dollars involved. I looked at my watch, seeing it was a few minutes before two in the morning. We drove to the docks where the ships loaded and unloaded metals of all kinds to Japan and China. Shags parked the car where they stack all the large empty crates as I followed Shags to a small building that was used for an office.

Shags went in the building shooting with me right behind him, then he quickly shot the two men but not before one of the men shot Shags in the chest. When Shags backed up against me I grabbed hold of him, but he was badly hurt and went limp, then I let him slowly fall to the floor. Shags didn't know what hit him, it happened so fast.

I looked around, not seeing anyone around, so I quickly grabbed the money and ran to the car. Just as I got to the car door to open it, I saw a dark figure of a man coming from the back of the office firing at me. I fell to the ground when I heard shooting, but it wasn't me shooting at him; it was the man that shot himself when he fell, then I heard a loud groan as the man was falling. I got up slowly. I went over to the man, seeing him looking up to the dark sky, but he was dead. I got in the car, and as I drove away I had to smile, thinking again that I didn't have to shoot anyone because they really killed each other when I said it out loud, "Three more rats dead!"

I drove about a half-block away from my hotel and left Shags' car there in some alleyway.

I got to my hotel room, putting the money under the bed. I then walked to the WALK-IN BAR, just two blocks away from the hotel.

It was almost three o'clock in the morning. I asked Liz for a drink and sat down with her. She said she was waiting for Walls, so I told her about my seeing Darlene and how she was coming along. I was just going to tell her about Shags, but I changed my mind when I saw Walls come walking in.

"I just came from the docks, Steve. I saw Shags there. Would you know anything about Shags getting killed with two other men?" he asked, watching me and waiting for an answer.

"Shags got it too, huh? What do you know? I wondered where he went to. You know, he was supposed to call me but he didn't. I told you about that, Walls," I told him as he gave me a suspicious look.

He got a glass of beer from Liz and sat down. Walls still wasn't sure of my answer; I supposed he still thought I was with Shags that night when he got killed.

Liz smiled as I got up looking at Walls. She told Walls about what I told her, how Darlene was coming along.

I took a cigar from my pocket and started to light it, saying, "I guess that makes it complete now, Walls; with Shags dead, that takes care of the gang as I see it. You come up with anything on your end yet? It has to be someone maybe from the police station," I told him again.

"I checked everyone at the station, Steve. I have no idea who, but I know one thing, Steve; it wasn't Miles and I'll put my life on that!" Walls told me, a little excited.

"Okay, it wasn't Miles! Then who in the hell did shoot Darlene? I know Darlene didn't shoot herself," I told him, getting a little irritated myself. I got another drink from Liz and changed the subject until Liz closed for the night.

The next morning, I took the money from Shags' job and took it to the doctor. I told him to use the money for anything he wanted to, telling him the money came from the drug gangs. He said he would use it to pay for those that couldn't pay for their bills. He also told me he put Darlene in another room under an assumed name for her safety because she would cringe every time the door opened. I was happy the doctor took good care of her.

I left the doctor and went in to see Darlene before I left the hospital. I saw that she was asleep. I stayed a few minutes, knowing she was okay and seeing she was looking better each time I saw her.

I got back to the mansion to see what was going on. It was quiet now that we had only a few men working the routes and the routine jobs. Sidney told me that Marie called saying she would be back by the next day. So, I got the books done by late afternoon, then I went to dinner. An hour later I went to the WALK-IN BAR, where Liz was busy with her customers. I had a drink when Walls came in.

"Okay if I sit with you?" he asked.

I smiled, nodding to him to sit. "I haven't bit you yet, have I?" I asked him when he gave me a look.

He sat down, taking a drink of beer, then he put the glass down, saying sarcastically, "Well, by the way you acted the other day, you think all cops are no good. You almost accused me, maybe you think Liz shot Darlene."

I asked Liz to bring me a scotch and soda, then I lit a cigar to calm down and not get too excited. I looked at Walls and said, "Think about it, Walls, the organization is about dead. The only one left was Shags, and I know he wasn't involved because he never knew Darlene, so he never had anything to do with her death. Someone from the police station is guilty, I don't know of anyone else, Walls. But don't worry about it; as soon as Darlene is able, we'll leave this damn city."

I looked at him knowing how he was feeling about it. I asked Liz to bring me another scotch and soda.

"Look, Walls! I know you did what you could, I appreciate that," I told him. "And I apologize, okay?"

He looked at me and smiled, saying okay. We had another drink and talked about other things until late that night.

The next morning, Marie and her friend she knew as Antone came into the office.

"Well, nice to see you're back," I said, looking at Antone.

He was a tall man with some baldness on top. Antone had a tan like he was in the Caribbean Islands for years. He looked strong, with the look of someone who couldn't care less if the world stopped or not. Marie introduced him to me as I held my hand out, but he just grunted and looked at Marie.

I sat down all the while he was watching my every move. It looked like Marie was wondering if I was ready to fight or something. I never said anything to Antone from that time on. I just waited and was ready just in case he had any ideas.

Marie sat down, telling Antone about our operation there while Antone just looked around, not paying any attention to her. Then he looked at Marie, telling her in a rough manly voice that he didn't like what he was seeing there in our operation.

Marie stood up, staring at him, not expecting that kind of remark, and asked, "Why?"

Antone sat there like he was in charge, announcing, "Starting right now, I'm the boss here, Marie. You came to me for my help. I will make this place bigger, and a lot better than you have now! But I will do it my way! I'm also going to change the operation! It will be the same as my place in Chicago. I have eight men coming in the morning to take over the men you have here! I'll throw out all those I don't want! Starting right now, I take half of everything that comes in here, that's for myself! Now I want to see your books!" he demanded.

I had to smile at the way Antone came here and demanded what was going to be, and that was that. I was looking at Marie all the while Antone was giving the two of us his demands. She let herself get into trouble by going after that big mouth, acting like he was the big boss over our operation. I could see the look on her face; she was very disturbed and very worried. I don't believe she expected that Antone would just take over, like he thought he would. Marie really thought he was the guy that would solve all her problems, but it backfired on her. Antone was out for himself; he was not there to help anyone, and certainly not for Marie. I believe she knew that now by the look on her face.

"No, Antone! You get nothing! I called you to help out, instead you think you're taking over, and that you won't do! You gave me the boot some time ago, and I thought you changed but I see you're still the same rat as before!" she shouted.

Antone looked at her with a stare, and his cheeks were twitching. His eyes got cold as he turned to look at me. I was ready for any sudden moves on his part. I then pushed the button I had on the floor near to my foot to warn Walls, by the back door, and also at the bar where Sidney could hear it. It was our way to be ready for any such emergency.

Antone stood up, taking his gun out, saying in a loud and very angry tone, "I'm here to take over! I will take over with or without you, Marie! No one will stop me!" he said, yelling louder. He looked at me with a growl and, still talking loudly, saying, "I'm taking over and nothing even you can do about it, buddy!" he shouted at me.

He bellowed again and waited for me to make some kind of move. But I just sat there and shrugged my shoulders, as if it was okay with me, while Marie looked very angry with me for not doing anything to stop him.

When I thought Walls was ready by the door, I told Antone, "I think you better put that gun away," in a loud, demanding voice.

He looked at me, pointing the gun at my chest and turning red in the face. "Oh! I suppose you will stop me, buddy?" he asked like he was ready to laugh, like it was all a joke.

"Ever since you were here, my friend, you were covered!" I told him in a low voice. "Now put the gun away and we will talk, or if you want you can die right there where you're standing, old buddy!" I said as I sat there staring at him while Marie watched Antone, wondering what his next move would be.

He seemed to be confused by me just sitting there and not moving, and at the same time he was wondering just how I was going to stop him.

Antone laughed as he pointed his gun at my chest, saying in a loud voice, "You're dead! You hear me, you're dead! Now die!" he yelled out.

Walls came in, telling Antone to drop the gun. Antone quickly turned but not fast enough; he had no chance. Walls fired and so did Sidney, shooting from the other door at the same time. Antone fell with a look of surprise on his face that we outsmarted him.

Marie put her hand to her mouth with a surprised expression. "I thought he was going to shoot you, Steve! You just sat there and did nothing, and I thought you were gonna be killed," she went on hysterically.

"Yeah, he thought so too, didn't he? But now we have his men coming in the morning, so what about it, Marie?" I asked, looking at her.

"I don't know," she said with a red face. "Maybe wait for them and shoot it out, or just tell them Antone went to California or something like that," she went on in an excited way, and not really knowing what to say.

"We can try that," I told her, then I told Walls and Sidney to have the boys take Antone's body out to the bay somewhere and dump him. I then told Marie we can take care of our own place. We didn't need anyone to come here to give us help, but she insisted on having Antone to come here, so now I thought she learned that wasn't a good idea.

"Thanks, Walls, and you too, Sidney, for your help. Just don't say anything about this; no need to have it spread around, and also to anyone else about this."

Marie was sitting down, lighting her cigarette, and then she looked at me, asking, "You were ready for something like this, huh? I don't know, Steve, you're something else. I seem to underestimate you at times. You make sure of things like this, and I would never have thought that Antone would do what he tried to do. He wanted this place for his own, and he would have taken it if you didn't have the men stop him," she told me with a stare.

She called for Sidney, telling him to send in her two men that she had waiting in the barroom. Marie got up and kissed me, then she slowly pulled away from me. She smiled, then her face changed to a different expression now. She stared at me with eyes wide with fury, and her cheekbones were now showing because of her biting down so hard with her teeth.

Her face was now getting red and showing a rage that I never saw before. She was going out of control, for some reason I was not aware of. I had no idea of what was happening, or why.

The men came in when Marie took her gun out of her dress pocket and pointed it at me. I slowly sat down, feeling like something was about to happen again, and I didn't feel too good about it. So I pushed the button on the floor again for Walls and Sidney to come in the two doors like they did before. By pushing the button, Walls and Sidney could listen to what was going on in the office. It was an idea I had when Marie left for Lake Placid, just in case she had ideas about getting rid of me, so I rigged this device that would maybe save my life if anything went wrong in the office. It was the feeling I had when Marie told me about Antone, and not only that, but I knew how Marie thought; she wanted money so bad she'd do anything to get it. Now I felt like I was in danger again, only this time she wanted me out permanently.

But I didn't really know why; we did well together, and she always seemed to be happy with that. But it was different now; she seemed a lot different ever since she came back from the Islands with Kendall. But again, she seemed happy that Kendall was killed, so what in hell was her problem? Why was she looking at me like she was now, with that gun pointing at me?

"What's the gun for, Marie?" I asked. "I thought everything was going the way you want it. You going to shoot me with that thing, or you just fooling around?" I asked, wondering what the next move was going to be.

The men she sent for were just standing there beside her while she held her gun on me.

Then she went on, saying in her nasty and unsteady voice, like she was about to explode, "I'm not playing around, Steve! Everything was okay until I found out that you were in love with Darlene! I knew that by the way you talked about her, and that hurt me because I thought you loved me. But in a way, I felt like you didn't really love me, long before this happened. But I was hoping it was just my own feelings. But it was the time Darlene was caught ratting on our organization, and we found out that she was a cop! You knew she was a cop! And you were in love with her, and you didn't care if she was a cop anyway, did you?"

Marie turned to her men that stood on each side of her like two statues, and she turned back to me as she got a cigarette from her dress pocket and her man on her right side held a light for her. After a puff or two, her face turned from red to a more calmness now. Then she looked at me again with her face changing again to a look of defiance and hate as she went on.

"The next thing you did wrong, Steve, was hitting Kendall without consulting me first. But that was okay if you done it for me or for us! You did it because your Darlene was killed! And again, I thought you did it for me, and then you had the audacity to accuse Kendall, but he had nothing to with it any more than I did. But to accuse me also, that was the last straw, you damn fool!"

She took another puff and let the smoke come out of her mouth and then her nose, looking hard and certainly not ladylike.

I was hoping that Walls and Sidney were behind those doors, like they were before, because I knew she was ready to shoot me very soon, by the way she was looking at me right now.

"So, you see, Steve, I can't trust you anymore! I think you're working with the police. When I talked to Antone in Chicago, I had the feeling that you were here for that reason. I know you are working for the cops!" She yelled it out loud. "That's why I made a deal with Antone, to get rid of you. But he wasn't as smart as he thought he was. I couldn't believe you outsmarted him like you did; it surprised me too! It's all over now and it's too bad for you, because now my men here are gonna take your dead body and dump it in the bay just like you had Antone's body dumped."

She looked at her two men while she raised her gun to my chest again and was about to shoot when Walls and Sidney came in shooting. Marie stood there stunned and couldn't move while her two men fell in hail of bullets.

Marie's face was red and distorted as the hate filled her whole being while she was looking at me and waving her gun, trying to hold it still to shoot me. Walls told her to drop the gun, but she wasn't listening; he fired twice, hitting her in the chest, with each bullet pushing her enough to make her drop the gun and fall backwards.

I never had my gun out and I don't think I could have shot her anyway. I knew she was a killer and deserved to die for what she had done, but I wouldn't have shot her myself.

I stood there looking at her on the floor with her eyes slowly closing, then she looked like she was just sleeping. I was seeing how pretty and how attractive a woman she really was. If only she had shown some of that beauty within her heart as she was on the outside. She would be alive now.

I was thinking about all the times she told me about going away from here and the many times she told me she never set foot from the big city. She never knew the real world that was beyond that crowded and busy city that she lived in all her life. But she could have, she could have done so many other things to make a living and to go where she always wanted to go. But instead, she chose all the wrong ways to make a living. She had done so many things wrong just for money; she never gave a thought to or even cared about the killings and those she had someone kill. She also went against all the laws of man and God just to satisfy her own needs. Now she would answer for what she had done, just like we all would do when that time came.

I went out to the bar for a drink. I sat down and took a long drink when Walls came in.

Sidney gave Walls a beer, then sat down next to me, asking, "What's going to happen now, Steve?"

Sidney was looking at me, and I could see he felt somewhat uneasy about Marie being killed. Everyone in the organization liked Sidney; he was a quiet lad that did his job well and bothered no one. But now was the time to talk to him.

"There is no more organization, Sidney; there is no more Marie, but there are still men throughout the city making the usual, bringing in the bets and also drugs that still will be coming into the office. But all that is coming to an end. I suppose our jobs here are just about done, Sidney," I told him as I took a drink. I patted him on the back, saying, "My friend, I got a deal for you, because you done a good job for us. You are a good man, Sidney; I want you to have some money, so you and your girlfriend can get married. Now, we are all leaving this place, and we have a hundred and fifty thousand dollars in the office that I want to split up between us. I know you can use it, but spend it quietly; you don't want people to wonder where you got it, okay? You go home and forget this place."

Sidney looked at me with a blank face as I went on.

"Yes, old buddy, forget this damn place! And all the evil that went on here, let it all go from your mind, Sidney. You and your girl live a good life," I told Sidney.

Walls puffed on his cigar and smiled looking at me when we went in the office. I took the money out and we each had our share of fifty thousand dollars. Sidney shook hands with us and went to the door and smiled.

"Thanks, Steve, and you too, Walls. you two guys are okay, and thanks for the money. Now I can marry her and get far away from here," he told us, going out the door.

"I hope he makes a good life for him and his woman, Walls; I like that boy," I told him as I finished my drink.

Walls went behind the bar and made both of us another drink. "Marie certainly made an about-face, didn't she?" Walls remarked as he sat down after handing me a drink.

"I can't figure her doing that, especially when everything was going so well. What in hell made her go so against you, Steve? And the way she changed so quickly to such hatred toward you. I can't understand that," he added, taking a puff on his cigar.

I nodded as I took a drink, then I said to Walls, "I guess you didn't hear what she said before she got nasty. You weren't behind the door when she said she was pretty sure I was a cop. Yeah, she said Darlene was an undercover cop and I must have known that. Because I was with her so much, so I must be a cop too. That was her thinking, and there was no way I could change her mind. Later she said she couldn't trust me anymore, and that's why she called that Antone guy; she figured that Antone would kill me and she would have him to work with.

"I was lucky, Walls, yes, I was lucky because in a way I had a funny feeling about Marie going to meet with Antone. They met for one thing, to make plans on getting me killed and out of the way. When Marie and Kendall left on their honeymoon, I heard about having a listening device before, so I did the same thing so you could hear what was going in on the office. It was my way trying to play it safe with people that kill for a living, and I didn't think I was safe to trust them. It was a safe way to be able to hear someone in another room. So, by installing that device, it really did save my life two different times. The first time was when Antone was going to shoot me, and you and Sidney shot him. The second time was when Marie was going to kill me, with her two stooges standing each side of her. I had no chance of coming out alive. It was a good thing I thought about having that hearing device."

We sat there talking and the only thing we had was to wait for the men to come in from their jobs, and that wouldn't be for some time now. So, we were not in any hurry now. We had seven men out working, and as I sat there I got to thinking about the men and that place, then I looked at Walls.

"I was thinking about something, my friend. What about the men we still have here? We can't just let them go, Walls; you think you could call Miles or someone there at station, they could come here and pick these guys up? It sure would help us."

Walls looked at me and smiled. "I don't really know, Steve; I have a problem with that. Yes, if I call them I know they will come. But do we really want that? You know as well as I they will be out on the streets again and doing the same damn thing. Besides that, Steve, they would also be out looking for us. It will be us looking over our shoulders. We can make them a deal, surrender or go for their guns, that's my deal I'll give them. They're killers, Steve, and we're still giving them a chance to be free, or it could even be us that will be killed. But I'd rather take that chance instead of letting the police take them."

"Okay, Walls, remember this, I was for taking them in like the good guy I am, but you're the one that wants them dead, the bad guy you are."

He almost choked while taking a drink. Then he laughed.

"We won't go into that right now. It's not that I want to fight them; it's what can happen later that's bothering me, Steve. I know for sure they will be out doing their rotten killings and putting more drugs out on the streets again. All the time them rats been here, in this mansion, they were doing whatever they wanted. it's time they pay for their crimes. I cannot let them just get away with it. I can't let that happen, Steve."

I knew what Walls was saying, everybody did, especially the police; they went through it all the time. It's a shame killers get out for all kinds of reasons; sometimes our laws should be changed to stop rats from getting away with their terrible crimes. If you kill, then you should be killed. But some people don't agree. Now these men that were coming in this evening were killers and drug pushers; they were as bad as they came. They didn't belong in any jail, but if they chose to give up then we'd take them in.

"Let's take all the drugs and flush them down the toilet, and all the whiskey and cigars we'll put in the car. We'll be ready to leave here after we take care of the men that are coming in."

We had the car packed and ready. I had a cup of coffee as we waited. We sat where we could see in all directions, with two guns each and two other guns on the counter, in case we needed them.

Now we were ready to get this over with so we could get along with our own lives. I knew Miles would like to be here with us, but it was best he didn't get involved. This way it would look like drug gangs fought it out and killed each other. Thugs that plagued our world, but Miles couldn't, so it was better for Walls and I to end this for good. And it was also better for Walls and I to make it look like a war took place between the organization and the gangs. It was better to make it look like they fought it out and done away with other. That way the media and the public wouldn't feel like the police were overpowering and too brutal, like they often do say about the police. They thought the police could stop crime by being mild and using kids' gloves. But that's not the real world!

In this real world, you have to fight fire with fire; otherwise, we'll be overrun with crime, just like it is right now! You have to fight them on their own terms! You have to fight violence with the same violence they fight us with! The sooner they knew that, the sooner we would have some peace in our NATION!

I knew Walls would like to end this also, he would rather be back to his police station, doing his normal job. And I would be waiting for Darlene to heal enough to take her away from this city that she had known for so long, and certainly far too long. Yes, the city she'd like to get away from, and wanted to for a long time now. The city where her mother and farther were killed! The place she knew of violence, gangs, killers and drugs that were everywhere. Yes, she was ready to leave and looking forward to a better life in a better place.

We both were looking forward to that place, our place in the woods, somewhere in the Adirondack Mountains. It was my place that was waiting for us to return.

I was looking at my watch when a car came up the driveway. Walls went out the back door to make it look like it always was.

Two men came in, seeing me there at the bar having a drink, when one of the men said, "Hey, Steve! Here's the money we got from New Jersey. Tell Marie we want to change to New Jersey to work out of instead of here."

The other man went behind the bar for a drink and asked about Sidney. I told him, "Sidney don't work here anymore, and you guys can't work in New Jersey either; that's not possible, men."

The man looked at me, asking, "Why, what's the difference? You got the money we brought in," looking surprised at me.

"For one thing, men, you two guys are going to the police. This place is no more my friend! Marie is dead, and her friends are all dead! Now you both have a choice! Either give up and take your chances with the cops, or go for your guns you both have on you. But make damn sure that's what you want to do! Because Walls is waiting for your answer!" I told them as I got up, watching them closely.

"Wait, Steve! Are you saying you are in with the cops? What is it, Steve?" he asked, getting very nervous as he stood there looking at me and then as Walls.

The second man started to back away, then I said, "Yeah, that's what I'm saying, I'm with the cops, and Walls there is a cop. So, men, give it up, you have no chance, guys!" I told them with a hard look.

Then one of the men started yelling out, "You no-good-bastard cops! You're not taking us in, you rotten, lousy cops! You and Walls are nothing but shit!"

That was when they went for their guns, but they both fell as one of the men got to fire one shot. Lucky for us they weren't that good with guns.

We dragged them to the back room, where they wouldn't be seen when the other men came.

I lit my cigar, which had gone out, as we heard another car coming up the driveway. As before, Walls went out to the back door looking like a guard, like the men were used to seeing. The men coming in had no idea what was going on here. They came in asking for a drink; they said they had a hard day making drug deals. After they had a drink, Walls came in just in time when I was telling the men that Marie was dead and also Kendall and the men he had. I told them they had to turn themselves in to the police. They looked at us and each other when they quickly went for their guns as I grabbed for my gun, but the man to my right shot me in the arm, making me drop my gun, then Walls got his man and turned to get the man that shot me.

My arm hurt so bad, it felt like a burning fire going through me. Walls got some towels and cut one to wrap around the wound, making it feel a little better.

About five minutes later, the third car was coming up the driveway. This time we decided not to tell these two guys anything about the others that were killed. I told those two drug guys that we were working with the police and they had to give up to us or go for their guns. One of the men that was near the bar quickly jumped over the bar and started shooting, but he didn't know his partner was in his line of fire, then I saw him fall without a sound. Now we had to flush the guy out from behind the bar, and that wouldn't be easy.

I saw a paper bag with some wet rags on the floor, so I got a bottle of whiskey and poured it on the rags and, using my lighter, I put it on the fire and threw it over the bar. I knew it would smoke up so much, it would make it hard see. The guy behind the bar couldn't catch his breath with all that smoke and ran out shooting when I shot him, trying to get to the back door.

That was the sixth man we had deal with, now we had one more to go, but what we didn't know was he was already here. He was right behind us, with his gun out. With all the smoke and noise, he came in without being noticed.

"What in hell is going on here?" he asked.

"Take it easy, Gil; we had some trouble with those two shitheads over there; they came in trying to shoot us and I got shot in the arm, but Walls fixed me up okay. Then the guy got behind the bar, and we had smoked him out.

"How did you make out with your job, Gil?" I asked him.

Gil put his gun away and went behind the bar for a drink. I looked at Walls while Gil was getting his drink. Then Gil sat down, telling us what he did all that day.

I lit my cigar, which had gone out, as I looked at Gil, then I saw Walls looking like he was getting ready for action again. After my cigar was lit, I said to Gil, "I have something to tell you, Gil. Since you've been here with us, you've been picking up the money from all the bets around the city. Now I want to give you a proposition: You take the money you got right there that you brought in, why don't you keep it? I'd say you got about ninety thousand dollars there, huh?"

Gil looked at me and then at Walls. "What you saying, Steve? Why would I keep all this money?" he asked with that questionable look about him.

"Well, for one thing, Gil, your only crime was that you only picked up money for us, so since Walls there is a cop and I work for the police, I think you should take the money and go away from here and try not get into trouble. If you do that, Gil, we won't have to take you in. Now is that a deal, my friend?" I asked, looking at him.

Gil looked at both of us, wondering what to say or what was really going on here. He couldn't believe what was happening.

"You say you guys are cops? Where are the others? Marie and the other guys?" he asked, getting nervous.

"Don't get nervous, Gil; right now while we have the chance, we are giving you a way out. The only reason we are is because you never hurt anyone and you're not wanted by the police. So, take the money and you're free to go. The others are dead, my friend; they had the chance to give up but they chose to fight. They were killers and drug pushers, and they got what they deserved. So, do we have your word, Gil? That you will be straight and be the man you are? If so, then have another drink and leave this place and forget this place."

Gil smiled, saying, "Okay," then took another drink, said "Thanks for the money," and left.

Walls smiled, saying he was happy that Gil took the money and left. Gil was a good man, and now he was free to live his life.

"Well, Walls, it's finally over! The men and the women are gone to where they should be! To the fires of hell, right where God will have the last word. As for the mansion, well, we'll set fire to it, because we should destroy what it was there for, all the hate and destruction of people's lives and murders that went on just because of money. I feel like it takes fire to destroy the evil that's in this mansion."

Chapter Twelve

It was the idea that it was used for everything, like deceit and corruption, killings and drugs.

It was also a place of death, that only darkness was its just reward. Yes, we set fire to destroy it completely.

For the next three weeks, Darlene was getting stronger as I visited her each day, but at night I followed Miles and the others until I made sure they were clean. On the fourth week, I told Liz and Walls I was wrong about Miles. I still had the feeling somehow there had to be someone in the police department that worked for the organization.

Somebody was still out there that shot Darlene; he or she was still on the loose, and I was hoping to find that person soon. But whether or not I found that person, I would still take Darlene away from this place as soon as I possibly could. I was spending more time with Liz and Walls at the WALK-IN BAR now because I liked those two people. It was a place to sit and talk and to just let time go by until Darlene was well enough to join me again.

It was Saturday night, about eleven o'clock. I started to get up when Walls grabbed my arm.

"You got ants or something? Sit! Liz, give him a drink," he insisted.

I sat back down, saying it was about time he bought me a drink. "Maybe I'll enjoy this free drink I didn't have to pay for, and besides, I'm broke."

Walls laughed, knowing only too well; we both had a lot of money from the drugs and all.

We had another drink and since it got quiet now, with no people around, Liz said she wanted to close up and go home early. I noticed Walls had a little trouble in getting up, so Liz and I helped him to his feet and into the car.

Back at my hotel room, I had to lie down quickly because my head was spinning and I didn't feel all that great. After a while I started to think about all the people I met since I had been there in New York City, and there were many. Then, for the longest time lying there on my bed, I started thinking again about who shot Darlene, but I got nowhere. Before I realized, I said again out loud, "Who the hell shot Darlene, and why?" Maybe it was someone that had it in for her, maybe this or maybe that.

The next morning I drove along the shoreline, taking my time just looking around. I stopped at a restaurant that Marie and I went to a few times. I sat at the counter for coffee, eggs and toast. It was few minutes later that some guy sat down that I recognized. I had to look again to make sure he was who I thought he was.

"How you doing, Curtis? Good to see you," I said, looking at him from three seats away.

He turned and laughed as he remembered me. "Steve! Hell, man, glad to see ya. Where in hell you been? I thought you got killed," he said, then he moved closer to me.

"I was lucky, Curtis; I was with Walls, you remember him, Curtis? He was with me when we went after those three guys you wanted taken care of."

"Yeah, right! So, you were away when all the shit hit the fan, huh? What really happened anyway, Steve? Did they all fight to get control, and what about Marie, Steve?" he asked, taking some coffee.

I told Curtis, "Marie got greedy and wanted the whole area to herself. She had Kendall try to take the men from the mansion, but it didn't work out; the men fought it out, and I suppose they killed each other. When Walls and I got back from our job we had to take care of, we saw dead bodies everywhere and places where they tried to burn the place down. We didn't know any more than you do, Curtis. So, what's going on with you?"

"Well, I still have three men I work with, and what about you, Steve? Why don't you throw in with me? We can do okay together," he said with a smile.

I took a drink of coffee, thinking about that, then I nodded in agreement, saying, "Why not, I got no other place to go. Sure, Curtis," as he held out his hand to shake hands with me.

I followed Curtis to his place, which wasn't too far from the restaurant. He worked from his house, which was close to the water. His house looked like it was very well kept up, with three bedrooms and a swimming pool. It was a pretty good-looking house, not too elaborate but very comfortable. He showed me around, then he got a bottle of scotch and we had a drink. He told me about the things he was doing. He was into drugs very heavily; he also knew the big people that were buying and selling it by the truckloads.

He looked at me, then lit his cigar. He took a drink and asked, "Got time to spend with me today, Steve? I got things to show ya. I need you, my friend; I need a partner I know I can trust, and besides, Steve, I know you don't fool around; you get things done. If you're in with me, I'll take you where we can get all the money we'd ever want," Curtis said, smiling.

"Show the way, Curtis, I'm with you. I can use the money now that I'm out of a job," I told him.

He patted me on the back, saying to follow him to his car.

He drove toward the city, then tuned to the shoreline, where all the big and expensive homes were along the water's edge. Yes, this was the place where the wealthy lived that had more money than they could ever spend in their lifetime.

He stopped close to an iron gate, which opened, and we drove over a long driveway. We got to a big house that seemed to have no end to what I was looking at. Curtis smiled as we got out of the car and went to the front door. It opened with the butler greeting us as we went in. I was impressed with the elegance of the place, as well as the high-class people there, acting like they were from some kind of royalty.

"Right on time, Curtis, my friend, and your companion, I trust, is one of us?" the elderly man questioned.

Curtis smiled and assured the man that I was his partner and certainly could be trusted.

We entered the study, where bookcases covered the walls on all sides of the room. And to my surprise, a large bookcase opened up to reveal another room that no one would even know was there. We went in to discuss business. Inside were three more men with guns showing in their belts looking at us. I was sure those men intended for us to know they had guns and were ready to use them. The elderly man's name was Francis. He was the man that had the connections with the drug people from the Islands. Exactly what island, I didn't know, but I was listening with both ears. It was very interesting how these people got the drugs to this place in the wealthy section.

I was amazed at the ingenuity of it all. They would get the drugs from the ships and boats that were dropped into the ocean at certain places and at certain times. But it was always at nighttime, because after the drugs were dropped a light would come on under the water, showing where to pick up the drugs, in the darkness by helicopter. It was a dim light that would be overlooked by anyone going by. They would then drop a man down by a cable and hook the drug packages and pick him up back in the helicopter. It was then carried to the backyard of the big house and dropped between the big trees that couldn't be seen by anyone. There was a heavy net between the trees that caught the drugs. And all this was happening in Manhattan, New York City, and no one was the wiser.

A shipment was coming in at eleven o'clock Thursday night. It was now Tuesday as I sat there listening to all this. I was wondering if I could get Walls to set up a welcome committee to be waiting for these guys. By the sound of that shipment, it sounded like the largest quantity of drugs ever to be shipped there.

After Curtis got his orders on the shipment, he told Francis he'd have his men ready and we would see him on Thursday at the designated time. We left them around three that afternoon. We got back to Curtis' house and had a drink. He told me he had another big deal in a couple weeks.

Curtis smiled, looking at me as he puffed on his cigar. "You can see I need you, Steve; I need a good man to help me get that shipment."

Curtis looked at me again as he puffed on that cigar again. He took a glass and filled it up and held it as he told me he had more to tell me, then he drank half of his drink.

"As you can see, Steve, this shipment is worth about twenty million dollars! Yeah, Steve, I want it for us, not for those guys we just talked to. I have a plan to get rid of them and to take the drugs to a buyer I already made a deal with."

I watched him as he told me all this. I got up and took a cigar from his desk and lit it. I then sat down, asking, "You sure you got this all figured out so we don't get ourselves killed, Curtis? Tell me about it; maybe I can help someway with your plan."

"Sure, I have a man that can operate the helicopter. He will kill the pilot and take over while my men take care of those you just met. Now Francis, the owner of the place, has a ton of money, but he wants more and more. If he had the world, he would still want more. Now the other three guys that work for Francis, they will be in the trees, taking the drugs out of the net, and we'll be there with our silencers to kill them. You know, we still have Francis to get rid of. Now you saw the butler and how he looked at me, well, he works for me, Steve. He's my man, he worked for Francis a long time, and Francis never knew that his butler is my friend; he's my ace in the hole. I planted him there over a year ago, when I learned that Francis' other butler died. That's when Len, my butler friend, started to work for Francis, and all that time Len was telling me what was going on there. So, that's it," Curtis explained as he had another drink.

"I see you got it under control, Curtis. It sounds good to me, but what about someone we don't know about, like someone that's watching out for Francis, or maybe a bodyguard? Or even a friend that's watching or something? There's always someone around watching that we might not see. I'm trying to impress on you, Curtis. I know it happened to me a while ago."

Curtis looked at me, then puffed out some smoke, still looking at me. "I never thought about that, maybe you're right, Steve; I better have two guys walking around and looking for such people around here; they can let me know what they see."

"I think for our protection, Curits, we should! You remember Walls, huh? He's a good friend, and a good man with a gun we can trust. We could have him close by, or we could have your man the butler for Francis to get Walls in the house, to keep an eye on what's happening. If Francis has a bodyguard guarding him, Walls will find out; that way if your butler don't get Francis, Walls will. We need the protection, Curtis, what you think?" I asked, and he agreed.

"Yeah, Steve, okay, have Walls ready." Curtis took a puff on his cigar again. He got up, saying, "Look, I got a job for tomorrow at four o'clock in the afternoon. You think Walls and you could take care of it for me? I have something else to do with my men. I'll give you half of what you get, okay?" he asked.

"Okay, if you want, we can take care of it," I told him. "What is it?" I asked, taking a drink.

He went to his desk and wrote down the address, handing it to me, saying, "Two men and a woman run a cocaine factory; they put the stuff into little bags and get them ready to be shipped out. They have a hell of a business, Steve; it cuts into my business. I want them out of business, and it's time they were stopped. I warned them before but they didn't take my warning, so take care of it for me, Steve."

"Consider it done! Walls and I will pay them a visit," I told him. "Okay, Curtis, I'll see you tomorrow night."

I drove to my hotel and parked the car. I then walked to the WALK-IN BAR and sat at the far end of the room. Liz brought me a drink, saying Walls wanted to see me that night, after he got off work. I told Liz I had to go and have something to eat. Then I'd be back and to tell Walls to wait for me.

I was having dinner while I was thinking about what I learned today. I was surprised to see Curtis again, and I was really surprised to see how much he was involved in drugs, also how big an operation it really was. I wondered how Walls would take all this and what he would do. Would he help me with this, or would he get the police in on it?

It was an hour later when I got back to Liz, when Walls was just coming in the bar. We sat in the back, far enough from other people so no one could hear our conversation. Walls told me that he was still looking for the ones responsible for Darlene getting shot. But so far, he had nothing to report to me. Then, I told Walls what I found out this day. He remembered Curtis, and he said he would like to be a part of this and would talk to Miles about it so he could get off the force until it was completed.

We had another drink when I told him I had another job to do for Curtis, and maybe he could help with that one too.

He smiled and shook his head, saying, "Hell, Steve! You find things going on that the police don't even know exist. Yeah, I'll call Miles right now; he has to get me off long enough to do both jobs." He looked at me like he was thinking. "You still got the silencers and dynamite at your hotel? We might need them, Steve."

Walls sounded a little excited about all this. I knew he was ready to join me; he sounded like he was bored with his job at the police station. He was ready for some excitement.

Before I could answer him, he got up and went to the phone to call Miles. In a few minutes, he came back saying Miles told him to go for it. Miles would take care of his absence at the police station. Then he looked at me again, asking if I had the dynamite and the silencers again. I told him I had both as he took a drink. I told him I had to go see Darlene before it got too late.

I got back at the hotel and changed. I got to the hospital just in time before visiting hour was over. I saw Darlene was awake and smiling; she said she was feeling better as I took her hand. She even looked happy, and each day she asked the doctor when she could leave. The doctor said in about another week. I told her I missed her. I also told her about the job Walls and I had, and she said she would like to go with us too. I could see she was a lot happier now, as she was getting her strength back. I told her again how I missed her not being with me. She smiled and I kissed her, saying I'd be back the next evening.

The next day I met Walls close to the place we were to take over. It was over by the Spanish section of the city as we watched the place and the people going in and out of the place. Two guys were looking at us that were supposed to be watching the back door.

I lit my cigar when I saw a cop go in, then Walls looked at me, saying, "I know that guy; he's in the narcotics division. What's he doing in that place?" he asked me.

"Well, maybe he's buying or he's in on it," I told Walls as he gave me a disgusted look. "Well, what do you think he's there for?"

"I don't know but I'll find out; Walls told me and is still keeping his eyes on the place."

I looked at my watch, seeing it was four o'clock; that was the time we were supposed to start moving in. I checked my gun to make sure it was still in my belt. We started walking across the street, seeing the cop that went in before was now coming back out.

The two men at the door were watching us as we got closer, then one of the men put his hand up, telling us to stop, yelling out, "Hold it right there, you guys! I told you guys to stop right now! You can't come in here!" as he stared at us.

"Why not? If Selby can go in, then I can go in, old buddy!" Walls told the guy and started to go in, when the man started to get angry and pushed Walls back, asking who Selby was. Then he pushed Walls again and told us louder to get away as the other man started to go for his gun.

I got my gun out, putting it to the man's stomach before he could use his gun that he was pulling out. Walls was already holding the other man, telling him to shut up. We both pushed the men inside, keeping them ahead of us as a human shield. The woman inside fired at us, killing the man Walls was holding as his shield. I shot the woman when Walls yelled out to the men that were there working not to move, then yelled out, "Police! Now take those guns you got there and let them drop to the floor, and be very careful," he told them.

The men dropped the guns, but they quickly grabbed another one from under the arm holsters and fired at us before we realized what was happening. They killed the man I was holding in front of me. Walls shot one of the men as I rushed behind a desk with bullets flying close to me. I looked around, seeing one man still shooting at Walls as I shot the man, but not before he shot Walls in the shoulder. As I started to get out from behind the desk, I felt my arm hurting. I looked down, seeing blood. I grabbed a towel from the desk and wrapped it around my arm.

I yelled out at Walls, seeing him leaning against the doorway, holding his hand over his shoulder. "Are you okay? How bad is it?" I asked.

"It's bad enough!" He looked at me and started cursing. "Damn, I had to get shot again! That's what happens when I'm around you, Steve."

I quickly pushed all the drugs I could find in a pile and set it on fire. Walls got the money and ran for the car. Before leaving, I put a stick of dynamite close to the fire so it would go off in a second or two. I ran out, yelling at the people that were close by to run for cover; the place was gonna blow up. People ran in all directions.

I drove and by the time we got to the next street, the place blew up and it was completely engulfed with flames burning the drugs, which made me happy. We got to the WALK-IN BAR, seeing Miles sitting there with a beer, waiting for us.

"Well, I see the city wreckers are back!"

I had to laugh; it was funny the way he said it.

We got a drink while Liz fixed Walls' shoulder. I lit a cigar when Miles told us he knew what we did, because he got a call just as we got there at that cocaine factory.

"I had you two covered, in case it went wrong; I had three men watching you guys. I told them not to interfere unless you needed help. You two guys work good together. I'm also glad that place is out of commission for good." Miles took a drink and lit a cigarette, asking, "Now tell me about the shipment coming in Thursday!"

I told him from the beginning about what we said and what Walls and I had in mind, that took about ten minutes in all.

Miles looked at us, then he smiled, saying, "Okay, gentlemen," and finished his drink, saying, "Be careful and don't take anything for granted." Miles looked at us again, saying, "You know that guy you named? You said Curtis, didn't you?

Well, I know him too! He lets you think you're his friend, and before you know it you are dead, my friend! He's good at shooting people in the back. Remember that, it might save your life. Now you guys take care, and before I forget, I have that helicopter that Francis has covered. I have a military copter standing by to follow their helicopter. I know Curtis will be in it, wherever it goes. I want the ones that are bringing the stuff in, as well as the drugs on that shipment."

Miles got another drink and he lit another cigarette, then he went on.

"When Walls told me about this operation, I got busy with the military people that I know and had them come in on this operation with us." Miles smiled and said, "I didn't think about having our own copter and our own men on this, because what if one of our men is in with these drug people, then it would jeopardize our men and this whole operation."

Walls interrupted Miles, saying, "Hold on a minute, Lieutenant; that place we just blew up, I saw one of our boys going in that place as we were watching the place. I think he has something to do with that place."

Miles looked at him as he puffed on his cigarette. He took a drink and seemed to look surprised about it.

"What's his name, Walls?"

"You know him very well, Miles; he's Selby."

"How about that, Selby, the guy that said he was doing all he could to do away with drugs."

Miles shook his head and told Walls he would check it out, then he turned to me, saying, "Now Steve, you stay in good standing with Curtis; it sounds as though Curtis likes you. He seems to have a lot confidence in you. Maybe it's because you did that job for him a while ago. Now maybe that job you and Walls did for him, I really think you are in solid, but watch your back, Steve, just be careful."

Miles left us as Walls and I sat there for a while, going over the job we just did.

Later I went to dinner and drove out to see Curtis like I said I would. He was all smiles when I got there, telling him how well he did the job.

"I know I can depend on you, Steve. I'm happy to have you with me, my friend. Now, what can I give you for doing that job for me? I know you didn't have the chance to get anything from there, because you and Walls had to leave there in a hell of hurry. Anything, my friend, you earned it," he said, smiling and getting a drink for me.

"It wasn't that hard to do, Curtis; why don't you wait until we take care of the shipment and pay me what you think? You know I don't mind helping a friend," I told him as he looked at me.

He nodded, saying, "You're okay, Steve! You're okay. After the shipment is taken care of, I'll make you a deal you'll like. Okay, here's to us!" he said as he held his glass to mine.

We drank, then I told him I had to go and I'd be back in time for the shipment. He smiled as I left him.

I drove back to my hotel and parked the car. I went to the hospital to visit with Darlene. She was awake and looking beautiful, and she seemed to be a lot healthier now. When she smiled, I noticed her eyes had that sparkle in them like before, when I first met her. I told her what I was doing and how Miles joined in with Walls and me on this coming job. I stayed with her a bit longer this time, telling her about our house that was being built by Ward and his friend. It made her happy to hear that, and it made me happy just seeing her getting better.

It was Thursday morning now, and I was at the restaurant I always went to for breakfast when Walls came in with Miles. I was surprised to see Miles at that time.

After they got some coffee, Miles smiled, saying, "Just so you guys will know, the military copter and I will be waiting for the ships to come in to the docks. Then our copter and I will go after the shipment those guys left out there in the ocean, but we will pick up that shipment and leave our dummy shipment there in its place. So, we'll already have the drugs. Like I said before, we'll follow Curtis in his copter, to where he tries to sell that dummy shipment. That's when we'll take them by surprise." Miles drank his coffee and said he'd see us later.

"I'm glad he's got that part taken care of, Steve," Walls remarked. "All we have to worry about is the guys at that big house Francis has. We know of one butler and a maid, along with those three guys we met, and of course Francis himself. There just might be more than we think in that place," he said, looking a little skeptical and worried.

"There might be, Walls; he could have a driver we don't know about, and maybe a few grounds people working for him also. Tell you what, if we have our silencers with us and an extra clip hidden under our jacket and maybe a stick of dynamite each for added protection, I think we should be able to handle it, don't you think?" I asked him while taking a cigar from my coat pocket.

"Well, I didn't think we were going to war," Walls told me, smiling.

"Yeah, I'd say maybe it is a war. If you think about it, Walls, we are outnumbered, my friend, and we have to be able to cut down the odds a bit somehow," I told Walls as we both went out to the street.

For the rest of that day, we got what we needed and hid it all around our body, under our coat and tied to our legs, out of sight. By eight-thirty that night, we drove to Francis' big house, where Francis with his three men were waiting for us. I lit a cigar as I stood by my car looking around the place when Francis called from the porch.

"Up here!" he yelled to us. "We need to go over the plan before we leave here," he said in a rough and unsteady voice.

I wondered about that; it sounded like he was very nervous for some reason.

Curtis drove in and parked alongside us and walked over to us, saying in a low voice to watch for him as he made a move against Francis and his three men as soon as we got to the meeting room.

Walls and I walked behind Curtis as we went through the front doorway. I told Walls to be ready for a double-cross, then Walls looked at me with a nod. We walked toward the meeting room as I watched the doorways as we passed by them for anyone waiting in ambush. I had that feeling something was going to happen, and very soon, because I knew Curtis was about to start shooting; he had it in his mind to take it all, with the help of Walls and me. But I wondered about after this was all over, would he try to put us out of commission also? Actually, I wouldn't be surprised if he would try! I knew Miles had the helicopter covered, and also the drug people that were waiting to buy the stuff. So it was up to Walls and me to take over whoever it was here at Francis' big house.

We got to the meeting room, then the butler that was a friend of Curtis nodded to Curtis, letting him know he was on his way to the trees, where Francis' butler was also the pilot of the helicopter and ready to take off. But Curtis' butler friend was supposed to kill the pilot that worked for Francis and to wait there for Curtis to join him after Francis and his men were killed.

Now we got to the meeting room and were ready to go over the plan again when Curtis started shooting at Francis as Walls and I fired at the three men that were trying to find something to hide behind, but they fell after being hit many times. I turned around, seeing another man coming from a bedroom shooting at Curtis, hitting him in the shoulder, then I shot the man before he could shoot again.

Curtis fell against a chair, then I yelled to him, "Get to the helicopter, Curtis!"

He looked at me and got to the stairs, going as fast he could for the trees to join his friend, the butler.

Walls and I started to check all the rooms from the top and worked our way downstairs, checking every room. As we got to the kitchen area, we could hear the helicopter taking off, then I could see it go over the rooftops and disappear. We finished checking the house and went out to the four-car garage, seeing two Cadillacs and a new Lincoln. Just as we started to open the third door, another Cadillac started up and ran right through the closed door as we both fired at the back window. The car knocked the door all to pieces as it went through, and then it glazed off the side of a tree and ran through the next neighbor's fence and into their swimming pool. We quickly ran to see if the men were dead or if they got away, but they were still in the car; they weren't going anywhere. They both were dead and covered with blood.

We got back, making sure all there were dead. We then checked for drugs and any other incriminating evidence we could find, but the place was clean. Walls picked the phone and called the police, then we got to our car and drove away. I lit a cigar, saying how well it all went; at least we got all those that were involved without getting hurt ourselves. But we came very close to it.

Then I mentioned to Walls about what Miles was supposed to be doing on his end of that job. I was also wondering if it was going as good as our job did.

We got to the bar, where Liz was busy with a few customers. We got a drink when Liz wasn't busy. She wanted to know what happened and was interested about it, because she knew the man that owned that big house. I was surprised that she even knew Francis and all his money. She said he was a good man and was well liked by everyone. She never knew how he made his money and she was very surprised to hear he was into drugs. Then I told her he was dead with all his people that worked for him that tried to kill us.

It was around midnight when we got a call from Miles. He said to meet him as his home as soon as we could. So half an hour later we were at his house smoking cigars, and Miles was handing us drinks. Miles told us what happened, he said the police helicopter got the drugs and destroyed all of them by opening the bags and throwing them all into the ocean. Miles said he didn't want to take it to the police station, like they used to do, but not this time because it would only be a temptation for some cop to take it for himself. He told us they watched for the other helicopter that Curtis and his butler friend were in and watched Curtis pick up the dummy shipment, thinking it was the real drug package. Then he flew to a place in Miami, to another wealthy home.

"We watched them through high-powered binoculars, seeing Curtis getting money from those people that bought drugs, and he took off quickly. We just let him get away. Because he'll only get caught sooner or later by those people he just screwed out of the drugs they were supposed to get. Either way he's a dead man!" Miles smiled when he told us that. He took some coffee and lit a cigarette, then looked at us, saying, "You boys are supposed to see Curtis in the morning, is that right?"

"Yes, at ten o'clock, Miles," I told him.

"Okay, be ready for action, because knowing Curtis like I do he might just figure on shooting you two guys and saving the money for himself. And before I forget it, I sent the narcotics boys to take those people in that accepted the drugs. I had those places surrounded, but maybe some got away but we won't know that yet."

Miles looked at us as he went on telling us what else happened.

"You know, those damn people weren't going to be taken in, so they fought it out until two of our men were killed and six of theirs dead, with three others badly hurt. So, you two be very careful! I'm sure some got away, and let me know if you need help. If not then I'll see you guys when this is over," he said with a smile.

I met Walls the next day and drove to Curtis' house. Curtis had a cigar in his mouth and was smiling.

"It went well last night, boys! We got the money and now I have that operation for myself."

He laughed and took a drink of his scotch as I watched him, thinking that he didn't even know those people were killed at that place he dropped off the drug package. And before he could say anything else, I asked him if there was another shipment coming, and when would our next job be?

Curtis smiled as he looked at us, saying, "I have to wait until next Thursday, before I know if they will send another package or not. But as for right now, I have a deal to pick up a package at the shipyard around two o'clock this afternoon. I need you guys to go with me; we have this deal every week. It's pure cocaine. I have to cut it and package it for selling it on the street. I have fifty thousand for each of you at this time. When I get straightened out, I'll give you guys a share of it," he said, then took a drink.

"Okay, Curtis, we will meet with you here by one-thirty or someplace else?" I asked.

"Yeah, Steve, here is okay. See you guys later," he said.

After we drove away, I remarked how well it went. "You know, Walls, I was ready in case he tried to double-cross us. So far, he needs us in his deals. I thought Leo and the others were big time, but this guy Curtis is just as big, and sometimes I think he does a hell of a lot better than Leo. And maybe Kendall ever did, and not to forget Ted!"

We went for lunch and talked about our next job with Miles after Walls called him to meet us at this small restaurant. Miles told us he would have some of his men around the shipyard, just to make sure we were safe. Also, he said he'd have that ship searched after we made our deal and were gone from sight. Miles wanted to make sure that ship never carried any more drugs of any kind. Another thing Miles was trying to do, he was stopping everyone that made deals with Curtis. Miles was watching every move that Curtis made.

At one-thirty Walls and I met with Curtis at his home, then we drove to the shipyard and walked to the cargo ship that was tied up to the dock. It was a large ship, and it was being loaded as we went up the steps to the deck, where the captain was waiting for us, and we followed him to his cabin. He handed Curtis a large package as Curtis gave the captain the money. We were on our way back down the steps when I noticed plainclothes men coming close to the ship, then they stopped until they saw us back on the dock. Walls gave me a look when he noticed them also.

We got in Curtis' car and drove off as I glanced toward the ship, seeing four men going up the steps and several men on the dock standing by. I figured the ship's captain was about to be taken. Curtis drove on, not noticing what was going on behind him. He made a big deal, and it went well for him when he picked up the drugs with the helicopter, and now the big package he just picked up from the ship. Now he must be thinking about all the money he had and how he'd spend it. But what he didn't know was the drugs he picked up with the helicopter was the fake package he got; Miles and his men switched the packages. So now according to my thinking, the drug people would be looking for Curtis, thinking that Curtis double-crossed them. I was sure they would just kill him. I knew they didn't fool around when they thought they got screwed by anyone.

I sat in the seat smoking my cigar, feeling good about all this.

"You got a good business going for yourself, Curtis. In fact, I think you do a lot better than Leo, Ted, and even Kendall ever did. I'm certainly glad to be working with you; we needed a job now that the old gang is gone."

Curtis smiled, saying, "I do alright. I know who to see for the best deals; you know, at times I have to eliminate a few so I can have more money to operate with," he said, looking at me from his rearview mirror. "Right now I need more men, and with the money I have now and the money I'm getting, I can buy men anywhere; everyone has a price for his services. I'm paying you guys five thousand for this job; you didn't have to work too hard for it, did you?" he said as he pulled into his driveway. He paid us as he also said for us to be back there at eight o'clock; he had another job to do.

Walls drove as I started to laugh, and I threw my cigar away, saying, "Curtis is something else. He told me that I was going to be his partner and I would get half of everything, but now I'm just getting paid like any one of his everyday men. He seems to have forgotten about the deal he made with me," I told Walls as I sat there thinking about it.

"You didn't think Curtis would part with any of the money, did you? You saw how he acted getting the money and the drugs; he was like a kid in a candy store. He wants it all and when he's through with us, what do you think he'll do? He'll kill us! That's what he'll do!"

Walls got a little excited telling me that. I knew Walls was right about what Curtis would do.

Walls looked at me, saying, "Well, anyway, I was surprised that Curtis paid us fifty thousand for the other job."

Yeah, Walls, I was surprised myself.

"Yes, the five thousand he just gave us isn't much considering what he just took in. But he didn't think about that either, did he? I was thinking, at least we got enough money to retire on that no one knows about, Walls. If I were you, don't say anything about it to Miles since you've been working with me." He smiled, puffing on his cigar.

We stopped at the WALK-IN BAR and had a beer when Miles came in smiling.

"Well, look here, my two vagabonds! And how did the deal go on that ship?" he asked as he sat down with a beer.

Walls told him what went on and remarked about the police going to the ship as we left the ship.

"Yes, I had them take the captain to jail, and we searched the ship and found more drugs, so now the ship stays at that dock until we make a complete search of it, then we'll let it go, and it's not to return to this port again," Miles told us.

We had another beer and told Miles we had to go and to be ready for another job at eight o'clock for Curtis. He asked what kind of job. I told him we didn't know.

"He never said, Miles, but you can have a backup for us if you want. By the way Curtis acts, I can't really tell what's on his mind. It's hard to tell if he's ready to kill or not. You know Curtis, he's all business and he's greedy as hell," I told Miles, and Walls agreed with me.

"Okay, men, be careful. I will have someone looking out for you, so we meet here after the job is over."

We went to dinner early and rested for an hour before going to see Curtis. By seven-thirty we were at Curtis' door.

Chet, who worked for Curtis, opened the door, saying, "Come in, gentlemen."

I asked, "How's everything, Chet?"

He smiled, saying, "Everything is pretty good so far, gentlemen. Curtis is in the study; he is expecting you."

I nodded to Walls as we went in seeing Curtis with drink in hand.

"Come in, Steve, Walls. I'd like you two to go to this liquor store and see the owner, he's a big guy, and tell him I sent you to pick up two large packages. Here's the address, and bring them here; I have someone coming here around eleven o'clock tonight to buy them."

We were just about to turn around and leave when two men were right behind us with guns showing.

"Hold it right there! Don't anyone move! Now, you will all put your guns on that desk right there, and be very careful!" the man told us, and we did what he told us to do, especially with guns looking right at us.

I was wondering what to do next. They had us cold, and we never heard them come in behind us.

The man talking was tall and very thin, like he didn't eat much. In fact, he was skinny with a drawn face with piercing eyes. The other man was heavy and very homely with shaking hands and looking sick.

"You, Curtis, you had the police raid us after you left us with our money! You get that money right now or I'll shoot you full of holes! You understand that, you son of bitch!"

I could see Curtis was starting to sweat and looked very uncomfortable with that guy's gun pointing at him.

"Okay, men! I have the money in my safe. I'll get it for you, just take it easy, okay?" he told them very nervously.

He went to a big table and took the top off, revealing the safe inside. Curtis opened it, taking out several bags full of money and letting them fall to the floor. Then all of a sudden, Curtis grabbed the gun he had inside the safe and fired at the two men. But I saw him fall as Walls and I dove behind the two big chairs just behind us, seeing Curtis trying to hold on to the side of the table and shooting it out with those two guys. But Curtis didn't make it, as we shot back and killed those guys; it was lucky for us that we had a small gun under our belts out of sight. It was a lifesaver for us, especially at times like this.

It was over and Curtis was dead, as well as the two men. We started to take the money when three more guys came in shooting as we dove behind the two chairs again just in time. But it wasn't easy to shoot back at those guys because of the angle we had to shoot from. Another thing we had for our protection, I had a stick of dynamite in my pocket, so I lit it with my cigar and tossed it just outside of the door behind where the men were shooting from. It went off, blowing them and the wall down with a deafening roar, and my ears started to hurt. Being behind the two big chairs saved us from the debris that fell all around us.

We then checked the men, making sure they were dead, but I looked out the window seeing two men in a car, waiting in the driveway. They got out and ran to the side door and came into the house as we waited for them. We were hiding behind the big chairs again as they came in slowly, looking around, seeing the dead bodies. They were looking at the study and the doorway blown away, making them nervous. Then they saw the money lying around the floor as they ran to it to take it, when we stood away from the chairs, telling them to drop the guns. They stopped and looked at us with a surprised look on their faces by not seeing us before. They just stood there staring at us and then at each other.

I yelled out, "Drop those guns, men! We got you covered; you have no chance! Now drop them!" I told them loudly.

They started shooting a bit wildly; they had no chance to make it, but they did hit Walls in the same arm, but it just nicked his arm but not bad, enough to make it bleed. We got two suitcases from the closet to put the money in and started to leave when the butler, Chet, came from a closet that held coats and hats for the guests at the side of the front door with a gun pointing at us and bleeding badly. He had blood coming down his arm and over his hand as he was shaking, telling us to get him a doctor, he needed a doctor, he kept saying over and over when I told him to sit down and I would call for an ambulance. He said he didn't have much time and to hurry, but I could see he was getting weaker as he dropped the gun and slowly fell to the floor while Walls was calling for an ambulance and the police.

In minutes, they were there taking Chet, Curtis' butler, away dead as the others were. Miles came in saying it was all over, saying we did a good job. According to Miles, everyone the police wanted was dead; he didn't think there were any more that we had to find. He felt like they were all killed and accounted for.

Walls and I had drinks at the WALK-IN BAR until it was time to close the place. He went with Liz as I went to my hotel room. I took a shower and sat by the window, having a smoke and looking around the city. Then I looked up at the sky, finding myself counting stars until I got tired.

The next morning, I was up around eight o'clock, having a good breakfast. After, I went to see Darlene. She was sitting in a chair smiling as I went in. She took my hand as I kissed her. She told me she was leaving the hospital in two days, and that sounded good to me. Now we could leave that place and never go back. There was nothing there for us. It was the new life we wanted, and to live in peace.

For the rest of that day, I got all of my things in the car trunk, ready to leave as soon as Darlene was released from the hospital. It was only two more days, but to me it seemed like it was the longest time I ever had to wait for anything in my life.

The next day I walked around the city and bought a few things and just let the day go by. I could walk a lot better now that my leg healed, and it felt pretty well considering how the bone was shattered like it was. It was close to noontime when I went into a bar on the side street next to 52nd Street.

There were four men sitting at the bar and talking as I sat at the far end, where I could see the front door, which led to the street. The bartender was coming to me for my order when two young guys came in looking around like they were casing the place. They must be amateurs, because they made it look so obvious they were up to no good by their actions. I sat so I could react quickly as they both got to the bar. One of the men was about two feet away from me as I took my gun out and held it in my hand where he couldn't see it, then they both pulled their guns out. I quickly jumped the guy and held my gun to his head, telling the other guy to drop his gun.

"You got just three seconds to drop your gun, or I'll blow your friend's head off!"

The man I held was sweating as I held my gun to his temple, looking at the other man, waiting for his reaction.

"What the hell you waiting for, you dummy! Drop that damn gun, you shit-head! He's gonna kill me!" the man yelled out to his partner.

His partner looked around and dropped his gun, but reluctantly. I pushed the guy I was holding away from me, telling them both not to move.

"You two just stand there and don't move, or I'll shoot you both!" I told them, and told the bartender to go to the phone and call the police.

Then one of the men pulled another gun from under his shirt and shot at the bartender, then I shot him and at the same time the other man ran out into the street and got lost in the crowd of people on the sidewalks. I then told the bartender again to call for the police right away as I went out and got lost in the crowd myself before the police got there. It was another hour before I stopped for a drink and sandwich. Later I just walked the streets, for next hour feeling the warm sun as I enjoyed looking in the store windows and seeing people in all directions. It was relaxing and restful for me, waiting for the time to pass.

It was only three o'clock that afternoon as I drove to the shore because I had a lot of time to relax and to enjoy the world; I had nothing else to do. It was a bright sunny day as I made my way over the Bayonne Bridge, when I was thinking about the gun I still had under my belt. I didn't need it anymore; I had no use for it now, my job was done, it was over. Like Walls told me, let the police find the one that shot Darlene and live my life. He was right about that, so I parked my car at the end of the bridge and walked to the middle of the bridge and let the gun fall. It was good to see it go; I even smiled seeing it sink into the depths of the deep water.

I was about to take my small gun out from my ankle when a car stopped right alongside me. I heard a voice I recognized. I turned to see Jed and Gloria. She had a gun, pointing it at me.

"What's the gun for?" I asked her.

"Get in the car! Don't you make a wrong move, you bastard! You no-good killer! You killed my father!" she yelled out. "I swore I'd get you, and you're gonna die for what you did! You're gonna die, Steve! You lousy rat! I'm gonna take pleasure in killing you!" she said in a snarling rage and in a nasty kind of tone.

Jed was laughing as he drove, and Gloria glared at me as she held her gun to my chest.

"When Jed told me you killed my father, I looked everywhere for you but I found your woman. I shot her going into her apartment. I shot her twice in the back! Now it's your turn to die!" she bellowed out. Then she laughed like she was in command now.

As I watched her, she sounded like her father, which made me think. Was she really like her father, and I never saw that in her before. I sat there hearing this. I wanted to grab them both, but they had a gun on me and I could do nothing. It was Gloria that shot Darlene, and the worst thing about that, it was me that let them both go. I couldn't believe I made that mistake.

Walls was right all along; he said someday it would come back to haunt me, and it certainly had. It almost cost the life of the only one that meant anything to me.

Just then we had to stop in the road, where the men were working fixing the curbs. One of the workers held up his hand for us to stop to let a big truck go by. I saw my chance when Gloria turned to look at the man. I pushed at the door and fell out. I quickly got up and ran to the back of the car as the workers were watching and wondering what was going on.

Behind the car I got my gun out from my ankle as Gloria jumped out from the car. I fired two shots, killing her. When Jed ran out shooting at me while running to get behind the workers, he wasn't fast enough when I shot him just before he got behind one of the men. He turned around and fell in the street, crying out, "You son of a bitch!" And he died.

I quickly got back in their car and drove out of there as fast as I could, before I had some explaining to do to the police, if they were around. And I didn't want to see any police; it would have been kind of hard to explain what I was doing there in first place. I parked their car just ahead of my car, which I left there by the bridge, and I drove from there quickly to my hotel. Then I took a walk to quiet my nerves; my heart was pounding as I walked trying to calm down. It wasn't that easy, because it was me that made that damn mistake of letting Gloria and Jed go in the first place, and Darlene was now paying for that mistake. I misjudged two people that were the cause of all this trouble, and almost caused my own demise.

I had to lean against the store window to rest as I stood there looking around. I couldn't help thinking again how lucky I was.

I walked to the nearest drugstore for cigars because I needed one right then. I began walking for the next hour, going over many things in my mind for the first time since I was there. I was now free to walk the streets without someone trying to shoot me. Besides, there were no more threats trying to kill Darlene. It was over; we were now both free again.

I felt like a new person now because I didn't have to go after killers or drug people. It was over for me and my lady; the police didn't need me anymore. I did their job for them and I was glad that I was able to it for them. But at the same time, I was happy that part of my life was over. There were many times I thought my life was over for me; Walls and I got into situations that were hard to get out of.

I went to New York for a vacation. I met a lady I just couldn't forget. I fell in love with her and tried to help her, but I had to fight to stay alive, and again I got into many situations that almost seemed impossible to get out of. At times it was like a bad dream, but it wasn't a dream; it was real. It was something that really happened.

As I walked along the streets, I remembered it all too well. We had some good times as well as the bad times, but all in all I guess I would probably do it all over again for that lady I fell in love with. Because she was worth it.

I walked a few miles that day, enjoying the warm air with my thoughts and my new outlook on life. Besides, Darlene, my lovely lady, would be ready to leave the hospital by the next day. I would be taking her to a better place, to live in peace and safety. That was my place, where she wanted to go back to, and to stay.

I stood at the street corner for a minute as that feeling came over me about all the killings. The feeling I'd been getting at times, and about what I did, and maybe I shouldn't have done. I knew I could not justify all that had been done, but who could in this kind of business? We know we shouldn't take it upon ourselves to eliminate those that threaten us, but what are we the people to do when threatened?

Why can't we fight them on their own terms? Why can't we fight them like the real enemy they are? We should fight them like we do whenever we're called into service of our country. We're told to fight for our freedom. Then what is this? Killers and murderers are not our enemy? They're not against our freedom? Well, I'll fight them whenever they threaten me. But I didn't fight those rats on my own, even though I was with Lenny and some others I was with; they did the killings, and they got killed. I killed only the ones that tried to kill me. Then the time came a little later on, I fought with the police, and for the police, which I was happy to do.

There are many things that people can do to better our way of life, to keep us safe. To start with is to vote for the right people in our offices that represent us. If they don't do their jobs, then vote them out; don't just let them stay in office! I've seen in my lifetime many people stay in office for many years before they are finally voted out. You can also go to school meetings; that way you see if your kids are safe or if they are properly learning, and if not then do something about it! Also go to town meetings; they are also important. I suggest if anyone sees things like someone getting hurt, then help them; maybe someday you might need someone's help. If you see someone in distress and if you don't go to their aid or at least call the police or anyone to help, then, my friend, there's something wrong with you! You are just as bad the ones hurting other people.

The next morning, I picked up Darlene, who was looking much stronger and healthier. She was finally ready to leave that hospital. Her beautiful self came back to life again. The sparkle returned to her eyes, like it was the first time I met her. She sat close to me as I drove away from that hospital. She smiled as she looked at me and asked if we could stop to see Liz before we left the city. I agreed because after all, they were very good friends for a long time and they should see each other.

Liz was surprised to see Darlene as she walked in and sat down. "Oh, Darlene! You look just wonderful!" she said as she came from behind the counter and kissed her. Liz asked how she felt and all that.

They talked for a while as I got a drink, watching them. Liz told Darlene that Walls and her were getting married next week and asked if Darlene and I were getting married. Darlene looked at me as I just sat there wondering what to say.

"Ask Steve, Liz," Darlene told her as she looked at me.

"Well, I don't know, Liz," I said as I looked at Darlene sitting there with a grin on her face.

Then Liz told us they were getting married right there at the WALK-IN BAR. They were inviting some of Walls' friends, and Miles and his wife would be there also. I could see the look on Darlene's face as Liz told us about all this. I knew then she wanted to be married, and now would be the time to make it a double wedding.

I didn't know what to say as they both looked at me, waiting for me to say something. I got up and sat down beside Darlene, asking, "Would you like to be married with them? I mean, would you marry me?" a little nervous about it.

She smiled and kissed me, saying, "It took you long enough to ask me. How long does a girl have to wait to be asked?"

She smiled and put her arms around me as I looked at Liz, saying, "I guess we're getting married, Liz. You mind if Darlene and I join you and Walls? Maybe by then Darlene will be stronger and feeling better."

I kissed Darlene when Walls was just coming in the bar. He laughed as he came to Darlene and kissed her, saying how happy he was to see her looking so well.

Liz told Walls about us getting married with them, making it a double wedding and how great that would be.

Walls looked at Darlene, saying, "I'll drink to that, and I would hope you thought long and hard about marrying Steve; I hope you know what you are doing, my dear."

Darlene smiled as she looked at me, saying, "Well, maybe I should think about it, huh?" She looked at me again, saying, "Okay, I thought about it. I guess I'll marry him anyway, no matter how many faults he has, and besides, I can't let anyone else have him. Maybe it's because I love him." She smiled, looking at me and squeezing my hand.

"I'm certainly happy to hear that," I said, then took a drink.

Darlene laughed, saying she wouldn't have anyone else.

We stayed for a while talking about the coming event. Then Miles came in and was surprised to see Darlene sitting there. He was happy to see her looking so well; he was especially happy to hear that we were getting married, with Liz and Walls.

It was about three o'clock when we left the WALK-IN BAR. We went to her apartment because, seeing we had to stay for another week, I had to take some things out of my car that I put in because I thought we were leaving the city that day. I saw the happiness in her eyes when I asked her to marry me. And I knew she was hoping I would agree to this double wedding, and I wasn't against it; I just thought we would, in time, get married up North at our own place.

I had Darlene sit by the window to relax and to rest. She looked tired and I didn't want her to overdo it. We talked until five o'clock that afternoon in her apartment. She was so happy to be here, away from that hospital. I felt wonderful to have her back with me, and I must have acted like a kid because I missed her so much.

"Feel like going to the New Yorker for dinner?" I asked. "I'll call for a cab so you won't have to walk too much."

"Okay, Steve, I am a little hungry."

I went to the lobby to call for the cab, also to make the call to the restaurant for our waiter that we would like him to be there. I told him we'd be there in a few minutes. The cab took us there to our special place we always went to. Ben, our usual waiter, was always there to greet us. Ben told her how happy he was to see her again. He had our same table with our usual bottle of wine on the table with the rose beside it. Darlene had a tear in her eyes as we sat down as Ben poured the wine. I told old Ben to bring us whatever he thought would be fine with us. We took a drink, then we got up to a slow dance that the band was now playing.

"I waited so long for this, Steve," she said softly as she held her head close to mine. "I missed you, my dear; I missed being with you as I lay in that hospital room. Thanks for letting me know you wanted me and for waiting for me like you did. I could hear you talking to me, and I wanted so much to tell you that but I couldn't do anything about it. I was saying to you, 'Don't leave me, Steve, don't leave me.'" Darlene started to cry softly as I gave her a napkin from one of the tables that was close to us.

When we got to our table, we were still waiting for our food and she said, "I hope you don't think I was forcing you to marry me, Steve; it's just that I would like to marry you. I love you with all my heart, and you made me love you, Steve. It was by the way you talked to me, the way you looked at me, and so many things. The doctor told me about how you felt and how you were getting sick worrying about me. Always love me, my dear; don't ever let anything happen to us. I will be so happy to be your wife, Steve. I hope with all my heart you feel as I do," she said as she kissed me.

"I'm sure you know how I feel; you know I'd do anything for you, and I'd do anything to keep you. Yes, I'll be happy to marry you too, beautiful."

After our dinner was over, I told her, "I don't want you to get too tired, honey; let's just take it slow and not do too much tonight."

She agreed and within an hour later, we got back to her apartment. I made her comfortable in bed as we talked about the things I did with Walls. She knew about some of the things I did, because Miles told her when he visited her in the hospital from time to time.

The days went by as we enjoyed being together again, going to places we hadn't seen before. Then she showed me around the city like she said she would do some time ago. The days passed by quickly until it was time for our wedding. We had many people there at the bar that gave us a party that we wouldn't forget for a long time. It was exciting. Darlene was very happy, but she was also ready and eager to leave; she wanted to go to our new home in the Adirondack Mountains.

We said our goodbyes to our friends, then we drove out of New York City. The city she knew all of her life. The place she grew up and despised, because of the crime she came in contact with. A city she'd leave without any remorse, or to even take the time to look back. She did her job, now she wanted to live in peace. And I thought she deserved that much.

There are many places to visit and to enjoy in the city of New York, but it's like all cities in our country. Because of the people that are rotten in so many ways, they prey on innocent people for their money. They enjoy doing those rotten things, but it's all over the world; it's not just here. New York is visited by people from all over the world, because it has a lot of history to share with people that are interested in how we fought and survived the wars and the harsh life that the people of our country had to go though. But there are many people that are hurt because of all the crime we have in that city, but isn't it so in all our cities?

We drove along at normal speed, enjoying the scenery, heading north. There was no need to hurry now; we had all the time in the world for this long-awaited trip. The trip we wanted to make long before this.

But at least we were on our way back to our place in the woods. It was a wonderful feeling as we drove the long hours back to where the animals and Mother Nature were at peace.

We walked to our new home, which Ward made sure would be ready for our return, and it sure was. It was far more beautiful than we both realized it would be. We walked the small path that led us to the lake that was always clean and waiting there for the animals to drink the cool water and for anyone that had need for it. We then looked up over the lake, seeing the top of the mountain just over the treetops.

We continued walking to it as it got bigger as we got closer. There it stood as the evening was beginning to give way to the night darkness. The massive tower of rock seemed to be looking down in all directions, watching its subjects far below.

I watched Darlene smile as she looked up at that magnificent creation with a growing look of happiness while she held my hand. The mountain that seemed to say "I'm here to watch over you" as we admired its beauty, like it had always done, looking over this land from the beginning of time.

I put my arm around Darlene's shoulder as she turned to look at me when I kissed her and told her, "Welcome to my home, my love. Just like that mountain up there, I will always watch over you."

Darlene: undercover cop
Lenny Barker: owner of the Coachman's Bar
Lieutenant Miles Cretchen: New York Police
Iris: Miles' wife
Walls: undercover cop
Liz: undercover cop
Wendel: Doctor Ward's construction man
Meggen: Ward's wife
Leo: boss of big mansion
Marie: worked for Leo
Doctor at the mansion
Doctor for Darlene
Tall hippy: robber on street
Cal the cop: did assassinations
Three cops: worked for Cal
Ted Belini: association boss
Gloria: Ted's daughter
Kendall Owens: association boss
Fat man: takes in bets
Two men with fat man
Third man with fat man
Short man: owner of bar
Man with rifle that shot Leo
Three men that killed Leo's men
Man in toilet at beach house
Two men playing cards at beach house
Two men shot in room at beach house
Man shot Tom at beach house and tunnel
Man at end of tunnel
Man behind Steve and Lenny at beach house and tunnel
Three men by the boats at tunnel
Black man: drug pusher and killer
Man with black man

Third black man: drug pusher
Tom: drug pusher and killer
Gus: drug pusher and killer
Beebee: drug pusher
Lon: drug pusher and killer
Micky: drug pusher and killer
First man with the money in suitcase
Other two men with the drugs
Tommy: drug pusher and killer
Phil: drug pusher and killer
Tony: drug pusher and killer
Greg: drug pusher and killer
Stan: drug pusher and killer
Aldo: drug pusher and killer
Hector: drug pusher and killer
Sam: drug pusher and killer
Ben: drug pusher and killer
Larry: drug pusher and killer
Man shot in restroom with Louie
Two men on yacht: drug pushers and killers
Lorie: Lenny's girlfriend
Marty: bartender
Sidney: bartender
Greg: bartender
Jed: bartender
Twelve men at meeting for new boss
Two men that took Lenny away
Shags' killer
Two men with truck with drugs
Three men at old house
Fat man and three guards at small store selling drugs
Milly: waitress at tavern
Fran and two friends at tavern
Sam Luchen: boss in New Jersey

Del: worked for Sam
George: worked for Sam
Ben: worked for Sam
Org: worked for Sam
Whitney: worked for Sam
Two guards: worked for Sam
Del's girl was barmaid
Guns: sold guns and ammo
His partner, Sandy, sold guns and ammo
Two men with Sandy
Bruce: picked up money from businesses
Wayne: picked up money from businesses
Timmy: picked up money from businesses
Johnny: armored car heist
Sid: armored car heist
Mark: armored car heist
Allen: armored car heist
Manny: fur warehouse
Trag: fur warehouse
Darlene: fur warehouse
Fats: bet collection
Moore: bet collection
Boggie: bet collection
Sims: bet collection
Mike: outside guard
Walls: outside guard
Gill: outside guard
Curtis: association boss
Two men Curtis wanted killed
Nine men at meeting at Kendall's house
Antone Agustis: Chicago boss
Six men killed after fight at bar
Gil: the last man at bar, free to leave
Francis: wealthy drug dealer

Darlene

Three men with Francis
Butler: worked for Francis
Selby: the bad cop
Two men in Cadillac: worked for Francis
The captain of ship with drugs
Two men that Curtis sold drugs to
Two young men: tried to hold up bar

Printed in the USA
CPSIA information can be obtained
at www.ICGtesting.com
LVHW010617011224
797923LV00015B/618

* 9 7 9 8 8 9 2 1 1 2 6 8 0 *